ABOUT THE AUTHOR

In the beginning, Golden worked the standard corporate rat race, completing college with a chemical engineering degree before starting a small photography company on the side.

Since then, the FuriousFotog brand grew into an internationally recognized brand, published in both domestic and international magazines, on websites, and trade/e-book book covers (even appearing on some himself). Having been in the industry since 2012, Golden has interfaced and networked with countless other authors, clients, and photographers to license and create over four-hundred romance book cover images, diversifying into other commercial work as well.

He published his debut novel, Homeward Bound (The Journeyman Series, Book One) in June 2016, completing the six-book paranormal adventure romance series in January 2017. Since then he has ventured into other genres, including contemporary, fantasy, and erotica.

Websites:
http://www.goldenczermak.com/
http://www.onefuriousfotog.com/
Facebook:
http://www.facebook.com/authorgoldenczermak
http://www.facebook.com/furiousfotog
Newsletter:
https://goo.gl/ZoLqC4

BOOKS BY THE AUTHOR

THE JOURNEYMAN SERIES
Paranormal Action, Adventure, Romance
Homeward Bound
Seal of Solomon
Made to Suffer
The Devil's Highway
Then Hell Followed
Running on Empty

THE STEAM TYCOON SERIES:
Steampunk Science Fiction & Fantasy
The Steam Tycoon

The Secret Life of Cooper Bennett

SWOLE SERIES
Erotic short stories (male-male)
Chest Day
Leg Day
Wet Wednesday
Triple Drop Sets
Flex Friday

THE SECRET LIFE OF COOPER Bennett

THE SECRET LIFE OF COOPER BENNETT

Published and written by: Golden Czermak
1st Edition

Cover Models: Joey Berry, Lovett Taylor, Andrew James
Cover Photography and Design by Golden Czermak, owner of
FuriousFotog
Chapter Drawings by Cassy Roop of Pink Ink Designs
Proofed by Ultra Editing
Edited by Kellie Montgomery
Formatted by Golden Czermak, owner of FuriousFotog

There are no secrets that time does not reveal.

{Jean Racine}

DEDICATION

Joey

My goodness man, it's done and out in the world! So surreal! Now, what can I say here that you don't already know? Are you like family to me? Check. My brother? Check. One of the best parts of my life? You better check!

You've managed to be there and inspire me not only for this book but also to be driven in my work ethic and my fitness (even though your hair and legs make me vastly jealous. Let's keep that between us...) You'll always be my Coop, Joey, and I'll always be there for you.

Drew

Ever since seeing you sing online, I was awestruck by your talents. Not only are you an amazing vocalist and songwriter (your debut single *To the Moon and Back* is wonderful), you have a drive for your health, body, and spirit that will always impress me. Thank you for being a great model and singer, but also a great friend I was blessed to meet and see rise.

Lovett

When I first saw you and that silver hair grace my newsfeed, and then posted those pictures on FuriousFotog that went on to become that the highest engaged posts on the page ever (let's forget they were selfies and not my professional shots), I knew that I had found a treasure. Not only as a client and cover model mind you, but a silver soul that completed the gold in mine. Thank you for being such a good friend and for everything else, Daddy :)

Stuart

Being the utmost professional in your sports, fitness, and your modelling careers makes you the perfect villain. Haha. Thank you for being such a longtime friend and for the opportunities to work together past and future. You're an amazing man, Stu, and I am truly lucky to know you.

Lastly, but certainly not the least, thank you to Eric – love of my life – and everyone that has been so supportive over the years, especially those who've stayed humble and true to yourselves. It's these kind of friendships and relationships that truly last forever.

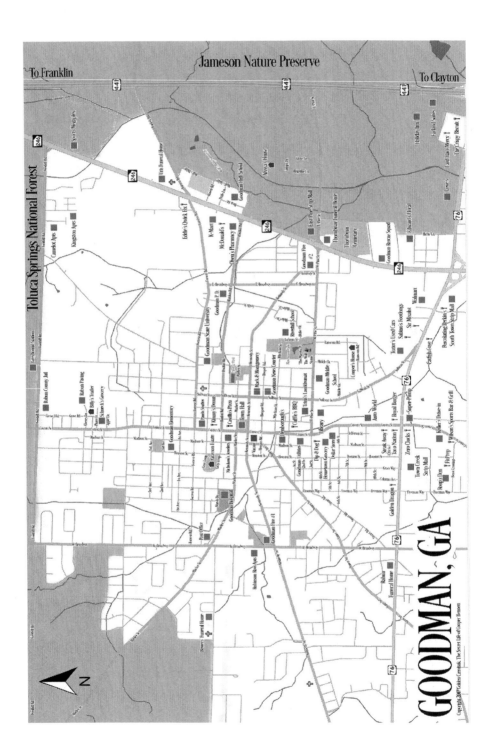

TABLE OF CONTENTS

PART ONE: LIFE BEFORE THE NIGHT TO FORGET

Chapter 1: The Shadow of Days Gone By

Friday January 7, 1994

1

You've probably heard it said that small towns hold some of the biggest secrets. In many cases, that statement is greatly exaggerated; nothing more than a prideful declaration made by cavalier citizens with only an anecdote or two masquerading as 'the truth'. However, despite the numerous falsehoods, there are a few cases – often in special places that don't even realize they are so special – where the statement is undeniably, and gravely, true.

Such was the situation in the sleepy town of Goodman, a sinister place despite its neighborly façade and well-mannered residents. It was a place that harbored far more than its fair share of dark secrets, both behind suspicious smiles and buried in deep places, bubbling up from time to time like a greasy stain on the Earth. There the muck would wait, biding its time until some unwitting soul stepped through it, spreading the darkness around wherever they went.

There was one such evening in early 1994, nineteen years before the horrible incident that would mar the streets of Goodman and its residents with blood. That cold night was the seventh of January, kicking off when the dim light of a waning crescent moon shone through a break in the clouds high above the Blue Ridge Mountains. Like a signal, the light drew out a long, somber howl from the evergreen trees. Another howl quickly answered, joining in song. Then came another, and another, until the entire valley was filled with a splendid chorus of unified wails.

It was countered by a storm of caterwauls, awful and discordant, tearing through the smooth sound like a ragged whip against bare flesh. The din of at least a hundred footfalls rose amidst the discord, forest debris cracking and snapping underfoot. Black and white shapes were darting between the trees, the dappled light glinting off fur slick with drizzling rain.

The shapes were that of wolves, two packs rushing toward each other bearing sharp teeth and mad cries. Yet there was something odd about these beasts. It was their eyes – each and every one of them – that spoke of something unnatural.

The forces crashed against each other like waves against a cliff, but instead of a surge of white foam and splashes of water, there were clouds of snowy fur and the splatter of crimson gore. Shrieks and wails echoed far off into the night, then ended swiftly when their sources were silenced.

It was the silvery wolves who had the first advantage against their adversaries, felling many with dagger-like quickness. Body after body fell, and victory looked to be at hand, but the luck of the pack changed in the span of a single heartbeat. A few dead leaves were flung into the air as the last black wolf toppled, taking their time to float back down to the floor of the shallow ravine as if to delay success.

Suddenly, more black wolves sprung over large rocks and decaying logs, others diving out from the dense overgrowth. Overwhelmed by the surge, the white wolves attempted to withdraw, but the endless stream of shadow surrounded them.

Observing the fray from the top of opposing embankments were two figures, larger and more imposing than the others. The alpha wolves' eyes shifted toward each other from the packs below (where a black wolf had just torn out the throat of a white one, the downed beast's comrades ramming the attacker against a nearby tree). They simply stared as the massacre continued; no growling, nor panting, nor other movements of any kind. The light one – standing with its back toward Goodman – appeared to have grief and contempt in his blue eyes. The dark one – his pack still streaming out of the forest – bore malice and victory in his vivid yellow gaze.

The soft drizzle had started to change into snow when a piercing shriek cut through the glares. The White Alpha looked down, watching six more of his pack fall dead against the enclosing circle of dark wolves. Anger had been brewing and at last he snarled, those cobalt eyes thinning to slits before lunging down the embankment, the cause of all this pain and suffering dead ahead. With a trail of saliva flowing from both sides of his muzzle, and tufts of weeds and bracken crumpling beneath thundering paws, the Alpha skillfully dodged and pushed through the gathered throng of lesser wolves. Their incoming swipes and bites were nothing more than a hindrance to him as he pressed ahead.

Reaching the bottom of the embankment, the soil was an off-putting shade of ruddy black. It squelched. Staring up at the Shadow Alpha, whose golden eyes had widened not with fear but encouragement, the White Alpha howled. Flanked by a team of wolves that escaped their confines (a couple of them limping badly), they yipped and yowled before sprinting up the slope together.

The shady creature drew closer, but a cluster of subordinate wolves had appeared, surrounding their leader, adding to their already solid and elevated advantage.

The charging Alpha did not waver though, spotting a fast-approaching tree to the left. He made a break for it, howling as his pack continued forward, a white arrow plunging into the heart of the shadow's defenses. A swarm of black and white fur exploded with noise, both teeth and claws locked in flesh as bodies went tumbling end over end down the slope.

The attack had worked and the Shadow Alpha was now in the open and unguarded. The White Alpha wasted no time, vaulting off the ground and against the tree. Pushing off and up, he soared through the air, his body now an incoming missile. Curling back his lips to bare his fangs, he was poised to howl again in victory, but this time no wolf sounds were uttered, only words…

"STOP THIS MADNESS!"

The wolves' bodies barreled into each other with such force that both hit the ground with a loud *thwack*! They rolled, then separated, continuing across the debris-strewn ground until the shadow wolf's hindquarters smashed against a protruding rock.

Breathless and panting, the white wolf was first to rise, having come to rest on a bed of withered brush and branches. A ringing in his ears subsided but all his limbs remained sore. One was adorned with clotted mats of red hair and there was a metallic taste in his mouth; it was surely bleeding.

Dammit, how did it come to this?

An ominous chuckle climbed over the sounds of fighting still happening down the hill.

"Stop what exactly, Grayson?" the Shadow Alpha said. "Winning? I think not –" He winced unexpectedly, realizing his back leg was sprained, perhaps even broken.

"By the looks of that leg, Lance, I think that's exactly what you need to do," Grayson Manning noted. He then sighed heavily. "It does not have to be this way; call off your pack and we can see if…"

Lance Goddard shook his entire body as if Grayson's words were vile, smearing him with a stinking residue that he had to get off.

"NO." Lance said presently. "I will not do anything of the sort."

"You must!" Grayson yelled, an inkling of desperation leaching out. He jerked his head toward the carnage below. "Look down there; those are our crews! Our families! Is having them slaughter each other like savages better than agreeing to live by their terms?"

Grayson looked back to Lance, who had not wasted precious energy looking down the embankment. Instead, he was staring directly ahead. There was a fire in his eyes fueled by so much hate that Grayson had to avert his own to avoid being burned.

"*Their… terms…*" Lance murmured, his voice slowly growing into a rough-edged shout. "You just answered your own question in the asking! Living under the rule of humans is the problem, you stupid, old mutt! We wouldn't be living free and *that* would be how the decline of our race begins."

"As if it hasn't been happening for years," Grayson challenged. "At least this way…"

"You would all but guarantee an end to our existence."

"While you've all but guaranteed the same for your pack. They will be hunted down like werewolves in the old days."

Lance didn't seem too bothered.

"I don't think we are in too great a danger," he replied. "The humans have an inability to see beyond their own nose, and that's something beings like us can use to our advantage."

"This is insane, Lance!"

"No, what's insane Grayson is that you don't see that it's *you* who brought on this butchery the moment *you* turned your back on your own kind!"

21

"Bullshit! This massacre is all on you and your temper, Lance! At least with my decision we won't be hunted down and killed like vermin, having a chance to exist peacefully, without fear of a silver bullet between the eyes. At least I can own that choice and its effects," Grayson said sternly. "Can you?"

"Oh, really?" Lance asked, and if his wolf form could smile it would be beaming. "You would be able to take ownership of *all* the effects your choice has brought to bear?"

Grayson recoiled at the callousness in Lance's tone. He wasn't telling him something and he knew that it was bad just from the look in that black wolf's eyes. Grayson didn't know it yet, but his heart would stop when Lance spoke his next words.

"Does Freya and that little runt Liam know how *heated* your actions have been?"

Grayson became cold, even though his fur provided more than enough protection against the cold wind. He turned back toward Goodman and between the narrowest gap in the trees he could make out a distant flicker of orange.

No.... Grayson thought.

Could his wolf-ears make out the distance blare of sirens?

No, that can't be the safe house...

His heart plummeted like a stone into his guts, splashing in the burning acid.

I need to get back!

"What have you done, Lance?" he snarled.

There was no reply, only that unrepentant yellow stare.

I need to see that they are okay.

"Lance! Answer me!"

The Shadow Alpha still did not yield answers. Grayson pressed him, his words becoming a string of shouts.

"I NEED TO KNOW THAT THEY ARE OKAY!"

"SHUT UP!" Lance roared suddenly, and a large part of his pack broke away from the assault. They scrambled up the hillside to assist their leader. "Your mate and son both suffered by the hand *you* shuffled, Grayson. I merely dealt the cards."

Grayson's eyes sparkled with tears, his pebbled nostrils flared.

"As for you," Lance continued, "do you think that the humans will not turn on you once your usefulness is spent? They do it all the time to themselves – it's in their nature – so who's to say they won't do it to some*thing* they view as inferior?" His voice suddenly broke with fury. "I for one am sick of being told by others – especially them – what is best for *my* pack. I will not bow before the throne of humanity while these

Journeymen and their wretched Order keep me from what is rightfully mine. Shadows will fall on them soon enough. But more importantly, my dear Grayson: I am sick... to death... of YOU!"

Grayson's eyes grew huge, bulging like great big sapphires as he looked down at the wolves fast approaching. They were not going to stop, their ravenous faces getting closer. There were so many of them (*no escape*), their claws tearing effortlessly into the soil (*no escape*) while the dark of their pelts blocked out what few blue pinpricks of hope Grayson could still see (*no escape*). They were replaced with the glimmer of bright fangs, slippery with fresh blood.

Soon it would be *his* blood.

"So be it, brother," Grayson said, his face falling to a look of solemn content. If his mate and son were indeed dead... "It's my hope, Lance, that down the road you realize the error of your ways..."

Grayson Manning then shut his eyes, patiently waiting for death to arrive in five... four... three...

2

"ONE!" A mighty voice rumbled across the forest. "CHARGE!"

The ground began to shake, the front line of onrushing wolves losing their grip. They fell on their bellies, unsettled and confused, while the monsters behind them had to stop their advance just to stay standing. The tremors continued and Grayson flung his eyes open. What he saw managed to lift his spirits.

The circle of black wolves had come under attack themselves, a large sleuth of bears erupting from the forest. Their powerful bodies and sluggish gait plowed through the lowly dogs, mowing them down like stalks of corn at harvest. Leading the charge was an enormous monster at least twice the size of the rest. His fur was shabby and dark brown (almost black), eyes the same color as the trees. The shadow wolves knew him, and fled his wrath.

"Ásbjörn!" Grayson whispered triumphantly, watching as the remains of his pack dashed west through a break in the circle toward the safe house and his family...

Then Grayson remembered.

Lance...

He turned, searching for the bastard amongst the chaos – high, low, and everywhere in between. Lance was nowhere to be found.

He must have bolted while your eyes were closed. Lance, you coward! Too scared to face punishment for what you've done?

Disappointed by the lack of justice for all the carnage, Grayson made his way toward the base of the embankment. The circle of shadow wolves was no more, the area now decorated with random (flattened) wolf corpses.

Grayson's stomach lurched, not only at the rancid smell of death already seeping into the air, but also knowing that all those bodies – in front of him, on the hill, and elsewhere – would revert to their human forms soon. He planned to be long gone before that gruesome event happened, checking on Freya and Liam.

"You look like shit," Ásbjörn said in a deep voice before Grayson had a chance to think too much about his family.

The shifter had been waiting for him, sitting away from the bloodshed (as much of it as he could, considering how widespread it was). Upright on a low stump, Ásbjörn was easily over a dozen feet tall, watching as the rest of his crew mopped up any straggling shadow wolves. They would also be the lucky ones cleaning up the area – so was the agreement struck with the Order.

"And you look bigger every time I see you, Bear King of the Blue Ridge Mountains" Grayson said. "And by bigger, I mean fatter, of course."

Ásbjörn chuckled and rubbed his belly.

"Ugh, you know how much I dislike formal titles, Grayson. Besides, I would be surprised if I were fatter. I love food, but Goddard's pack has cleared out most of the wildlife in this area and east into our territory. Probably feasted so they'd have enough energy to launch this little attack against you. Times ahead are going to be rough as we work through the food shortage."

"I wish that this attack was so insignificant," Grayson lamented, seeing a flash of Liam's chubby infant face in his mind's eye, and then his mate's beautiful smile. Both were then engulfed in flames. "Any sign of their Alpha?"

Grayson settled into position at the base of Ásbjörn's massive feet and took a seat, easing the hefty pain that was plaguing his front right leg.

Ásbjörn shook his head.

"No. Given fight or flight the little shit took the opportunity to flee. I sent a couple of my best scouts out east and up north to see if they can pick up a trail. They might, but you know as well as I do that Goddard knows ways to counter that."

"Dammit." Grayson's head hung low, his lame leg lifted slightly off the forest floor.

"You really should shift and take a look at that injury," Ásbjörn suggested. "Human form will give you a better grasp of the healing time, depending on what's left after the Change."

"I know," Grayson replied, trying not to snap. He winced instead. "I'll look later when…"

"You have some fancy suit to change into?"

If Grayson's human cheeks were visible they'd be bright pink.

Ásbjörn didn't wait for a retort, having no qualms about anyone seeing him naked. He shifted right in front of Grayson, his large bones made a crinkling noise like a hand rifling through a stiff plastic bag. His heavy coat began to withdraw into his body and as he stood, his burly limbs creaked and bent unnaturally as they reformed into a more mannish shape.

"So, tell me," a gruff but handsome man continued. All that was left of the bear's fur was a head full of messy hair, a bushy beard, and a smattering of fuzz across his muscular chest (complete with a trio of enchanted scars that would not heal). He was still quite tall – six-foot-five – and there was a tattoo sleeve along his entire left arm. "What does our naughty puppy want so badly in that town of yours?"

"I wish I knew exactly," Grayson replied. He searched his memory, but if anything was there to give him a clue, it had long since been forgotten.

At that point, all the two of them knew was that there was something in Goodman that the shadow wolves had become aware of – likely due to the Order's presence. Things before their first appearance in the late 1950s were fine, but ever since that alliance of humans and supernatural creatures took interest in the town, stress on the local paranormal population, especially shifters, skyrocketed.

However, Grayson knew there had to be something that happened recently to trigger Lance's fervent obsession, which just happened to coincide with the Accords he was so adamantly against.

The agreement laid out in the Accords would, in 'simple terms even a beast could understand,' allow shifters of the Blue Ridge Mountains to live free and clear under Order protection, but only if they registered themselves, keeping their numbers in check to maintain a low and manageable profile. Other duties had also been specifically called out in the documents, but were FOR ALPHA EYES ONLY.

"I'm in no way agreeing with his methods," Ásbjörn said, certainly no fan of the Accords himself, "but Goddard may have a point about the Order not being fully trustworthy."

"Well, neither are we," Grayson replied. "No matter how much we wrap ourselves in a blanket of honor and security. Life in general is out to survive, whatever the cost may be."

Ásbjörn agreed, taking a quick second to adjust himself; he insisted that it was because the stump was rough on his bare skin. Grayson didn't care and tried not to watch, turning his attention back west.

The safe house...

"Ásbjörn, my friend, thank you for coming when you received my call."

"Do you think it'd have been any other way?"

"No, because as stubborn as you can be, it's in your nature to fulfill your duties."

Ásbjörn smirked, his green eyes brighter.

"Speaking of duties, I should g-go and ch-check on th-things i-in t-town…" Grayson continued, the last words stuttering with raw emotion. He dreaded what was coming.

"Go on then, Snowy," Ásbjörn replied, trying to lighten the mood. "We'll take care of things up here."

Grayson didn't need to ask anymore, knowing that Ásbjörn would deliver like he always did.

"I'll stay in touch then and let you know if I hear anything."

"As will I," Ásbjörn said, then after a pause: "You think he'll be back?"

"Yes," Grayson said. A cold chill washed over his wolf-body.

"Any idea of when?"

"No," Grayson said simply, wishing the answer was different.

He would also be wishing for a time machine within the next half hour, specifically at the moment he arrived at the safe house on Center Street (which had been tucked away inside of an old clothing store between Kennedy and Hooper Road). There he would find his two-day old son safe and sound, rescued by the heroics of one of the human emergency responders. The fate of his mate was a completely different story. Her scorched remains – so badly burned she looked more like the remnants of a bonfire than a person – would haunt his waking memory and fuel his desire for revenge against Lance Goddard for many years to come.

"Regardless of when he returns," Ásbjörn said, "we'll be ready. I don't think he's going to be generous and give us another chance to gain the upper hand next time."

"No, not one bit. But if there was ever a team that could handle it, we're looking at each other right now."

"Damn right," Ásbjörn said and nothing more, watching as Grayson walked away into the woods. He then swaggered over to his crew, gathered by a trickling stream short distance away. "Okay fellows," he said, those stout arms bent with hands on his hips, "we best move quickly – some of the bodies are starting to turn. There's a lot of work ahead of us if we hope to get this mountain looking halfway decent again…"

Chapter 2: Happy Birthday to You

Friday January 7, 1994

1

The night of January seventh was certainly an eventful one up in the mountains of the Jameson Nature Preserve, bordering Goodman just east of U.S. 441.

Ásbjörn and his crew of black bears were busy beneath the trees, clearing away the aftermath of battle – the details of which nobody ever thought to ask, nor did they want to stick around to witness. There were, of course, plenty of rumors swirling amongst the Order and shifters alike. A lot assumed that without bonfires, which would be visible in town and beyond, the bodies were simply drug away and buried, scattered across a wide expanse of country. Others presumed, rather gruesomely (but somehow more fittingly), that the bodies had been drug away, stockpiled in cold caves, and subsequently eaten during the food shortage that afflicted the region over the ensuing year. Whatever their methods, Ásbjörn and his crew were always reliable, working quickly and efficiently.

The same thing could be said about another individual across town, or at least of his quick temper and efficient fists, who hours earlier was pissing into the toilet of a Goodman Hospital bathroom. There for what should have been a joyous occasion: the birth of his only child, Roland Bennett had no idea that his boy would go on to become entwined with the events that were building in the surrounding mountains.

Not that Roland cared. You'd die sooner than finding the man giving two shits about anyone other than himself on a good day, never mind a depressing January one that had done nothing but piss rain on the whole damn town.

Draining the lizard in that small and sterile bathroom for what seemed like the last thirty minutes, Roland ignored the slight burning in his urethra and ripped a loud one, catching a glimpse of himself in a small mirror off to the side, just before the stink rose to his nostrils and singed his eyes. There was a tiny chink in the glass, sitting at eye level. Unavoidable and annoying, that imperfection made him think about how harsh his features looked. He looked older than thirty-three. Decades more.

Old as shit.

His five-foot-eleven body wasn't all that appealing either, melting into its current, calorific state over the years. Roland would often boast that he'd just "slipped off the wagon" and could "easily get back into shape" – something he'd yet to attempt in ten years of saying the same shit on different days. He wasn't lying though. He *had* been in decent shape back when he met Agnes Bennett née Moody in June of 1983. It was at a bar up in North Carolina where she was working as one of the bartenders. Their relationship ended up being a zinger of a deal for him and a hopeless one for her. Other factors had taken over after their first year together and the resulting dynamics liked to encourage, or rather demand, that she stayed put.

Still staring at himself, the smell of gaseous Mexican food mixing with a six pack of brews started to curdle his senses. Through a veil of wet eyes, Roland saw the mismatch of parts staring back at him as if that bug-eyed mortician over at Thornbriar's Funeral Home had spliced him together from the worst possible remains. He had an egg-shaped head (hard boiled, then dropped) with tufts of wiry black hair sticking out from the sides. That all rested atop a sinewy neck that would tighten at the slightest nuisance while his torso, thick with burly slabs for limbs, often carried the smell of perspiration obscured by splashes of Old Spice. Literally rounding out his look was a large beer gut that stretched out the front of his wife-beater, resembling a balloon shoved under the fabric.

Conflicted with feelings of pride and disgust at what he saw, Roland stifled a cough. Shaking his junk twice, he reached for the fan switch, flipped it, and waited as the unit jostled and buzzed loudly. Roland shallowly breathed while tucking himself into his jeans. Zipping up, he took deeper breaths as the air cleared.

Fuck that was a close call, he thought, scratching at his bloated belly. The shirt's color was reminiscent of grimy dollar bills.

Then it dawned on Roland, bright like the fluorescent lights above: he'd missed out on nearly an entire day of pay. Being a warehouse worker at Preston's Building Supply (a sprawling yard with rundown brick buildings just north of the intersection of Sullivan and Forrest), he would have earned nearly thirteen dollars an hour. That was no chump change considering all the bills – and final notices – that were already screaming his way for this... well... *her* pregnancy.

Exiting the bathroom, he entered the hospital room proper but stopped just outside the door.

Bee-beep.

He liked it better inside that small room. Things were quieter in there. Out here, the constant drone of medical equipment and beeping of monitors were like crowbars trying to pry open his skull.

Bee-beep.

Then came the cries from that pink *thing* Agnes had basically shit out of her. At least she managed to do that without them having to cut her open and yank the thing out, costing more money. Shrill and piercing, the baby's cries helped those imaginary crowbars pop off the top Roland's skull and scramble his brains.

His thoughts might have been addled by the noise, but Roland knew that once they were home, he would have to remind his wife – for posterity – about staying on those goddamn pills. By the time he was done teaching her the importance of this particular lesson, she may have needed an unspoken prayer request at church all for herself. She'd always been a stubborn idiot in his eyes, making stupid choices despite his warnings. Like when she'd wear all that whore-paint on her face to "look good" in town (doing so to cover the bruises left behind from Roland's brand of open-handed teaching), or when she'd smoke those expensive *fucking* Marlboros.

At nearly two dollars a pack, he'd told her to stop, more to spare his wallet than her health, but she wouldn't listen, slowly inviting the throat cancer in. It would, within the next two years, seal her esophagus and windpipe up tight, releasing her from that miserable life at last. But the baby had given her a new outlook, too late as it was, and she did stop smoking the moment she knew she'd gotten pregnant.

Bee-beep.

"All for the baby," Roland grunted, feeling slighted by the memory. He was insulted that the *thing* got her to obey *his* commands. Something about that pissed him off and the fact it did showed unabashedly on his face.

But it wasn't all bad for him, the truly blessed one of the two. She could cook her man a good three meals a day (*not while in that hospital bed*) and pay him decent attention while on her knees or back (*could still happen in that hospital bed if I wanted it to*).

But Hell's bells Agnes! Why couldn't you remember to take those pills?

His eyes drifted over to her and the child. They narrowed. He glared.

Bee-beep.

Because she hadn't listened to him (*yet again everybody!*), look at the mess they were in now. His temper flared thinking about the monetary drain that crumpled turd in her arms would cause.

Bee-beep.

Looking for a reprieve, anything to take his mind off things, Roland scanned the room. Options were slim: the chairs were hard, the magazines old, and the television mounted to the ceiling was nothing but a kaleidoscope of distorted color due to the weather. If he didn't know better, he'd swear she'd timed all this on purpose so he'd be missing *Walker, Texas Ranger* on the box.

With the prices these people are charging, why can't this hospital spring for more than an antenna on the goddamn roof?

With no recourse, he started to walk up to the baby.

Bee-beep. Bee-beep. Bee-beep.

Agnes' eyes grew wider the closer Roland got to her. Heart thumping hard in her chest, she looked afraid.

He looked crazed.

Bee-beep. Bee-beep. Bee-beep.

"Wh-what are y-you doing?" she rasped, voice low but still submissive. Her throat had become sore over the last few weeks of the pregnancy, and she found it difficult to swallow, even when drinking. "Ro-Roland, p-please..."

Roland didn't answer, extending his arms. Wrapping his rough-skinned hands around the baby's silky smoothness, he pried it out of her weakened grip. There was a screech, causing him to nearly drop the thing in her lap.

"Ro-Roland…"

Bee-beep. Bee-beep. Bee-beep.

"Hush, little baby, don't say a word…" he whispered callously. It sounded more like an order than a lullaby.

It continued to cry, and the cords in Roland's neck tightened hearing that jarring noise again. His teeth clamped together in his jaw, and he began to tighten his grip like he was wringing out a washcloth.

"… or Daddy's gonna make you pay for thinking he slurred…"

The baby screamed, its cries defeated by the rapid dinging of Agnes' monitors.

Bee-beep. Bee-beep. Bee-beep. Bee-beep. Bee-beep. Bee-beep.

The door to the hospital room abruptly flung open. One of the nurses came rushing in. It was the pretty blonde Roland had dubbed Betty With-A-Nice-Rack. He'd fantasized about her quite often in the bathroom just behind him (and even the one down the hall, around the corner). She reminded him a lot of Agnes when she had the banging body of a twenty-one-year-old.

And what a lot of banging that body could do, he'd ponder, and if feelings could drool, he'd be standing in a puddle needing a "Caution: Wet Floor" sign permanently tattooed on his body.

Likely expecting to see a seizure or heart attack underway, Betty was surprised to be greeted by the sight of a gentle-faced husband returning a baby to his wife's arms. Despite the serenity the scene tried to portray, both mother and child were crying heavily.

"Is... everything alright sir?"

"Hmm? Oh yes, everything is quite fine," Roland replied gaily. "I think the stress the wife's been under is catching up. She's been quite emotional with these female hormones running wild. Hell, I'm probably preaching to the choir though, you probably see things like this every day."

"Ah yes, those infamous *female* hormones," Betty quietly said as she swept over to the monitors.

Bee-beep. Bee-beep.

Her eyes indicated that she was suspicious of the intensity in Agnes' readings; that something other than hormones was the cause. But unless Agnes said something (anything) there was nothing more Betty could do.

Agnes stayed quiet, save her sobbing.

On the other hand, Roland's eyes indicated that he was aroused, casting intermittent glances at Betty's namesakes. He loitered on them, imagining himself peeking under those scrubs while planting his nose right between those voluptuous breasts to take a whiff.

"Might I suggest a little bit of a break?"

Betty asked the question as if she could sense him looking at her; she didn't need turn in his direction.

"Yeah, that might be a good idea," he replied, moving to grab his denim jacket off the coat rack. He then reached for the door handle and cracked it open.

Bee-beep. Bee-beep.

Betty asked him another question out of the blue, catching Roland off-guard.

"Do you two have a name picked out?"

"A name for...?"

"The *baby*..." Betty said with a light flourish of disappointed laughter. She used her index finger to gently press against the infant's nose like a button and miraculously the crying started to subside. "He's got some gorgeous brown eyes, Mr. Bennett, but we can't keep calling him "the baby" now, can we?"

We certainly can, Roland thought.

"No. No name picked out yet," he said.

"Oh, that's a pity. Perhaps this little break will help you focus on one from your list?"

"Yeah," Roland replied, yanking the door all the way open. "The *list.*"

Bee-beep.

Taking one last look at the two miserable wretches in the hospital bed, and an even lengthier look at Betty's perky body as she resumed working, Roland stepped out of the hospital room.

He walked down the waxed checkerboard hall toward the elevators, planning to head down to the parking lot for some much-needed fresh air. More importantly, it would be quiet there under the night sky, and that's exactly what Roland Bennett needed.

2

Roland walked through the large, double glass doors at the front of Goodman Hospital, met by a cold snap of wind. The temperature plummeted a good forty degrees Fahrenheit in the span of three steps, the change so drastic Roland imagined himself as a cartoonish thermometer, mercury levels falling through his feet while his entire body iced over.

What are you, five years old?

Roland would often discipline himself mentally; working men didn't have time for juvenile fancies.

Rubbing his hands vigorously, he attempted to warm them. Another icy blast of wind made sure it didn't work. While Roland's added bulk helped shield him from the cold, his hands didn't have much insulation and were the first to freeze, followed quickly by his nose and cheeks. The pockets of his grubby work pants were unusable, his thighs far too big to allow anything thicker than a business card to slip into the side pockets. However, if that incessant beeping upstairs hadn't affected his memory, a pair of leather work gloves were sitting in the passenger seat of his truck.

Goodman Hospital had always been a relatively small place since opening in the early summer of 1951. At fifty beds, an expansion program would start in early 1995 to double the capacity and transform it into a state of the art, high-tech facility. Roland complained about it the entire time, citing the ever-increasing costs he paid as the (only) reason they could afford it. Thus, whenever he was there and no matter the ailment, he would strut about as if he owned the place, condescending to whoever got in the way.

But before all that, he was still cold, briskly making his way across the darkened parking lot. As he slid in and out of the orange light from overhead lamps, their shafts seemed to sparkle as fine drizzle wafted through in sheets. It was almost magical – if Roland had time for such juvenile fancies – but it was also quiet; peaceably so.

Looking around, still rubbing his bare hands, Roland only saw a handful of parked vehicles. Most of them were forgettable, but a bright red Lotus Elan stood out. Roland wished, with an ample dose of envy, that it was *his* car, but his '83 Chevy C10, complete with faded blue paint, was waiting at the far end of the lot.

When he arrived on the passenger side, he glanced inside and spotted the gloves. He got slightly warmer at the thought of putting them on, but still shivered as he plucked a ring of keys out of his jacket pocket. They jangled as he shook, the truck key finally entering the hole.

That's when the noise started, a distant chatter that came from the east, but also everywhere at once. It sounded like sirens. Maybe an accident or arrest up on north Madison? No, upon listening a little more Roland realized that the noise wasn't sirens, but howling.

While reaching inside the truck, Roland dropped his keys onto the pavement. They made a short, metallic *clunk,* but instead of going after them right away, he went for the gloves instead. Slipping his hands into their warm interior one by one, the howling seemed to intensify.

I hate dogs, he thought. The racket was starting to irritate him just like those damn hospital monitors. The imaginary crowbars were out again, coming for his skull…

Bee-beep.

"What the fuck does a man have to do to get some peace and quiet around this town?" he snapped.

Letting out a long stream of steaming air, Roland looked a deflating balloon that had mated with a whistling kettle. He squatted once able, scrabbling for the keys. Using gloved hands might not have been the best idea, but at least they were warm, and eventually he managed to pluck the keys off the pavement by their large Falcons keychain.

Damn duds, letting those candy-assed Cardinals win last Sunday, at home no less!

A whimper rose to his right. Roland turned. He half expected to see some monster sitting there (*again with the childish thoughts?*), or at least one of the mangy mutts that had been making all that infernal racket. He didn't see either. A disheveled labradoodle – or whatever pansy breed this *thing* might be – had walked up to him instead. It might have been cute at some stage, but as it meekly stepped forward, it looked abandoned, tired, and hungry.

"Aren't we all…" Roland muttered at it, sneering. "Now get the fuck away from me. I'm only going to tell you once."

He started to stand, but the dog, seeking the littlest bit of attention, persisted. It jumped playfully onto Roland's leg, its tail starting to wag, and for a moment it looked happy. That's precisely when Roland flung the poor creature with a swift kick that only Agnes could relate to. It careened into the side of the truck then fell over onto its side, whimpering and winded. It's tail was no longer wagging, tongue hanging out of the side of its mouth.

"I warned you," Roland whispered, approaching his temper's latest victim.

While looming over the dog like a specter, he spied its collar, a tag glinting off the light of one of the overhead lamps. Breathing out again so he could bend over, the repugnant man lowered himself, snatching the entire collar off its neck once he was low enough. He held it in his hand like a prize, reading out the name embossed on the small, blue tag.

"Cooper."

The dog whined again, and the distant howls were joined by others. The new ones were messier, discordant, and vastly more annoying to hear. Something heavy was going down in the woods, and Roland felt glad he was away from it. As for the dog lying beside his truck, he had business to finish. Roland Bennett didn't shirk his duties, no sir, no way! The mutt didn't listen to him after all, and there was *always* a price to pay for that.

Reaching out his meaty arms, Roland's hands grasped the dog's fur. It was soft, as was its skin as he tightened his grip around whatever he could hold. Looking up at the cloudy sky, breaking to let the dim light of a waning crescent moon shine through, Roland started twisting his grip. There were cries of pain, and he whispered back at the dog so softly that only he could hear…

"Hush little baby, don't say a word…"

Chapter 3: Cooper Bennett Has a Run-In

Friday August 31, 2012

1

Eighteen long years passed over the Blue Ridge Mountains, Goodman growing into quite a bustling community by 2012. Somehow, despite the influx of new people and businesses ("We're getting a Lard Have Mercy!" the freshmen students would shout cheerfully), the place still managed to hold on to its small-town roots.

Cooper Bennett would have loved to see those roots wither and die, growing into his eighteenth year like a resilient weed. His bullied school life, along with that at home (when he could muster enough drive to call that prison home), were akin to herbicide, both unrelenting as ever in keeping him down. Christmas break was always a welcome reprieve from the scholastic side of his torment, but that was a good four months away. But there was a silver lining and that was the upcoming Labor Day holiday. He'd definitely be making use of the time off.

As Cooper sat front and center in his desk – more for protection against projectiles and insults than good learning – he looked up at the classroom's wall clock. Rubbing a sandpapery buzz cut (one that he had to self-inflict every week or two because there was no way in Hell his dad was going to pay for one of those popular, queer haircuts on his boy), Cooper adjusted his glasses and squinted though the thick, coke-bottle lenses. It made him look constipated, a necessary evil to bring things into full focus. A clock just like the one he was peering at could be found in every classroom, each office, the lunch room, gymnasium, and hallways. All of their bright white faces and black numbers, once focused, read the same time. It was half past noon.

Ugh, that means half an hour to go, Cooper thought glumly. Thirty more agonizing minutes of listening to the aging Mr. Reid ramble on about the town's history, which he seemed to find vastly more interesting than the prescribed curriculum.

I guess it all fits in the post-Civil War timeframe, but I'm sure the finals won't be asking which stores went out of business downtown in 1976...

Cooper sighed as Mr. Reid continued, certain now that he had been born before Jesus Christ with all the historical facts and anecdotes he spouted. Propping up one of his lanky arms, Cooper's tee shirt billowed like an oversized white sail. Weighing in at some whopping one-hundred-forty pounds sopping wet (from tears), Cooper listened and waited patiently for the bell to ring.

You see, living in Goodman was both a blessing and a curse, all wrapped up in a neat little package that Cooper wished he could gift to some passerby in exchange for a one-way ticket out of town. He was a small-town kid with big time dreams, but Goodman seemed to do its best to keep him down. Outside, in the wide world, nobody really knew of Goodman, and people would often reference Gainesville, Greenville, or Gatlinburg for geographical reference. Goodman was roughly in the center of a triangle formed between those three cities.

Cooper couldn't go very far downtown without running into someone he knew, especially when hanging out in the streets, on the sidewalk, or in the parking lots was a common form of entertainment for the loser crowd.

It was a good thing if he liked the person (Mrs. Murphy, for example, would give him a handful of creamy Werther's Original candies from the never-ending supply in her purse) and awful if he didn't (every encounter with Liam Manning ranked high on that scale).

It was because of Liam – now a hunky star quarterback for the Goodman Wolverines that every mom would be proud to see their daughter with (and even happier to have grabbed his tight end themselves) – that Cooper spent much of his middle school years coasting on his bike up and down Goodman's crisscrossing streets. It allowed him to make a quick getaway should he come under fire from Manning's Army and, for the most part, it worked as long as the escape routes were clear. It stayed that way right up to Liam's sixteenth birthday. That's when the cocky shit got a car from his dad and his terrorizing took on a whole other level.

Cooper would frequently tell himself that he wasn't jealous of the rich boy nor all the attention lavished on him, but considering *he* got the old one two on his sixteenth birthday just for forgetting to take out the garbage that morning, he was, in fact, very envious – depression skirting his thoughts as his eyes became puffy and somewhat discolored. Thankfully, the thickness of his lenses helped mask the full brunt of that beating, which was also the reason his glasses were taped on the bridge of his nose in the first place. It was a consistent reminder of how shitty his life was; a loving gift from your

Pops who likes to pop.

Sometimes Cooper would leave the downtown area, his feet pedaling north toward Foothill Road and beyond, right to base of the mountain trails at Toluca Springs National Forest. Cooper never went further. Not that he didn't want to, but a gut feeling always told him that if he were going to venture up into the mountains, he should do it with a big group of friends and… well… since he only had one friend in Billy Arnett, he was shit out of luck.

Cooper probably could have met more people doing things outside his comfort zone, but most of the townsfolk were engrossed in things that he had absolutely zero interest in. The first hunting day of the season was so popular it evolved into an okay excuse to be absent from school (and probably should have been declared a holiday so the few remaining students could at least have a day off doing things they enjoyed). Cooper also made sure to avoid the ritualistic Friday night football games, where he'd feel not only out of place but stressed while on the lookout for Liam's goons.

Cooper squinted at the clock again; fifteen minutes to go.

Mr. Reid had moved on from talking about the downtown area. A question from Margaret Smith – also in the front row – had lead him all the way back to its founding.

"Why couldn't you have waited fifteen minutes?" Cooper groaned.

Margaret must have heard him, casting a spiteful glance over her right shoulder. Her lips were puckered as if she'd just sucked on a slice of lemon.

According to Mr. Reid, the region was settled back in the early 1800s by a group of Europeans that came upon a trio of Cherokee trails in the mountains just south of the Georgia/North Carolina border. Over the years, the settlement grew to consume the area, and in 1821 it was incorporated as Goodman, the county seat of what would become Rabun County.

Margaret had been listening intently, Cooper unsure sure if she was being genuine or not. Regardless, he watched her turn all the way to the right. She was looking directly at him now, wearing a bitchy smirk.

"How *fascinating*, Mr. Reid. But, can you please tell us who the town was named after?" Margaret chirped. She sounded like a bird and Cooper wished he had a slingshot.

"Oh my!" Mr. Reid exclaimed enthusiastically. "It's so good to see people your age interested in the town! A shame they aren't teaching this to you in elementary school anymore. To answer your question Miss Smith, his name was Walter P. Goodman..."

They *were* still teaching local history in elementary school, it's just most of the kids didn't remember all the trivial details after thirteen years. Most couldn't remember what they'd had for breakfast the day before and Margaret, with her expressions, told Cooper that she didn't care presently either.

Nonetheless, Mr. Reid continued regaling about the past as excitedly as his heart would let him. Licking his dry lips (Cooper swore he saw his teeth move), his old voice was similarly parched. Just looking at him made Cooper thirsty. Involuntarily, he cleared his throat and swallowed.

Mr. Reid told them that Goodman was arguably the most prominent member of the community at the time, rescuing several students and teachers from the community's very first schoolhouse. It had been surrounded by ravenous wolves and allegedly he'd killed most of them with a shotgun before wrestling the last one to the death. Monument Park would ultimately be built where that schoolhouse once stood, and Cooper finally connected the dots that the fight between Goodman and the last wolf is what the large statue in the park represented.

He knew the physical details of that statue very well, passing by it nearly every day on his way to and from both elementary and middle school. But there was one day in particular that stood out in memory more than all the others. That day was ten years ago, back when…

2

Thursday April 4, 2002

Cooper was eight, riding his trusty and rusty blue mountain bike home from Goodman Elementary. The April air was warm against his skin as he cruised southward, its humid touch slightly sticky from a brief rain that had stopped less than an hour ago.

He whizzed by many of the stores, their colorful signs and window displays calling him inside like the ice cream man's jingle, but there was something about today – a good feeling that rarely came to him but nevertheless stayed – that kept Cooper pedaling. His little feet, encased in a pair of raggedy, second-hand sneakers, moved so fast that his little heart threatened to burst from the pressure.

Center Street soon intersected with West Pine and Third, Cooper turning the handlebars sharply to the left. The bike did as it was told, shooting off in the same direction but Cooper had misjudged, cutting the corner tightly, his tires fighting for purchase on the asphalt. He ended up in the wrong lane.

A car blared its horn. The driver slammed on the brakes, seeing an oncoming projectile in the shape of an eight-year-old bike-riding boy heading straight for her.

Swooping off to the right and out of her way right before his front tire hit the car's bumper, Cooper giggled, then waved playfully as he passed.

She didn't look as jovial, the string of cursing flowing out of her mouth was loud enough to hear through the closed window, making his eyes expand and cheeks flush. He drove his little legs faster, racing down the street (in the correct lane this time), deviating only when large puddles that had collected in low spots called out for his tires and lots of splashing.

Sploosh!

Closer to home, Cooper passed by Monument Park. It was off to his left as he traveled east. There, just short of the turn onto Hanscom Road where his house – and surely his dad's belt – would be waiting, he stopped for a breather near the centerpiece of town. A large bronze statue of a mighty warrior wrestling what looked like a giant dog towered over him. Cooper had heard someone at school call that creature a wolf, but it didn't look like any wolf he'd seen before – either in person (thankfully), on the television at Billy's, or in the school library (where he'd search for non-educational things like *Spiderman* and movie reviews).

As Cooper analyzed the nasty beast (the sculpture's snarling jaws, long front legs, and oddly shaped body didn't do wolves any favors), something vivid – almost golden – flickered in the corner of his eye. He turned, and they widened to take in the beauty of what he saw.

It was a little girl, possibly the same age as he was, standing diagonally across Jackson Street at the top of the steps to Riverhill School's entrance.

It was a private elementary school, separate from Goodman, used by the more affluent in town to pamper their children (or rather offload them) before they were thrust into the general population for middle and high school. That practice was always rather jarring, setting up social cliques at an early age.

It was her blonde hair billowing in the breeze that caught his eye and her eyes (the color of which he couldn't see but imagined as blue), happened to be looking over in his direction. She was wearing a cheerful smile on her rosy lips, along with her purplish-blue pastel dress.

Cooper didn't know it at the time, but her name was Alyssa Noble and indeed she was the same age as he was. What he *did* know was that she was the prettiest thing he had ever seen, and he wanted to get a closer look. He started to make his way over, pushing his bike across the well-manicured grass ("Keep off the grass" signs be damned!)

It seemed to take an eternity to get there. She was already some distance away from the statue, and he grew more nervous the closer he got. Her bold features came into view.

Her eyes are *blue!*

It was the way she looked at him with through those jewels – cool, yet still warm and inviting – that kept him moving forward instead of running away like the thumping in his chest wanted. As the sun peeked out from behind the overcast sky, a fire was set in her golden hair that was simply, for lack of a better word: striking.

Cooper continued his admiration of her and that smile, his heart moving from rapid thumping to calm fluttering before it sank like a stone.

When Cooper got to the edge of Jackson Street, preparing himself to cross, a young boy marched over to Alyssa's side. Cooper had seen him many times before, mostly in passing but a few times up close. Too close. There was something about the kid that Cooper found very weird. He couldn't put a finger on it right away, but it reminded him an awful lot of his dad, especially seeing the way he put his arm around Alyssa's waist like someone much older would do.

The boy leered in Cooper's direction, his blue eyes twinkling even though the sun had been covered by clouds again. It was none other than Liam Manning, just as much of a handsome jerk then as he would be over the next ten years. Seeing those eyes look at him like goading cattle prods made Cooper mad and part of him extremely jealous.

Not jealous in a sexual way, since he was far too young for that. However, over the next few years he would hear about the birds and the bees in whispered conversations at school, the street, and even in his ear at church from one of the choirboys. It wasn't until he was fourteen that he *experienced* anything of that nature. That's when his thing, he'd told Billy one day in the softest voice imaginable, had grown stiff and about twice its regular size one night. He'd been thinking about Alyssa and so with curiosity he touched it, then grabbed it, and after a few minutes a strange feeling took over. It was like he, or more so his thing, got sick, spitting up a lot of white junk after he'd thought about actually kissing Alyssa. It scared him at first, but since it also felt good, he figured it couldn't be too bad for you. (With hindsight, and the current state of his vision, Cooper supposed there was something to what Father Ryan was saying after all, in that "doing such devilish activities will make boys go blind.")

Billy disagreed, following up with his own stories of choking chickens and spanking monkeys, all of which neglected to mention who or what he'd be thinking about.

Those fourteen-year-old teenage feelings were nothing like Cooper's eight-year-old self was experiencing as he watched Liam Manning and Alyssa Noble that hot afternoon in 2002. It was like Liam had received a ton of nice toys – not for his birthday but just because his rich daddy wanted to spoil him – and then flaunted all those toys in front of the other kids as if to say, "Look what I have and what you don't!"

It made Cooper want to punch Liam right in his fetching face, but Liam was bigger and probably much stronger than he was. Perhaps one day Cooper could follow through with that, but for now he was left to watch as...

3

Friday August 31, 2012

The school bell sounded, yanking Cooper away from his vivid memories. Looking around, Margaret had already left, as had the rest of the class. The only other person in the room was Mr. Reid, sitting at his desk like someone's grandpa, rocking away in his chair like he was on a wooden porch instead of in a humdrum high school classroom.

"Ah, I thought you had another block, Mr. Bennett," he said. "Staying behind to talk more about..."

"Oh gosh!" Cooper exclaimed, interrupting Mr. Reid as he shot to his feet. He snatched his bag off the back of the chair, its contents nearly spilling out of the undone zipper. "You're right! It... it must have slipped my mind. I better get going... I hope you have a wonderful day Mr. Reid! See you after the holiday!"

Cooper did one final check (he didn't want to risk having to come back later and be ensnared by old people stories). Once he was sure he had everything in order and that his bagged was zipped and over his shoulders, he zoomed out into the busy hallway. His clothes flapped wildly as they barely clung to his rail-like frame. "Goodbye!"

Mr. Reid was unfazed, maintaining his lethargic rocking pace. He turned his head and stole a long glance out the window.

"Kids these days," he said, licking his dry lips again, "always too busy to just relax."

"Excuse me! Hey watch where you're going!" Cooper said, his voice lost in the babble of hallway chitchat, his body bounced around like a pinball at Dip N Dog's.

Along the way, Cooper met up with his best friend, Billy Arnett, spotting him in the sea of students. He had just appeared out of a perpendicular hallway, beaming from the high he got from a more technical and science-based syllabus. Cooper was happy to see Billy in good sorts (he hated chemistry and biology with a passion), but Cooper didn't think he'd get used to the two of them having separate classes this year. Having been inseparable for years, something about that felt... final, like a nail in a coffin, and Cooper didn't want to dwell on the fact this was their last year together.

So, he didn't dwell on it one bit, and smiling in Billy's direction the gesture was returned. The two maneuvered through the swarm – people whose brains were thinking more about what they'd be doing in fifty minutes when school was out instead of right then and there – finally catching up to each other.

"These people are like zombies!" Cooper exclaimed, his thin shoulder knocked forward by a herd of students eager to get to math class.

"Um, Walkers..." Billy corrected with nerdy fervor. He was addicted to *The Walking Dead,* which he just happened to catch a month or so back. "At least that's what they're called on the show. I can't believe you haven't watched it yet."

"No TV, remember," Cooper said, and Billy's strong smile became an awkward one.

"Oh, yeah, sorry. I forgot... blame it on the biology high," Billy replied sheepishly, about to sling his heavy backpack – ladened with science books – over his shoulder.

"You're so weird," Cooper laughed, placing a reassuring arm around Billy to intercept. "Come on bud, one more class to go before we race out those front doors and into the fall!"

The two walked as best they could in the still crowded hall, and Cooper mulled over what Billy said. The ironic thing about him forgetting Cooper didn't have a television (or a mattress, or a lot of things others took for granted) was that Billy's family was just as poor, if not slightly more, than his. Cooper based that assumption on casual observations during his frequent visits.

He was on the right track. Even given Mr. Arnett's ownership of Rabun Paving, the reality was it was a lot of hard work for a negligible amount of money, not to mention contracts were getting hard to come by with increased competition from the surrounding area. By the time Mr. Arnett's employees were paid, the company's recurring expenses (rent, utilities, etc.) addressed, and the litany of taxes, insurance, and healthcare premiums withdrawn, there wasn't much left at all. Certainly not enough to afford a better house (and a mortgage) in a nicer, more southern part of town (where more taxes would be waiting).

Cooper slid his arm off Billy's shoulder, stretched, then used both hands to adjust his backpack.

"Maybe I'll be able to catch up on those episodes with you a bit over the weekend?" Cooper suggested. "I'm sure you have all the DVDs to date."

Billy beamed.

"You bet your ass I do! I did some extra yard work for the neighbors, and even helped Mr. Schneck for the cash. It'd be awesome if you could, but only if you have the time…"

What else am I going to do? Cooper thought. *Hang with the ol' man and enjoy getting tenderized like a steak for the grill?*

Of course, he didn't say anything of the sort out loud. Instead, he told Billy: "If there was anyone I'd love to hang with over the long weekend, it's you."

Billy perked up; he'd been slouching before. Standing a little taller than Cooper, he was also bigger in that "I do manual labor for my chores" kind of way. Perhaps if Cooper had inherited a fraction of those genetics, he'd be able to combat the unfortunate conditions he faced at home. Regardless, their mutual stresses were a key factor in helping the two boys bond over time.

Billy took to rifling through his jeans pockets, looking for change so they could stop by Kimmy's Donuts after school. The *clink* of quarters as Billy counted up reminded Cooper of his dad's tendency to deliver bruises instead of cash for an allowance. Then Cooper shuddered, realizing he hadn't yet been paid for the week, and the lingering pain from last week's compensation flared up.

Billy glanced over as Cooper rubbed his arm, noticing a large bruise sitting about halfway between Cooper's elbow and shoulder. It was mottled blue and yellow in color; not the first Billy had seen but definitely the freshest.

"Coop, you're eighteen now... why don't you just leave?"

"I... wouldn't have anywhere to go," Cooper said, his eyes restrained but desperate.

Billy stopped mid-stride.

"You've got our place."

Cooper was tempted to say yes, but would end up telling Billy that he didn't want to impose, since the space in their trailer was already tight. The real reason he didn't want to go: fear. Fear that his dad, in some kind of crazy rage, would come calling and possibly hurt Billy and his folks for helping. Cooper couldn't expose them to such a risk, or live with himself if something were to happen.

"Besides, I think I'd have to go further than your place to get away, Billy," Cooper said, "and leaving Goodman behind is too much to think about."

"We'll all be going our separate ways once college hits," Billy said sadly.

That weird feeling of finality came back.

"That may be true," Cooper muttered, "but like I said, let's not think about that just yet. Graduation's still months away, so let's make the most out of our time now."

Billy nodded, and turning down another hall he wasted no time resuming his jabber about zombies (*new episodes coming in October!*)

Despite his words to the contrary, Cooper was still thinking about the end of the year. His mind fell back to Alyssa and then, like a jab from Pops right in the guts, he realized how much time had passed and how distant he'd remained.

"Maybe I should ask her to the prom?"

A few words spilled out of Billy before he realized Cooper had spoken. A couple more before he'd processed what he said.

"Prom?" Billy asked, quite puzzled. "I thought we weren't thinking about that. Who are you talking about anyway?"

"Alyssa Noble," he replied, his tone of voice saying *as if there would be anyone else.*

Billy let out a tremendous, snorting laugh, unable to hold any of it back.

Cooper pouted when he heard it, then thumped Billy's shoulder. The lighthearted plan didn't go as intended, Billy tumbling backwards under the weight of his bag... right into a couple girls who'd been leaning on a bank of lockers.

Oh shit...

"Alyssa!" Cooper exclaimed, realizing one of the girls was her. He hoped – no he prayed – that she wasn't hurt.

Alyssa had been talking to one of her friends, teasing her light and silky hair between those slender fingers when Billy came crashing into her. She wasn't hurt, and much to Cooper's surprise she didn't look upset at being interrupted. The same couldn't be said for the other girl though; her face was so creased it looked like a puce baseball mitt. Alyssa giggled as Billy staggered away embarrassed. Her creamy skin aglow, lightly smattered with the faintest freckles, she sent a warm smile from her rosy lips to Cooper. It was exactly like the one she wore back when he'd first laid eyes on her ten years ago.

Relieved and blushing, Cooper smiled back.

That's when a hand came racing toward his face, sudden and unexpected. Cooper jerked his head back in time for it to miss, Liam Manning's open palm whooshing by in slow motion until his skin slapped against the lockers, snapping time back to normal speed.

The star football player bore a smug look, his hand starting to swell up larger than his...

"Dickhead!" Liam shouted, eyes alive with an unbridled temper. "How many times do I have to tell you, you little shit, to keep your scrawny eyes off *my* girl?"

"I'm not your property, Liam," Alyssa snipped before Cooper could reply.

Liam gave her an intense side glance and she recoiled. Looking to Cooper with worry, her pulse was visible in her neck.

"No you're not," Liam told her softly, "but that doesn't mean you aren't *mine...*"

Liam moved his hand from the lockers to Cooper's chest, his rough fingers slowly closing around Cooper's tee before yanking the fabric – and the boy – toward him.

Billy tried to step forward, but two of Liam's best ass-kissing goons moved in. Blocking the way, their strong hands came down on Billy's shoulders, locking him in place.

Mark Brown was one of them. A decent-looking kid who didn't *appear* to be a troublemaker, he was lanky and one of the tallest people at Goodman High, possibly the whole town. The only other person Cooper knew that was taller happened to be a large man with an equally large beard he'd spotted at Castillo's from time to time. He hadn't seen him in almost a year though, so assumed the beastly man must have moved – or at least found better pizza elsewhere.

Derek Wilder was the other boy. Known for being slightly crazed (easily living up to his nickname Wild Wilder), he was built like a locomotive. Derek could have been halfway attractive with his mocha skin and curly top fade resembling smoke from a stack, but his very yellow teeth canceled everything. They were decayed like old railway ties.

"Aw, is your little bitch-boy trying to help?" Liam's voice was a mocking falsetto, breath hot and minty as it blew across Cooper's face. "You're so weak *Coopie* that it's pathetic. What's the matter, don't have anything to say – cat got your tongue?"

No, the cat doesn't have my tongue, Liam, but if it did, I'd recommend it take lessons from your goons since they have such a firm hold of your nut sack.

Liam continued to mock Cooper, and with each of his subsequent taunts, Cooper felt emotion swelling in his chest. It wasn't the chicken-heartedness he normally had, or anger. It was courage... actual courage! Not enough to challenge Liam outright, but sufficient to ignore him *and* blurt out his invitation.

"Alyssa, would you like to go to the prom with me?"

Her concern turned to flattery and a smile came back to her lips.

Then Alyssa's friends started to laugh at Cooper's absurd request. *No way she would ever tell that loser yes*, the gaggle of laughter said.

Cooper didn't care about the laughs directed his way, knowing Liam had to be seething at the thought of *his* girl being hit on by a scrawny nerd in front of the whole damn school. The fact Cooper was that scrawny nerd filled him with even more spirit.

Liam shoved Cooper into the lockers, rearing back his free arm. The next punch was locked and loaded.

This was a familiar view for Cooper, one nobody should get used to but it was something he had seen far too often at home by the time he was three. The fist came barreling at him again, then – as if guided by instinct – Cooper jerked himself out of the way for a second time.

Liam struck the hard metal. There was a loud *clang* but no scream, and judging by the blank expression on his face, pain had not yet reached his brain.

Surrounding students let out gasps and shrieks on his behalf, some with their mouths agape in shock, others shutting their eyes tight after seeing Liam's fingers crumpled like paper. A large dent remained in the locker.

Mark and Derek had been laughing before, cheering on their boss. Now that he was hurt, they were just gawking, and in their stupor, had let Billy go.

Cooper didn't waste the opportunity with everyone distracted. Heart beating excitedly, he pulled double duty; continuing his conversation with Alyssa while working himself free.

"You didn't answer my question," Cooper said to her.

"Probably because it's awfully early to be asking about the summer just before Labor Day!" she replied with a promising tone.

"You can never be too prepared."

"True," she replied, eyes flicking between Liam, still nursing his injured hand, and Cooper, nearly loose of the other one. "But a lot can happen between now and then. I mean who knows if we'll still be friends by then…"

Cooper wondered if he heard her correctly; there was *no* way she actually considered themselves friends, right? Then, as if to say, "of course she does you idiot," he was free.

"Oh, that won't be a problem for me," Cooper replied, but Alyssa didn't look as happy as he would have expected. She looked dismayed.

"Oh, I think it's going to be a *major* problem for you..."

Cooper didn't need to look around to know that it was Liam talking, majorly pissed off.

"I don't know how you plan on still being friends if you're DEAD!" he snarled.

Another swing shot toward Cooper. Deftly, he dodged it and Liam overbalanced, meeting the glossy floor face-first.

Some of the crowd, formerly aghast, began laughing again, but not at Cooper this time. No, they were chuckling at *Liam's* expense. It was like karma had come home to roost, at least for a short time.

Cooper shot down the hall like a bullet, waving at Alyssa the entire time.

She said yes!

Discreetly, she raised a waving hand back at him.

Oh my God she actually said yes!

Billy would probably tell him that technically she hadn't answered either way, but the fact her answer did not include "gross," "get lost," or anything remotely sounding like a "no" fueled Cooper's feet as they tapped merrily down the hall.

Speaking of Billy, he was already waiting outside the classroom door when Cooper got there. The class bell rang seconds later, its sound overcoming the raucous laughter still going on down the hall.

CHAPTER 4: BEST FRIENDS WITH BILLY ARNETT

1

An exit door on the southern side of the school burst open, both Billy and Cooper escaping the confines of the cold hallway into the warm afternoon air. Billy was thankful, today more than ever, that their AP math class was far from whatever block Liam Manning and his boorish sidekicks were taking.

He's probably at the school nurse or the hospital by now, anyway, Billy thought, though he maintained a high level of caution.

Liam's injures were the worst he'd seen at school since Marcus Cole, a junior, lost his front two teeth and lodged a third deep inside his torn lips last November. Marcus asserted that he'd fallen on some icy steps in front of school, the claim causing a lot of problems for Mr. Simmons, who was in charge of the school's custodial services at the time. Billy knew in his gut, especially since there was no ice until at least January, that Mr. Simmons was a scapegoat. Marcus probably *did* fall down the steps in front of school, but he was certainly helped on that trip by a certain quarterback who always seemed to get away with too much.

Neither Cooper nor Billy had cars, so on any normal day they would have taken the school bus closer to home, yet after that day's events thought better of it. Liam was cunning and even though he might have been undergoing medical treatment, Billy wouldn't put it past him to have set up some kind of ambush. Shielded by the throng of students pouring out of the hideous red-bricked building like cheerful ants from a mound, Billy led Cooper southeast past the band room and tennis courts. Archery Park and its array of practice targets was to their left and Wolf's Ridge Greenway, a long walking trail used by hikers and joggers, snaked its way through the woods further to the east.

"I don't think we'll need go too much further down," Cooper said as they reached a small picnic area set beneath a pavilion.

Billy agreed.

After taking a few seconds to look around, he started to walk back west. The two reached, then crossed over Georgia 246 a short time later, continuing towards the downtown area along Hanlon Road. They planned to go to public library first, knocking out their one and only assignment from Mrs. Sanderson so it wouldn't be looming overhead like a depressing cloud the whole weekend.

"I can't believe she gave us work to do," Cooper said, kicking a small piece of trash out of his way.

"I can. You know she's the most unrelenting teacher prowling Goodman High," Billy said, going on to mention that he'd found out she was due to retire after they graduated.

"She probably stayed on just to torment us, then," Cooper said, remembering her intimidating stares from their freshman year as if it were yesterday.

"At least future generations will be free of the Sanderson Stare," Billy replied, shuddering. "Besides, this assignment isn't all too bad. With both of us working, it shouldn't take but an hour I think."

Billy slid his hands along the straps of his backpack before popping them in the pockets of his thrift store jeans. Looking around, he was always amazed by how quickly the monetary landscape of Goodman changed. It was most noticeable when walking along the sidewalks of Hanlon Road, middle-class houses and stores lining both sides of the streets beneath rows of old maples and oaks. When looking along the north-south cross streets, things to the south things stayed the same more or less, but to the north the financial gap widened, transitioning to lower-than-low class within a block or two. It was exceptionally bad when heading north on Center and Sullivan Streets. As fate would have it, that was the way to Billy's home.

Living up on that end of town made Billy feel ashamed, even when around Cooper who was in no position to judge (nor ever would). It was a personal issue that he struggled with – nearly every day – and more times than he cared to admit, it won, leading to stretches of depression and anxiety. Those feelings were made worse when face to face with Liam, who Billy knew deep down could do whatever he wanted and never get the punishment he deserved. Daddy-Manning bucks were aplenty and always there to buy his way out of trouble, trouble that would land someone as low on the totem pole as Billy Arnett directly in the county jail. Do not pass go, do not collect two hundred dollars. Thankfully, even though the despair was harsh and frequent, it never lasted. Billy had enough gumption to send it away while he focused on classes with the goal to get out of dire straits. Out of Goodman for good.

Billy was leading the way and as the two reached the intersection of Sullivan and Hanlon, he was really tempted to forgo the school assignment and stay on the road... Castillo's and Kimmy's were only a few blocks up ahead. His stomach agreed.

While Billy was busy debating with himself, Cooper had already made a left turn, heading south.

"Hey, come on," he said over his shoulder like a dog owner would to a puppy, "after you spent nearly all of math class convincing me to do this damn assignment first, you're not backing out of it."

But it'd be for pizza and donuts, Coop! Billy thought, successfully justifying it to himself.

Yet Cooper didn't stop.

"Seriously, come on Billy!" he called again.

Grumbling out loud instead of arguing, Billy fell in behind and they walked a couple more blocks. On the left was a curved bank of glass bricks making up an entire wall of Mack and Montgomery's, one of four law firms that had popped up around the downtown, and the only one with women as partners. (No representation is made that the quality of legal services provided by Mack and Montgomery are better than the quality of legal services performed by the other three misogynistic firms combined.)

Billy reached out to touch it, like he did habitually every time he'd pass by. The rough surface was deceptively smooth – the coarse part of the design sandwiched between two panes of smooth glass. As his fingers swept over it, his eyes were already ahead of Cooper, looking across Hooper Road toward the disheveled two-story façade of the Goodman News Courier. There was a large sign with big black letters stuck to the downstairs window with blue painter's tape. UNDERGOING RENOVATIONS, it said and Billy counted on his left hand the number of previous times the building had undergone extensive work. This time things looked more permanent though, as if the place was about to breathe its last newspapery breath.

While turning his attention back to Cooper, something caught Billy's attention. It was off to the right in a narrow alley, which was darker than the surrounds and overflowing with heaps of rubble and sprigs of weeds. Amidst the trash was a sharp piece of metal glinting in a thin beam of sunlight. The pinprick of light twinkled in Billy's eyes, reminding him of…

2

Saturday October 31, 2005

… sunlight dancing across his face as Derek Wilder's big head bobbed maniacally overhead in that very same alley seven years earlier.

Billy was cringing at the far end of the passageway, getting mercilessly punched and kicked by a pair of stinking, shit-caked Pumas.

"Softer..." Derek muttered. His dark eyes flickered oddly blue, hypnotized by thumping sounds against red, jiggling flesh.

"Stop it!" Billy shouted, shielding his face from attack. The maroon bricks were weeping with something rancid. The walls seemed to close in around him. "Get away from me! Stop!"

Derek did not listen.

"Softer... must... be... softer..." The pauses between words were drawn out in long, raspy breaths.

What does he mean by that? Just make it stop! God please... make it stop!

Billy would remember the eerie way Derek repeated those words with a wanton yet deadpan expression, over and over like a mantra. Even as he reflected on it so many years later, the memory would still send shivers down his spine.

Billy was grabbed, Derek's grip tight on his forearm. It hurt, the pressure nearly snapping the limb in two.

No! No! No!

"Soften... the... MEAT!"

Please God don't let him get closer!

"GET OFF ME!" Billy was now screaming at the top of his lungs. His eyes were wide with terror and his nostrils curled in disgust. "Help! HELP!"

Looking toward the mouth of the alley, Billy couldn't see a soul. Nobody was walking by that Saturday afternoon. Where were they?

I'm alone... all alone!

It was like he was trapped in a nightmare, the only thing he could feel – apart from the great pressure on his arm – were the beats of his heart pounding in his throat.

I'm going to die alone...

"Meat..." Derek began drooling slightly, adding a gurgle to his words. His gnashing teeth drew closer.

Billy started to cry. He was covered with smears, a large brown swipe across his cheek stopping a hairsbreadth away from his upper lip and chunky, footprint-shaped stamps all across his stomach. His guts heaved at the smell. His tears cut a path through the rank gunk. His strength, along with any chance for freedom, fled.

It was like Derek was trying to bite Billy that Halloween afternoon. No, as those teeth bared once more it was more like the eleven-year-old was trying to *eat* him.

"Okay, okay, I've learned my lesson," Billy said, pleading, grabbing at something... anything to make it stop.

Surely Derek was just embellishing his rounds of ass-beatings with this zombie vibe because it was Halloween, trying to get a little extra shit leaking out of fearful kid's assholes.

Yeah, that has to be it! This is a joke! Joke's on Billy Arnett again!

Regardless of Derek's intent, Billy wished it all would stop.

But Derek was only getting worse. His eyes were glazed with starving purpose and were piercing blue at certain angles. Billy had seen Derek up close many times over the years and his stare had always been the darkest green. But today they were blue and cold as ice.

"They better to see you with!" Derek said like some nightmarish version of *Little Red Riding Hood* come to life in that narrow alley in Goodman.

Then he started drooling profusely between those crooked yellow boxes in his mouth. It wasn't clear spittle like a normal person, but a river of dingy, almost creamy goo that had the odor of festering boils. It hung in long strands, grotesquely herky-jerky.

Billy's stomach lurched again as Derek *smiled* at him. His teeth had become huge and sharp. The hand still grabbing squeezing like one checks the ripeness of fruit.

"You're ready now. Time to EAT, kid!"

Billy wanted to scream, but the sounds were stuck behind the heartbeat in his throat.

Derek let out his own noises. They were like a series of eerie howls. His mouth hung open like a monster, and Billy tried to pretend it wasn't wide enough for his whole head to fit inside. That's when Derek's dark shadow – the final curtain – loomed overhead, and at last a horrific scream managed to escape.

"NO!"

Before Derek's jaws clamped shut, something struck him in the back.

Billy didn't want to take his eyes off his attacker, but they slid around and saw a young boy, rail thin, wearing some of the thickest glasses Billy had ever seen. The boy was wielding a thick piece of scrap wood that was better than half the size of him. He must have he found it on the street; there was a lot of scrap around these parts – wood near the multitude of stores undergoing renovation, rocks and bricks closer to home at Billy's dad's paving business. Billy could have done some serious damage with a rock…

The boy reared the scrap wood back and with a shout hit Derek again. Though he barely flinched, Derek redirected his attention that time, pouncing at the new target. He slashed at the boys' white tee shirt, cutting it with what must've been a knife.

No, he's not wielding one, Billy thought, but didn't have time to think on it again before the boy was knocked hard to the ground. Billy desperately looked around, spotting a metal pipe that was leaning loosely away from the opposing wall.

A quick tug could free that...

He moved with speed and purpose, wrapping both of his trash-juice and sweat covered hands around the metal cylinder. After the first pull, Billy lost his slick grip. After the second, with a better hold, the pipe groaned and began to give. By the third, the heavy section was free. Slapping it in his palm like a baseball bat, Billy turned and moved for Derek, just as the young boy reached into his skinny jeans pocket.

The next events happened so fast that had either of the boys blinked, they'd have missed them.

Billy pulled out every ounce of strength still in him, lifting the pipe above his head before bringing it down across Derek Wilder's back. The force of impact was so strong it also sent Billy falling backwards onto his ass.

Derek overbalanced, collapsing headfirst in a strange dance. He stretched out an arm to brace himself, the other moving to a defensive position across his face.

The thin boy had plucked out a little knife and Derek was heading right for it. Without delay, the boy slashed, sending a sharp line of silver across Derek's dark forearm. There was blood and it smoldered.

How is a wound... smoking? Billy's mind desperately sought for logic

85

where some should be.

Derek's shrieks cut through so loudly you'd think he'd been stabbed multiple times instead of with a single swipe. It sounded like he had two voices at one point, strange and discordant. It was off-putting, another thing that could haunt even the sanest person's dreams for years to come.

Tumbling briefly to one knee, Derek crawled a few feet before scrambling upright, kicking up dust as he tore away without so much as another word or even a look back. He was holding his bleeding arm tightly, blood splattering the pavement all the way to the mouth of the alley. Each drop steamed for a few seconds, then stopped. He was gone.

The thin boy walked up to Billy, extending a hand to help him off the ground. It didn't look like he'd be capable of pulling up Billy's weight, but he managed.

"Thank you," Billy said, now shaking the hand that pulled him up.

"No problem," the boy replied, dusting Billy off. "But geez, what kind of drugs was that kid on? He looked sort of familiar. Did you know him?"

"Sadly, yeah," Billy said, remembering all the past instances of bullying.

"Well, my name's Cooper," the thin boy said. "Cooper Bennett."

Cooper sounds like a dog's name, Billy thought, but figured it was better not to insult the boy who'd probably just saved his life.

Instead, Billy breathed a deep sigh of relief, smiled, and said, "Thanks Coop! Pleasure to meet you. My name's..."

3

Friday August 31, 2012

"Billy!" Cooper called, snapping his fingers a few times with no effect. "Hello? Earth to Billy Arnett! Hello?"

Something about the last snap close to Billy's face did it and he blinked a few times, looking like he'd been on a long journey.

"I'm so sorry!" he said. "Something must have come over me."

"I couldn't tell one bit," Cooper said sarcastically. "What were you thinking about, anyway?"

Billy was still looking across Hooper Road at the alley. The sun might have disappeared behind a cloud, but things seemed brighter than before.

"Old times," Billy replied. "It was back on the day we first met..."

Cooper was quiet. Billy fell that way, too. They hadn't talked about the events of that Halloween for nearly as many days it was in the past. It was almost like their minds had locked those events behind a wall, for what purpose Billy had no idea, but that flicker was like a key that unleashed it.

I wonder what else might be tossed away in the dark corners of my mind...

There was that shudder down Billy's spine, right on queue.

Soften... the... meat...

Trying his best to shake it off, Billy looked over to Cooper, who had taken up position by his side. He had a couple of items in his hands.

"Now's as good a time as any," Cooper said, immediately handing them over.

"Are... these for me?" Billy asked, and the corners of his wide eyes sparkled in the afternoon sun. There was a pair of plain sunglasses and black and white bandana in his shaking hands.

"Yup!"

"Oh wow, thanks, Coop!" Billy replied, leaning against the glass wall of the law office.

Cooper chuckled, watching his friend's mad rush to put on the headband like a kid that was ten years younger. Billy's thick fingers struggled to tie off the folded strip of fabric, hemming and hawing.

Glancing across the street once again, his face irritable, Billy didn't look to the rubble – something else seized his attention. It was Mr. Bradley Kensington, owner of the *Courier*, who had appeared in an upper floor window. He was staring keenly, those permanently squinting eyes (from a combination, both his doctor and pharmacist would say, of old age, poor vision, and never-ending bouts of constipation) checking to see if the boys were doing anything interesting. Sadly, they were just being senior high school boys – the boring type that didn't like to cause a commotion or do anything newsworthy. Kensington wished, as he peered through the dust-coated window, that they were more like that Manning kid.

Billy's dad had mentioned one day that the *Courier* was on the verge of closing, holding on stubbornly against the tide of online news sources because old-fashioned places like Goodman clung to tradition like shit to a shovel, and people (well over sixty years old Mr. Arnett supposed) were still buying enough to keep the place afloat, though leaks in the hull were evident and the large sign in the window would not be enough to save the sinking ship.

Secretly, Kensington hoped that one of the boys – preferably the bigger one wearing that gang-ish bandanna – would vandalize the eyesore that was the law firm's exterior. That would bring the police, force the blemish those two snooty bitches owned to be redecorated, and generate a meaty story full of the kind of juicy stuff that sent papers flying off the stands. Recent weeks had been quiet – too quiet – and most people around town thought that was a good thing. Perfect, crime-free Goodman maintaining itself as a pinnacle of society, showing how tradition could triumph over change.

But Kensington knew in his old bones that the silence meant a whopper of a story was lurking just beneath the surface, ready to spring itself on the town. It'd happened before, not in Goodman (though there were a couple of instances that popped up before the 1950s), but over in Big Stone Gap, Virginia back in 2010. After a time of serenity and quiet, the town suddenly went up in flames, large sections of it reduced to smoldering ash while the entirety of Wallen's Ridge State Prison collapsed into a giant sinkhole.

"At last!" Billy exclaimed, finally able to tie off the bandana. Using the sunglasses, he checked his reflection and found that tears had spilled down his cheeks, framing his quivering smile.

Cooper smiled back much more securely.

Would it matter to Billy if he knew those glasses were some cheap knock-off Cooper had spent three bucks on from some store display? No. Just like it didn't matter the headband was Cooper's dad's (though Billy might have felt guilty of the hurt Cooper would get for that later.) All that mattered was that he had a good friend like Cooper – his only friend. Moments like these were not locked behind mental walls or cages, kept in darkness like the Halloween of 2005. They were brought out to be enjoyed beneath the afternoon sun on a warm August day, where people like Billy Arnett could remember them for the rest of their lives.

4

As Billy predicted, they only needed an hour to finish their assignment at Goodman Public Library. Leaving the large monochrome building, boxy like the books inside, the two boys walked along Center Street. The scenery shifted as they continued up the gradual slope, stopping along the way to snag a couple of donuts with the loose change Billy had counted earlier. Things transitioned out of middle class pretty quickly after that, becoming borderline slummy when they reached Cherry Lane a mile and a half north of the library. It might as well have been the distance between the Earth and moon with how different Goodman felt on that end of town, even the sidewalks seeming to give up and sag.

It was less dense up on that end of town, the homes and businesses spread further apart. That left a lot more room for junk to occupy, filling the poorly maintained spaces.

They got to Billy's trailer just before five o'clock. It was situated on the corner of Cherry Lane and Grove Road, just past a long and wobbly privacy fence that didn't stop the neighbor's two Rottweilers from barking at everything that passed by. A single-wide unit made of gray aluminum, there were maroon accents painted along its edges. Air conditioning units jutted out from various windows and a ragged porch, about the same width as the trailer, had been added. It ran a third of the way down the front, giving the place a homier feel. Despite all those improvements, Billy glanced

91

embarrassingly at his un-improvable home, then down the street where the chain link gate to family business was open.

Walking over gravel and sparse grassy patches, Billy went up the creaking wood stairs. First to shed his backpack, it dropped to the timber with a heavy *thud*. With it went the encumbered feeling of school, replaced with one of freedom, though it was quick like a swift breeze.

Cooper followed suit a few seconds later and both boys plunked their butts down on a worn, but surprisingly comfortable couch. Propping his feet up on a makeshift ottoman (sparing no expense by using an upturned bucket from the hardware store), Cooper folded his arms behind his head, closed his eyes, and relaxed in the silence of a yell-free zone.

Billy was also leaning back on the couch, his eyes still open. He'd been thinking about Cooper and the new gifts he'd received. Removing the sunglasses, Billy turned them in his hands and then stared at his reflection for a while – lost in thoughts about friendship, the future, and home.

"You should relax a bit," Cooper said, one of his eyes popped open. Nearly half an hour had gone by since they'd gotten there.

"I'm trying to," Billy answered, unsure why he couldn't just unplug himself today. Maybe it was because he got these gifts – nice and unprompted – or maybe it was the fact he had bought so many DVDs with the money he'd saved and felt guilty about not spending any of it on Cooper.

Cooper could tell something was up.

"You know, friendship isn't based on the things we buy for each other, Billy. It's based on the more intangible things we get from it... like how one feels when around their buddies."

"In my case *buddy*," said Billy, holding up a single finger.

"So?" Cooper was quick to say. "Quality over quantity any day of the week. I think you ended up with one of the bestest around."

"You're right," he replied, chuckling. "I just don't see what I have to offer anyone. I'm just lowly me..."

"Well I have to take back what I said now," Cooper replied. Billy looked confused. "You didn't end up with the best friend around... I did. What you just said right there, my friend, tells me that you have no motivation to be anyone besides yourself. *That* is the hallmark of someone you definitely want to have around in your life. Count me blessed."

Billy was smiling, barely able to hold on to his emotions.

Jesus, if you cry again today William it's going to be the first time in history that someone kicks their own ass!

Cooper laughed a little before his face drew down like the sun. It was hovering above a sparse line of trees and buildings to the west, the faintest hints of orange taking over the sky.

"Hey, do you know what time it is?" he asked, Billy telling him about

93

a quarter to six. "Damn," Cooper continued, dejected, "I better start making my way back to the house."

"Hey, this may seem last minute, but you could always stick around for dinner."

"I don't want to put your folks out."

"Nah, it won't," Billy persisted. "Besides, Mom will make sure you're filled right up! She's always happy for a chance to show off her cooking skills."

Cooper couldn't disagree, Billy's mother was an ace with the stove, her talents in home-cooking unparalleled even by some of the five star eateries in Goodman and the tri cities.

"You'll be home by seven-thirty at the latest, I promise. We can start watching a few of those episodes tomorrow," Billy suggested. When Cooper still seemed hesitant, he switched into an alluring tone of voice. "We're having roast beef..."

Cooper got up from the couch, taking a couple of steps forward. He leaned his forearms against the railing, air sputtering between his lips.

Billy waited for an answer.

"Roast beef you say?" Cooper asked just as his stomach growled.

5

The inside of Billy's trailer was compact, but felt less cramped than an eighteen by ninety-foot rectangle should. That was more to do with Mr. Arnett's tendency to keep things well-organized and clutter-free, along with Mrs. Arnett's keen eye for dust, than anything Billy contributed. His room, after all, was the untidiest part in the place.

Upon entering, one was greeted with a well-furnished living area. Carpeted in beige there were cozy seats, a low coffee table, and decorative lamps perched on matching end tables. To the right was the master bedroom, its door normally closed when visitors were there. Billy's bedroom was on the other end of the trailer (the DANGER ZONE, according to a traffic sign mounted to that door). Right outside his room was the household bathroom, shared by all three but occupied mostly by Billy – his appetite fueling those all-too-frequent visits to the porcelain god.

The only places left in the trailer were the kitchen and dining room, appropriately together at the center of the trailer – its heart. The family would spend most of its time together there, all their important celebrations and life-changing decisions – good, bad, and ugly – made in that neat, square space.

Small and made from an octagonal piece of dark wood, the dining room table saw Billy's dad sitting there for hours at a time filing taxes and paperwork, his mother had wept there for days after losing their second child and would cut Billy slices of chocolate cake each birthday up to his sixteenth. As for Billy, he'd often be there doing his homework or reading a comic book. On days in past years when he would be an ornery little shit (Mrs. Arnett far too polite to *say* things like that, but that didn't stop her from *thinking* them), his mom would gently let it slip that he might have been conceived on that very table, changing the location depending on which chair he was occupying at the time.

That evening, they were all enjoying a well-cooked meal at the table with their guest, the smell of roast beef, green beans, and mashed potatoes filling the air and their hearts.

"Thank you so much Mrs. Arnett," Cooper said, pushing away the empty plate that had seen two helpings come and go. "That was delicious."

Nodding gracefully, Brenda Arnett could see the happiness in Cooper's face, bringing some to her own. Voracious teenage appetites aside, her mother's intuition told her Cooper hadn't eaten that well in quite some time and – she was admittedly supposing here – that he felt more at home with them than his own father.

The wretched bastard, Roland Bennett, she would think whenever she saw Cooper, but never say aloud.

Cooper Bennett had turned out nothing like his father (thank God) and over the years had evolved into a surrogate brother to Billy. That part was abundantly clear, yet a long look in her eyes would indicate there was another piece, something niggling that she kept locked away. She thought, again with intuition, that Billy might feel *more* than brotherly love for Cooper. Not that it would have mattered to her one bit (her one and only son would be that for all her life), but it was the actions of others against her treasured boy that she feared.

She wasn't keeping it from her husband because he belonged in that category, either. No, Branson was the furthest thing from it. He might come across as conservative and macho at times, but that was mainly due to his appearance and preconceived notions of men with said appearance rather than the actual man he was. Mr. Arnett had always been loving and understanding, especially when it came to his wife and his son. The reason she didn't tell him was to keep him sane. He had enough stress going on at work, trying to keep meals like they were enjoying that night on the table. So, she kept trivial little things to herself, facing those *other* people in town who claimed to be loving and charitable when in fact they just wore it as a badge, often doubling as a mask. They would show their true, leprous faces to things they did not love nor care about, because it was far easier to dismiss and lob hatred at things than accept it.

Scum of the Earth, Mrs. Arnett would think, and in many cases not have any issues saying right to their faces.

Despite her meandering thoughts, dinner proceed pleasantly and there were a lot of laughs (mainly at Billy's expense). Through it all, Cooper kept glancing over to a fat chicken-shaped clock that was mounted above the sink. Mrs. Arnett thought he seemed nervous, especially when he couldn't go a full minute before looking at it again. Looking herself, it was just past six-thirty.

"It appears we've reached the best part of the meal!" she said, examining everyone's bare plates and the nearly empty serving dishes. "Dessert then?"

Though she said it in the form of a question, if anyone was going to say no they would have stood no chance – her beaming grin evaporated those silly notions. Everyone at the table nodded, even Cooper, after taking one last look at the clock.

Mrs. Arnett stood up, humming *You Are My Sunshine* as she collected their dirty plates, returning a moment later to clear away the glass serving dishes.

"You okay?" Billy asked Cooper, who was fidgeting in his seat.

His eyes weren't on the clock, instead looking over to his bruised arm.

"Hmm? Yeah, I'm okay," Cooper said. "It just itches."

He scratched at it, stopping when Billy's mom returned. She was carrying three plates: two scoops of vanilla ice cream melting like molten sin on top of the thick slices of pecan pie.

"Here you go dear," she said to Cooper, gingerly putting the plate down on the placement in front of him.

The wrinkled sleeve of his tee shirt caught her attention as she withdrew her arm. Cooper's bruise was clear as day.

Billy noticed his mom and gently tapped the side of Cooper's foot with his own beneath the table. Cooper turned his head and saw Billy nod in the sleeve's direction. He quickly straightened the fabric before yanking it down, slowly returning to his former position.

But Mrs. Arnett had already seen it, her expression, at first, dismissive – like it was a typical boy-bruise from horseplay. However, once she sat down she continued to ponder...

That bastard Roland Bennett.

... she wondered why a random horseplay bruise would be shaped like anything other than a random blob. Cooper's was in the loose shape of a hand, like someone had grabbed him hard like a vice.

She leaned toward Branson, whispering something to her husband. Her voice was deliberately low so the boys could not hear what she said.

Mr. Arnett's kind, brown eyes never left Cooper as she spoke, even when he rested his arm on the table. He lifted his stout and hairy forearm as she wrapped up, resting a hand in his bushy beard once she'd finished.

"Son," he said, Billy immediately looking at him.

He noticed that his dad was not speaking to him, so he nudged Cooper again under the table, tilting his head this time in his dad's direction.

Cooper's eyes followed, crossing Mr. Arnett's coveralls before getting locked in his stare. It was still kind like before, but an underlying fire was burning.

"Son," he repeated, confirming that Cooper was looking in the right place. "I just want you to know that if you need a place to stay, you are welcome to stay here."

Billy shrank back into his seat. Hearing his dad offer the very same thing to Cooper that he had earlier at school was overwhelming.

Mrs. Arnett bobbed her head approvingly, sending Cooper shrinking into his seat as well. He glanced again to his arm, extremely tempted by their offer, and tried not to cry.

Mr. Arnett was so much the dad Cooper wanted to have in his life (even Billy had no idea the weight that statement carried) and given a fair fight, if things came to that, he could hold his own. Mr. Arnett was bigger than Cooper's father, stronger too from a life of handling asphalt, concrete, and masonry. But then the fear came back and Cooper sank even further in the chair, so far that his back started squeezing through its gaps. The question that entered his mind hit him, ironically, like a ton of bricks before sending him into a silent, but brief, state of depression.

When was Pops ever fair?

With unsympathetic reality dumping on him, along with a brief flash of his dad's shotgun, Cooper stabbed the first bite of homemade pie with his fork. He used the soft piece to mop up pools of melted ice cream from his plate. Popping it in his mouth, it tasted like home. Home as it should be.

"I really appreciate the pie, Mrs. Arnett," Cooper said, feeling all eyes on him. His voice crackled. "But as much I want to stay here... I can't."

Chapter 5: The Darkness Returns

1

A large and fine house sat proudly on a neatly trimmed lawn framed with flowering gardens of lilies and rose. Its solid gray stone basked in the warm hue of an oncoming sunset. It was serene.

Grayson Manning wished the same could be said of him, seated inside his office with a few beads of nervous sweat clinging to his brow. His human form was that of an attractive, middle-aged man – almost regal in appearance and mannerisms. Hair, white as fresh snow, rested on top of his head in a stylish forty-five-dollar cut and filled his beard with softness that his fingers often found comfort in caressing. This evening, they were doing just that.

The room itself was decorated with grand wood paneling, a large stone fireplace off to the side. Antiques were placed on the mantle and displayed on surrounding shelves. Paintings had been mounted all along the walls like a jigsaw puzzle, lending an air of history to the space; one of depth and austerity.

"Sir," came a voice over hidden speakers mounted in the ceiling. "Your appointment has arrived."

"Thank you Fridolf," Grayson replied, fingers now raking his beard.

Turning away from his Cherrywood desk, Grayson looked out one of the arched windows from his leather chair, his piercing blue eyes following a muddy utility vehicle – used by Toluca Springs park rangers – as it pulled into the gated yard.

I hope this is some kind of mistake, he thought as the ironwork closed. Then, rising slowly, he sighed. *But something tells me it won't be.*

Leaving the office, Grayson hurried down a wide hallway. Patent leather dress shoes echoed off the polished marble floor while their ombré effect caught light off scrolled wall sconces. Entering the foyer – a large set of neo gothic wood doors ahead, an equally majestic double staircase behind – Grayson tried to brush out some of the fine wrinkles that had worked their way into the fabric of his blue suit.

Fridolf emerged from a parlor to the left. He was a youngish man with slicked back hair, clothed in a tailored custom black suit with faint skull-patterned lapels. He hastened to the front door, looking back to Grayson.

The old man nodded. Fridolf opened the door.

Standing in the rectangular frame was a gruff forest ranger with a satchel slung over one shoulder and a black plastic bag in the other. Grayson didn't like the look of the glossy plastic, bulging and sagging with something weighty. It resembled a huge blob of tar. Whatever was inside also had a pungent odor, even with the end knotted.

"Please, come in," Grayson said, moving over to a circular table in the middle of the foyer. On it was a large vase full of fresh and colorful flowers. "Can we get you any refreshments? Water or…"

"No," the man replied bluntly, causing Fridolf to purse his lips.

The ranger walked into the house, his campaign hat low on his head while his dark green jacket and jeans rubbed against each other with every step.

Swish.

There was a gold badge affixed to his left lapel, while a thin tag on the right twinkled. DON SMITH, it read.

Swish. Swish.

Fridolf's eyes began to twinge when he noticed the heavy and deliberate mud prints Ranger Smith was leaving on the floor with his boots. He tried his best not to groan, but a little slipped out.

Smith cast him a foreboding look from beneath the brim of his hat, his eyes spangled with shades of cobalt.

"Very well," Grayson said. "To business then. I gather whatever you have in that bag is the reason this meeting was necessary?"

Smith stopped his advance with a final *swish* and raising his arm, dropped the black bag indifferently on the tabletop. It made a *thud* so loud that he might as well have thrown it from the front door.

"Yep," he replied sternly. "I got your evidence right there."

"Perhaps the ranger could afford some formality to go with his cheap attitude?" Fridolf said as he closed the front door. "You are speaking to the Alpha, *subordinate*."

"I got your evidence right there, *master…*" Ranger Smith repeated.

"Thank you," Grayson replied politely enough, though he would have liked to show the brazen wolf why the Mannings were still Alphas of the white wolves and had been for centuries.

Grayson didn't hold his anger for long. Smith's attitude was the tip of a very jagged iceberg, one that had grown over the last eighteen years in a sea of misfortune. Life for the pack since the Accords were implemented had been tolerable, but didn't come remotely close to living up to the great promises made by the Order. There had been several instances – the ones in 1998, 2005, and 2010 the worst – that left huge marks on the shifter population. Grayson maintained his end of the bargain, loyal some would say to a fault, in order to make amends for some cases and show leadership in others. The undercurrent of contention in the pack, felt to that very evening, stemmed from that.

"What have you found?" Grayson continued.

Smith flipped up his brim and began to untie the bag.

"Our team was returning from the forest this morning," he said, the bag rolling – sloshing – around as Smith fidgeted with the knot. "We came across a group of hikers down in the brush, quite close to Foothill Road. There were eight of them in all, at least we think there were eight."

"You think?" Grayson asked as Smith was able to get the knot loose. He hooked a finger into it.

"Yeah, we think. The place was brutal when we found it. At first, we thought wild animals had attacked the hikers. Their bodies had been mutilated, but nothing was eaten. The parts… there were so many parts… had been ripped off, broken off, bitten off, then thrown around like confetti at a kid's birthday party."

Fridolf looked green, taking quick and shallow breaths. Whoever did that to those people were savages.

"All of the bodies had been decapitated. We couldn't find any of the heads around, except for one. It was easy to spot."

Smith unfurled the bag and a ripe, bitter stench filled the glorious foyer of Grayson's home. He reached inside and after a few seconds of groping and splashing, he raised what was inside.

It was the head of a woman, long strands of her brown hair drawn tight in Smith's fingers. Caked with blackened gunk that dribbled fat, stinking drops back into the plastic bag, her face was forever locked in an expression that said, *true horror had come for me, and this is my very last moment alive.*

Grayson didn't recognize her – the poor thing and her friends were probably in the wrong place at the wrong time.

Just like Jordan Parker. We should have acted sooner!

All this could have been dismissed as the work of a cold-blooded human. Grayson wanted to do just that, and would have, if not for one final detail that etched itself in his memory like the sight of his mate's burned corpse did so many years ago. On the woman's forehead, carved deep with a sharp claw, were the words: LIGHT BEARER'S FATE.

Lichtträger schicksal... the light bearer's fate. My *fate...*

Grayson remained stoic, but his skin had grown unpleasantly cold and damp. Regardless of his wants, there was no mistaking this sign for anything else: Lance Goddard and his shadow pack were playing the first card in their hand.

"I… thank you for bringing this evidence so I could see it with my own eyes."

Smith smirked as he nodded, lowering the head back into the bag. Even after tying it off again, making his way for the door, the smell – grislier now that the source of it was known – persisted.

"Fridolf," Grayson said hastily. "I need you to send word immediately to the Order and also to Ásbjörn. The day I told them we've been waiting for is upon us."

"Yes, Alpha," Fridolf replied, gulping noisily. "As for Ásbjörn, he is still in the Jameson Preserve, correct?"

"That is where he told us he was headed after his last visit to Goodman." Grayson lowered his voice to a whisper. "But it has been some time since we heard anything. Have a few scouts go up there to check on him, starting at Sky Valley. And Don, as for you…"

The ranger stopped, already over halfway to the door. Turning, he popped his neck before looking Grayson in the eyes.

"Don, our pack needs to be aligned, more now than ever before. I promise that if we manage to get through this urgent matter, I will reconsider our positioning in the Accords and fight to bring some amendments to the terms the Order has put on us. Perhaps they are more willing to listen now."

Smith didn't say a word as Grayson looped around the table, biting down on his thumb as he approached. A stream of red ran down his skin, pooling slightly in his cupped palm.

"A blood oath…" Fridolf murmured, entranced as he watched Grayson extend his bloody hand toward the ranger. There wasn't a single drip.

Tipping his hat, Smith extended his own arm, grabbing hold of Grayson's waiting hand. They shook. It was sticky and warm.

"We will make the shadow pack suffer for those we lost, my Alpha," Smith said, an assured look across on his face. Pulling away his hand, it was coated in Grayson's blood – a symbol of the promise made and the honor binding it. Smith closed his hand and thumped that fist across his chest, resuming his exit. Moments later, he was gone.

"And so it begins…" Grayson sighed as the front door closed. Then, he spotted Fridolf still standing over by the archway to the parlor. "Why are you still here?"

Grayson's voice snapped the young wolf's out of his stupor.

"I… I'm on it!" Fridolf stammered, racing out of the room the same way he came in.

Grayson looked around, stopping on the grim bag that had been left on the central foyer table. Above it, motes of dust danced in warm shafts of light. It reminded him of snow... cold snow...

2

Sunday January 8, 2012

... that was falling over the woods of the Preserve nearly nine months earlier.

Grayson was taking a stroll that evening to clear his mind, the last few weeks of juggling ongoing issues with the pack – along with Liam's endless tendency to let his ego get himself into trouble – weighing down on his shoulders like a ton of bricks, or ten, it didn't matter at that point. Normally finding solace in the silence of the woods off the beaten path, things the night of January eighth felt different, and that made Grayson uncomfortable.

The woods were dark, teeming with more shadows than there should have been with a full moon overhead. Grayson dismissed the odd feeling as fatigue, trekking further east into the forest. Perhaps there he could find the conditions he needed for reprieve. That was when another feeling crept in:

the unmistakable sensation of being watched. Watched by eyes that did not fear him. Watched by eyes that had been following for a long time.

Grayson couldn't see or sense anyone beyond the veil of gloom. That concerned him even more than the feeling itself. He picked up his pace – the twigs snapping and dirty snow crunching beneath his shoes.

I hope I don't have to transform and ruin another perfectly good suit, he thought, half attempting to lighten the mood, half wishing to save a couple thousand dollars in tailoring. *Maybe I can convince the tailor for a bulk –"*

Grayson stumbled over a rock, his words cut off, falling face first onto the snowy ground. There he lay motionless for a few minutes.

"Well done, Grayson, you ruined the suit anyway," he said, spitting out a few leaves. Some were still stuck to his tongue when he looked briefly over his shoulder. His heart sank and his face grew white like a freshly laundered sheet.

It was not a rock that he'd stumbled over, but a body. The tiny, mangled one of a little boy who had been featured in the *Courier* over the last week, headlines reading: JORDAN PARKER, 6 – MISSING SINCE NEW YEAR'S EVE. The accompanying photograph of the kid had been a recent portrait by his mother (an avid photographer assisting at Panda Studios, wishing to open her own business one day): bright green eyes sparking beneath a sweep of ginger hair, wearing a smile that dimpled his freckled cheeks. It was a stark contrast to what Grayson saw lying there on the forest floor – cold, lifeless, no sparkle.

While Grayson was distracted, a new shadow appeared out of the darkness behind him. It lunged for him, but Grayson was faster, scurrying forward then spinning up and around with lightning speed. Grabbing the figure, Grayson charged forward, pining it against the trunk of a nearby tree.

"*Who are you?*" Grayson shouted.

There was no reply, just curls of steaming breath escaping from beneath the hooded cloak.

"*I asked you a question!*" Grayson yelled again and this time his claws emerged, piercing the fabric. "Who are you? Did you murder that innocent child?"

"Now you've asked me two questions…" a man's voice said. It was distant and uncaring.

Grayson dug his claws further into the cloak, puncturing the skin underneath. He could smell him now, blood dribbling out of five holes in his chest.

"Come on… just make me ask you *one more time…*"

Grayson squeezed… and the man yielded.

"No, I didn't touch the kid! His fate just led him to the wrong place at the wrong time." The man paused. "As for who I am, you first, Fido."

Fido? FIDO? This human is slinging insults when I'm about to turn him into a meaty pincushion!

"I don't think so," Grayson said, flexing his fingers again. "You obviously know more about me than the other way around. How did you know that I'm a werewolf?"

The man chuckled beneath the hood.

"I didn't, but thanks for telling me. I assumed you were a vampire at first with those claws and people-tossing skills, but when I didn't see the fangs, well, assumed you were a lost rougarou."

A goddamn rougarou! Grayson thought, a look of disgust on his face at the double insult. *You happen to be talking to a purebred alpha!*

"It seems that I struck a nerve, my apologies."

"Indeed," Grayson replied, loosening his grip but only slightly. "You're speaking to Grayson Manning, Alpha of..."

"The *Lichtträger* pack..."

"Yes, that is correct," Grayson said, taken aback that a human was familiar with such a title and also enamored by it. He let go of the man – more out of shock than sense – and stepped away from him. "But that title does not refer to the pack. It refers to me."

"Well then, Mr. Light Bearer," the man said, gripping the sides of his hood with both hands. The sleeves tumbled down his tattooed forearms, fingers wearing many rings, and letters on the knuckles spelling out: STAY TRUE. "It seems your wolf brothers are starting to make moves around the fringes of that town at the base of this valley. Goodman, is it? More like Goodbye, should they attack."

Sliding back this hood, a plume of dirty blond hair appeared, catching an icy blast of snow-laden wind. The mottled moonlight shone through it, highlighting the man's sharp facial features and rough, unkempt beard. His ears were full of glittering piercings, while a pair of thick-framed glasses rested in front of his eyes. They were almost werewolf like in their cunning.

"Who exactly *are* you?" Grayson repeated, this time with added adoration. It worked.

"My name is Ty Sheridan and I'm..." The man swiftly dropped his gaze to the ground. The snow was beginning to stick. "I'm just passing through."

"Passing through?" Grayson asked. He had so many questions.

Where to?

Where from?

Who have you met?

Who are you meeting?

How did you avoid me sensing you?

He settled on the first one, asking Ty: "Where to?"

"As far from anything related to the Order as I can get," Ty replied.

Grayson saw the truth in the man's eyes, also weighed heavily with something deeply troubling and personal.

"Mr. Sheridan... Ty..." he said, "you seem to know more about what is going on in these woods than my own scouts. That's no small feat. I gather from what you just said that you have no love for the Order?"

Ty scoffed, looking up toward the sky. He laughed again as snow filled his view.

"I did once, perhaps, if ever... Regardless things changed for me in 2010." Ty shook his head, a single tear working free and rolling down his cheek, "Though my brother Marcus would gladly scream his love for them from the rooftops if he could."

"That was the year of the Incursion..."

"Yes." Ty nodded. "That was when our parents died – when they were killed – and the Order took away my only remaining family with false promises."

False promises like the Accords.

"A lot of your kind died that year," Grayson said. "Some of my kind, too. We are living in dangerous times."

"With more dangerous ones to come, if what I hear is correct."

"How so?"

"It's about…" Ty paused, then reconsidered speaking any more the matter. "No, that's not your concern at the moment. Your concern right now is that town; am I right in thinking the Order has your pack guarding things for them?"

"Yes," Grayson said, clearing snow from a nearby log. He sat, offering the spot next to him to Ty. "I need you to tell me all that you know."

"It's not all too much," Ty replied, taking a seat, "but I'll do it… then I'm done and out of here. Deal?"

Grayson's fingers found comfort in his beard again.

"Deal."

So it was that Grayson Manning and Ty Sheridan continued to talk well into the night about what the former Journeyman knew and what he'd seen during his travels across the Blue Ridge Mountains.

"*How* many do you think there are?"

"I couldn't count all the tracks, too many of them were overlapping. But, one night about two weeks back, I was up in Toluca Springs at, oh, Cliffside Lake. I saw a damn herd of wolves around the lake. They were using it as a watering hole. I'd guess their numbers around two hundred at least."

Grayson tried to recall if there had been any mass reports of disappearances in the area, which would account for people being turned.

He couldn't recall, at least anything more than usual.

Lance, you've been quite the busy boy...

"That's all I know," Ty said as he began to get up. "I followed the herd out this way after that. They've stayed pretty distant – using the forest for cover and food – but with little Jared over there..." and Ty pointed to the child's body, getting buried under the snow. "They've started testing the perimeter and your response. My guess is that it'll be the fall before they make a formal move, continuing to build their forces with one last litter this spring and some Turning if need be, all while assuming you have no idea they're here."

Grayson didn't know it then, but Ty would be spot on with his estimate, that horrific, carved message arriving on the cusp of Labor Day.

"Ty," Grayson said, "if what you say is true, I wish that we could take them out now, but with the other shifters still spread thin after the Incursion..."

"And the Accords limiting your own pack's numbers," Ty continued, "it's not a pretty picture. You'll need all the help you can get. But like I said already, I can't offer you any more help than I've already given."

He went on to tell Grayson that if he wants any favor with the Order, he should forget the name Sheridan and that he was ever there.

"Keep them at arm's length, too," Ty warned. "Ever since the Incursion things on the inside have been unstable and dangerous. I can't underscore the need to *cooperate* with them – hell, use them for resources – but only as much as needed under your own terms. Thankfully for someone like me, there isn't a need anymore. For you, all this couldn't have come at a worse time."

"And for Lance, the best time," Grayson said, closing his eyes. The cool night air against his skin was refreshing. "Very well, you can go, Mr. Sheridan. The help is greatly appreciated."

Ty collected his belongings, scattered over the course of their conversation.

"Ty…" Grayson said softly. "If I am to leave out your name in all accounts, do you have anything I can use as proof, short of an old wolf's ramblings, to the Order? If it's as unstable as you suggest, then I'm sure skepticism and pride are at an all-time high."

Ty nodded; Grayson had a valid point. Removing his outer cloak, there was a fur coat enrobing him underneath. Unfastening it, then slipping it off, Ty pitched it over to Grayson before rushing to put the cloak back on. It wasn't doing anywhere near as good of a job keeping out the biting wind.

Grayson deliberately turned the fur over several times in his hand. It was soft and black as midnight on a moonless night.

"Is this… a werewolf pelt?"

Ty nodded, a weird mix of timid pride. He went on to explain.

"I had to kill one of the subordinates in self-defense," Ty said, puffing out a couple clouds of steaming breath from his mouth, "else you'd be talking to a steaming pile of dog shit right now. I also needed some added protection for that ice storm that came through about the same time after Christmas. I skinned him before he could shift back into human form."

"How did you delay the Change to do that?" Grayson asked, astonished. Even after the battle of 1994 where transformations were delayed due to heartbreakingly long deaths, they still transformed back to humans.

Ty shook his rucksack and the unseen contents jostled, breaking Grayson's train of thought.

"I have a talent for those kinds of things," Ty said. "The world around us offers solutions all the time – doesn't matter if it's natural or supernatural. You just need to know where to look and then figure out how to apply what you've learned toward a solution. Quite literally in this case."

As Grayson held the pelt in his hands, he could not help but be impressed. "Does it last…"

"Goodbye, Grayson Manning," Ty said urgently, and with the slightest of smirks raised his hood.

"Goodbye, whoever you are…" Grayson replied, watching the strange, hooded figure of a man turn before getting consumed by the snowstorm.

CHAPTER 6: LIAM MANNING GIVES CHASE

Friday August 31, 2012

1

Dusk had crept across the sky as Cooper was leaving Billy's home, the

boy taking one last, longing look at the trailer he could so easily see himself

living in. Suddenly, the scene shifted and the north-south cross street of

Grove Road crumbled into a bottomless chasm. Cherry Lane morphed into

a rickety bridge right out of an action-adventure movie, swaying

precariously over the great divide. It was a manifestation of the fear Cooper needed to overcome if he wanted life with the Arnetts to become a reality.

But for now, Cooper turned away, unable to cross. The surroundings shriveled then blew away like flakes of paint on a breeze. The mundane (*but safe and solid*) pavement of Cherry Lane had reappeared and Cooper plodded along that road then left a couple blocks to Schneck's Grocery, where he stopped in for some much-needed bubble gum. He found that gum helped pass the time during long walks and improve his focus, despite what other kids said.

Fo-eyed Coopie and hiz always bwoken gwasses, they'd taunt. *Maybe if he learned to walk and chew gum at the same he'd be able to keep a pair...*

As Cooper pushed through the single glass door, a little bell (taken from the toe of an old Christmas stocking by the looks of the bits fabric still attached) jingled to announce his arrival. Mr. Schneck appeared at the back of the store. He was a nice man, if not a bit eccentric, always greeting patrons with a smile like that, no matter the day, time, or weather.

"Hello there Mr. Bennett! Did your friend like those sunglasses?" Mr. Schneck asked, wiping his hands on a paper towel before making way for the front.

"He sure did!" Cooper beamed, coming up to the counter with a pack of classic pink gum and a bottle of soda. He rifled through his backpack for some cash and paid. "Thank you for your help with that."

Mr. Schneck smiled again at the words "thank you" (heard far too little these days), only charging him for the gum.

"I think you made a mistake," Cooper said.

"No, no, I insist! Now off home with you, Mr. Bennett!" he said, shooing him away with his hand. "Be safe and we'll see you again soon!"

"Thanks again Mr. Schneck; you bet!"

Cooper popped a handful of pink cubes into his mouth, started smacking, and yanked the door open. The bell jingled merrily again and he stepped through, continuing his journey south on Center Street.

In less than a block, what should have been an uneventful trip home took a turn for the worse. Parked in a gravel lot across from Apple Lane was a car – a sleek, black BMW. In the driver's seat was Liam Manning, dressed in his favorite gold and black Wolverine's jacket. He'd been waiting for who knows how long with Mark Brown.

Why are they here? Why is HE here and not in the hospital?

Leaning on the far side of the car near the trunk, his back toward Cooper, was Derek Wilder. He was hunched over as if shaking his tube after a piss (or doing something far less savory; Cooper couldn't nor did he want to make it out). Whatever it was, those broad shoulders rolled and jostled with a groan as he wrapped nature's business.

Are they here... for me? Cooper wondered, heart beating faster when he realized Liam had probably stewed over things for hours.

How'd they know where I'd be?

He imagined Liam harassing other kids for information, his goons beating them senseless regardless of their replies. All to teach Cooper-fucking-Bennett a lesson for embarrassing him earlier that day.

How long have they...

"Shit!" Cooper shouted. He'd dawdled too long.

Liam had spotted him. Mark was shouting something indiscernible, but sweet enough to foam at the mouth. Derek raced to zip up his pants, ambling into the back seat of the sleek, black bullet.

Cooper wasted no time. Dropping what was left of the gum and soda, he dashed north, leaving the bottle fizzing and spinning as it spewed all over the sidewalk.

Behind, Cooper could hear the car's engine revving amidst a storm of hollering and laughing. Ahead, his thin shadow grew wider; the headlights getting closer and closer before...

Plum Lane came up on the right, Cooper turned and was on it before his mind had time to catch up. Continuing north on Grove Road, he saw Billy's trailer passing by. Longing once again to be inside, that damn bridge of fear appeared again, not because of his dad this time but because he couldn't fathom bringing Liam all the way to Billy's front door. Slipping both arms out of his backpack, Cooper slung it into the yard where it landed in the damp grass (*I hope Billy finds it!*) and kept running as fast his legs could take him.

Liam was still in pursuit, but his rich man's car was less than effective on those poor, potholed streets.

Lucky for Cooper, who was a blur as he bounded through back yards and over fences like a jackrabbit, gaining distance all the way past the prison to Foothill Road and beyond. He didn't look back as he started up the mountain, throwing years of caution right into the rusty trash bins at the Greyhound bus station below. He didn't need to look back as he climbed up the trail, hearing the brakes of the BMW squeal as the tires skidded on pavement, the car doors opening then slamming shut, angry feet scrambling to catch him...

"You won't get far!" a voice roared. It was Liam's, more animal than man. "I'm going to break you in half, skinny fucker!"

Cooper kept running, his heart thumping as the incline started to take its toll. He couldn't believe people hiked these wandering trails for fun.

Tha-thump.

"They're going to catch me!" he wheezed with barely enough air for his next breath. Evergreen trees had sprung up all around him. He had to lose them; get off the trails.

Tha-thump.

"They're going to…"

A small opening through the overgrowth caught his attention ahead. Cooper beelined for it and crashing through the branches – striking him like a flurry of whips to the face and arms – he stumbled. The ground was quickly sloping away. A large embankment had been hidden from view.

"Ah shit!" Cooper cried, unable to recover his balance.

Falling forward, he hit the muddy ground, rolling onto his back before coming to a stop. Covered in leaf litter, he looked up at the trees. They were whispering old stories to each other, bobbing and swaying in serene bliss. They were adding the tale of skinny Coop to the list, the boy who was throttled to death by three untamed…

Shit! Liam!

Snapping to attention, Cooper leapt to his feet then collapsed again. One hurt something fierce; it might have been sprained in the tumble. Little did Cooper know that would be the least of his concerns. Wincing, he listened, and over his low breaths could hear Mark Brown calling "Cooooopie…"

Placing trembling hands on his already shaking knees, Cooper struggled to his feet then limped on. He had no idea where he was or where he was going in the darkening forest.

Why the hell did you come up here?

He could hear his pursuers, wishing he couldn't. They were gaining fast and Cooper had exhausted most of his reserves. He looked around for anything that could help. There was nothing... except a twinkle in the distance. They looked like eyes. Cat-like and yellow between two entangled trees.

What is –

A fist suddenly struck him in the back and once again Cooper was unwillingly kissing dirt and sipping water from a shallow creek bed. Winded, he looked around, seeing nothing but forest. The eyes were gone.

Derek grabbed Cooper's shirt by the neck, yanking him up with a single, powerful jerk. The shirt ripped, its torn edges flapping like a pair of giggling geishas waving handkerchiefs. He clamped one of his large hands on Cooper's shoulder and spun him around just in time for Mark to swoop in and deliver a hefty punch. Just like Cooper's good ol' dad.

There's no place like home, right? You all should bring him next time!

Cooper collapsed to his knees, bloody and defeated. The energy to fight had left like his hope. Derek didn't care, landing a swift boot right in his stomach. Mark joined him, both boys going to town as if Cooper was one of the punching bags at Roop's Den on the south side of town. Except those punching bags didn't bleed. Those punching bags didn't cry either.

"Aww, look at the wittle baby!" Mark teased, Cooper swaying like a reed, propped up only by the slight breeze that was cold against his scratched and bruised skin.

Derek was muttering, paste-like drool flying from his lips.

"Soften... the... meat..."

Liam was just watching it all from a nearby tree, one of his athletic arms propped up on its trunk. He chuckled while his goons did the dirty work. He'd mop up whatever they left, which made him wonder exactly...

2

Friday July 4, 2003

"HOW MUCH?" Grayson Manning shouted at the top of his lungs. He had just been told the total cost of damages his son had accrued with his latest confrontation with the good people of Goodman.

Many Independence Days ago, Liam had been a terror (and many would say, if they weren't so intimated to do so, he had been every day in between). However, on that particular day Liam had set off a large number of fireworks in the dairy section of Hometown Grocery, blowing up everything from milk and eggs to blocks of cheddar cheese, making them into a new variety of Swiss. If that weren't enough to swallow, his father also received word that his son was a suspect in another, more serious incident.

"Allegedly," an officer had said to Grayson, "on the night of July 3, 2003, Liam Manning approached a young boy – six years old – by the name of Brad Farrell. After a brief and apparently heated exchange of words over an action figure, Mr. Manning placed a handful of cherry bombs and said toy inside Brad's jeans before lighting them with a lighter."

The series of explosions had caused severe third-degree burns and tissue damage on large parts of Brad's body. Ironically, the police would not have pinned the earlier crime on Liam if the Hometown Grocery incident hadn't occurred.

Grayson closed his eyes and did *not* allegedly smack the back of Liam's head with the full force of his hand.

After a couple days of high stress, reprieve came for Grayson and karma neglected to visit his son once again. Liam was cleared of all charges in the Farrell case, the event swept away by the Order. (Brad had actually been injured while playing with rune stones he had crafted himself as a burgeoning mage. He had been whisked away to New York City, undergoing medical treatment and evaluation at the headquarters building.)

All that was left for Grayson to do was to settle the physical damages to the grocery building and lost property, along with the medical expenses for a mother and daughter who were taken away for minor smoke inhalation. Like many instances before and many to come, Grayson would always manage to keep the press and police at bay.

"Liam!" Grayson said angrily one evening after the school had called (again). "You must stop this insanity! As Beta, you must learn when and where it is appropriate to show force, otherwise we are no better than rougarou or the shadow…"

"But they are lesser than me, Dad," he replied from an ornate armchair with the ease of blinking. His blue stare was unyielding and true.

Grayson sighed, folding his arms as he propped himself up on his office desk. Staring at Liam, he saw a son that had the appearance of a well-mannered and dressed boy, but his words were always that of a spoiled brat, laced with venom.

"That they may be, son," Grayson continued, "but it is still the place of a Beta, and the Alpha he becomes, to be unprejudiced and worthy of the position, else the pack tear itself apart from the chaos."

"When will that be?" Liam asked coldly and eagerly.

"When I determine you are ready…"

Eventually, Grayson succeeded in convincing Liam to channel his anger into skills that could be developed into a fine point over time. He had doubts but as a father and as Alpha, he held out hope (even if Grayson would never admit it was the smallest amount).

Liam seemed to listen and as such became popular in middle school, once joining the ranks of "the other people," as he still called them. Using his honed talents, Liam skyrocketed in popularity, becoming the star quarterback at Goodman High School. Although that didn't sound like much to write home about yet, he had speed, accuracy, and (arguably most important) good looks on his side. He even started attending church with his father, getting a tattoo across the right half of his chest that said, "I am the way, the truth, and the life. No one comes to the Father except through me." It was a reflection of his struggle to better himself, though how successful that endeavor would be needed the prism of time to see.

No doubt all of those things, along with Daddy's continued money and influence, would take Liam to the next level and beyond. Much further than some lowly waste like Cooper Bennett could aspire to, or the worse-off schmuck Billy Arnett, whose north-side roots all but locked him in a hard future of gritty nails, callouses, and busted body parts.

Liam was poised for greatness, but despite all he had going for him, his obstinate temper and superiority complex both kept him chained to Goodman. It would stay that way until he could find the appropriate key, or a saw to cut through.

3

Friday August 31, 2012

Liam reveled in the sight of Cooper getting the shit beaten out of him. His bruised body was now swelling thanks to contributions from Mark Brown and Derek Wilder. His lip had been split like a fillet of fish by a branch, foliage sticking to the upper one like garnish. Thick, red blood trickled down both sides of his mouth. Derek wiped it with a finger, licking it off yearningly.

"Can... I... do it? Can I?" he wailed.

"No, you can't you lumbering dolt!" Liam said, approaching.

Mark and Derek backed away, but not before Mark delivered one last kick to Cooper's gut, causing him to bite his tongue. Blood sprayed like a red water fountain through the air.

"Hi there, Coop. So, you wanted to play ball with the big guys," Liam said nicely, crouching beside the pulpy mess that was once a boy. He took a finger and scooped up some dank mud like peanut butter right out of a jar, spreading it like eye black across Cooper's cheeks. "There, now you at least look the part. Well, barely. Tsk, tsk, tsk. When are you going to learn that you really shouldn't mess with monsters?"

Liam wiped the rest of the mud off on Cooper's buzz cut.

Snap.

The sound of a twig snapping caught Liam's attention and he spun his head around, looking into all corners of the forest. He didn't see anything; perhaps it was just a deer. Derek would have to get on that later. Liam returned his attention to his victim.

"I'm not sure how you pulled off those quick moves earlier today, or grew balls big enough to think you could even breathe the same air as my girl but –"

"Sh-she said sh-she's nuh-not y-your puh-puh-property," Cooper cut in. Even his voice sounded swollen.

Liam punched Cooper, sending his glasses flying off to God knows where.

"Don't interrupt me again, Coop. Jesus, fuck my hand still hurts, but at least it's healing well."

Cooper's face was bewildered. *What did he mean healing well? It should be broken*, the look said.

Liam was elated, standing up to gloat over his browbeaten buddy. He started chuckling, Mark and Derek joining in.

"You have no idea what you're messing with."

Cooper's face shifted, forming a proud – and still pleasingly battered – smirk.

"W-well, I was th-thinking th-that the oh-only t-thing muh-monstrous about y-you three is h-how luh-low your I...Q...s are. Duh-do y-you think you're guh-going to g-get away w-with t-this?"

Liam's nostrils flared.

"I get away with a *lot* more than you know, prick..."

"Muh-more like Duh-Daddy lets..."

Liam lost control, kicking Cooper in the face. A tooth flew off into the forest. His two goons seemed surprised, their laughter dead as they shrank away.

"You see, it's one thing to embarrass a man in front of his lessers, and another to bear the consequences of those actions. Now, whose IQ is monstrously low, Coop?"

Cooper muttered under his breath; Liam couldn't hear what he said. When he leaned in close, Cooper spat blood his face, mixed with mucus and snot that had accumulated at the back of his throat.

That was the final straw, Liam entering an animalistic rage.

Mark and Derek leapt further back as Liam flung off his jacket, then the shirt as he began to change into something... else.

His bones cracked and he howled madly. Fur that was white like snow sprouted from his skin – slow at first, almost invisible, then in streams. His blue eyes seemed to glow in the light of the full August moon.

Cooper thought that he was hallucinating, scurrying backwards while on his ass (*you've been playing* Altered Beast *too often at the Dip & Dog,* he thought), but his rapid heartbeat and breaths told him what he saw seeing was real enough. Then he couldn't go any further, stopped by a stump or maybe a rock. He didn't look, instead transfixed on the Liam-monster as he... as it... reared back and howled at the moon, spit flying in a horrible plume into the night sky.

Then with lightning speed it crouched, claws and teeth bared, lunging headlong toward Cooper at breakneck speed.

Cooper raised his feeble arms up in front of his face. They would be useless against what was coming for him but he did it nonetheless. He closed his eyes and could still hear the thing's footfalls, smell its musky odor coming at him. The end was close!

Then, a messy noise mixed with a loud *thud* echoed through the forest, followed by a whimper. Cooper risked a peek, lowering his arms for a better view and his eyes grew huge at the perplexing sight playing out before him.

There were two *wolves* fighting, Liam the white one from before but now there was a black one, too, its eyes piercing yellow. Glancing off to the right at the sound of a terrified gasp, Cooper saw Mark Brown and Derek Wilder still locked in their stupor, dismayed by what they were witnessing.

The fight continued for a few minutes, the wolves locked by claw and jaw. The noise was loud and painful to listen to. For a while, Liam appeared to have the upper hand, but the black wolf gained it during a lapse in Liam's concentration – a fit of careless anger the cause. The black wolf grabbed Liam by the neck and with tremendous force flung him to the side, the furry body rolling through the brambles before striking the trunk of a tree.

Liam shifted back into human form almost immediately, his tight and muscular body naked in the night as he scrambled to collect his clothes. Liam was limping as he plucked his designer jeans from a bush; they'd been torn from the Change but his shirt and beloved jacket were intact. Gathering them all in his arms, he hauled himself over to his goons, both miraculously able to move again.

"You okay boss?" Mark asked, receiving all of Liam's clothes with an angry push against his chest.

"Where the hell were you two?" he shouted, spinning around to look at the enemy before either could answer.

The black wolf had stepped out in front of Cooper, snarling toward the three boys. Derek seemed to panic, muttering something that sounded German – like the words "shittin" and "trouble" had been smashed together into one guttural, stammering word.

Not knowing what was said, but judging by Derek's expression (and the one Liam was trying to hide) Cooper didn't feel comfortable at all. His heart had already gotten its fill night. *No more please, I'm full!* it screamed.

136

"Shut up Derek!" Liam yelled, pointing to Cooper. His chest was heaving, sweat now pouring down it and over his rippled torso, mixing with blood and plasma. "This isn't over... either of you!"

The black wolf barked ferociously, Cooper shuddering as Liam, Mark, and Derek raced into the gloom.

Once they were gone, the forest fell silent...

4

Until Cooper coughed into his hand. There was more blood. His head was spinning like he'd been riding a Round Up at the fair for too long. That drew the wolf's attention. It turned. Its panting was quiet, yet deafening all the same.

Cooper tried his best to calm the beast down (forgetting entirely to do so himself first). Not making any sudden moves – his body wouldn't have let him anyway – Cooper attempted to speak gently and understandably.

"It's o-okay..." he muttered. "I'm nuh-not g-going to huh-hurt you..."

That's rich! Cooper thought. *As if!*

The wolf's fairly benign pants transitioned to a low growl, growing more menacing with each step.

Woah, woah, woah!

Cooper could feel warm piss pooling in his lap before running down the sides of his legs. It was the only fluid he had left to drain.

"Now w-wait a m-minute, puh-poochie!" Cooper said, this time more sternly.

It worked!

The creature paused, letting Cooper breath an all too short sigh of relief. It began advancing again, angrier from an apparent dislike of being addressed like a puppy. It was close now, making it to Cooper's feet where it became clearer in his vision. He could now see its clumpy, rough fur, glistening eyes, and a thin strand of drool swinging like a pendulum from...

It attacked, jaws clamping around Cooper's lower right leg. It took a moment for what was happening to register, a moment for the pain to link up with his mind and let a scream out of his throat.

"Stop!" Cooper struggled, but he was weak.

You'll always be weak Coopie! Liam's voice echoed, unwanted, in his mind.

Dirt and leaves slipped between his fingers when it didn't collect under his nails. He was being dragged away for what was destined to be a long, agonizing, and humiliating death.

Dog food becomes dog shit, after all!

There was more rustling in the dark foliage, Cooper pulled over rocks, sticks, feces, and oh God what else? He could feel more eyes staring at him as he was drug up another steep incline. More yellow eyes in the dark – all watching. Penetrating.

"Gah! Stop! I said let me go!"

The wolf didn't care and Cooper's imagination was set loose. It went down every grizzly possibility until, as suddenly as it all began, everything stopped.

Am I... dead?

No, he wasn't. Cooper could still feel the throbbing pain in his calf muscle, smell the dirt and decay of the forest around him, hear the wind blowing through the trees (probably still telling those she old stories to each other), and taste the blood and vinegary bite of stomach acid that had tried to vomit itself up.

He wasn't dead yet, but certainly on the brink.

Cooper realized that the beast had let him go, seeing that he was back on the main trail at the cusp of the decline toward the Greyhound bus station, the town's lights twinkling down there to the south and beyond.

"Owwwooooo," came a low howl, joined by a discordant throng of others.

Cooper watched the black wolf wander away through his blurry and quickly fading vision. A searing pain shot up Cooper's leg; it was having a spasm, flopping around like a fish that had leapt off a hook to the deck of a pier one hot summer afternoon. At last his stomach unburdened itself of its contents, a rancid collection of blood, stomach acid, soda, and pecan pie spilling out beside and on him.

Oh Jesus I have rabies! Cooper thought, turning away from his vomit to lie on his opposite side. *Fucking rabies...*

"We'll see you soon," a voice howled on the wind. It seemed to come from all directions, repeating twice more before Cooper was finally overcome by his injuries and everything faded to black.

CHAPTER 7: ALYSSA NOBLE

Friday August 31, 2012

1

Earlier at Goodman High on the Friday before Labor Day, Alyssa Noble watched as Cooper Bennett tap danced merrily down the hallway toward his last class of the day. He was waving to her, Billy Arnett grabbing hold of his arm before pulling him inside the AP math classroom.

Alyssa lowered her own discreetly waving hand as she turned back toward her school friends, beaming from a giggle with hints of rose on her cheeks. Her color was drained almost immediately by their faces; uninterested in her happiness – all interest in Liam's.

Mary Sue Ellen (posh enough to have *three* girl's names bestowed upon her) was in a tight white top that looked about to burst, her short pink skirt barely hitched above her cootch. Becky Prince (another suitably royal name) wore a similar number but with an open sweater over her, likely to hide the fact her tits were not as large and fake as Mary's. Last but certainly not least was Virginia Crawford, who had bold braces bared on her buck-teeth. Most people claimed not to notice them, but Alyssa couldn't help but see (*you'd have to be blind not to notice, but chances are even then your other senses would compensate to keep those massive chompers from causing any damage*). Alyssa felt justified in her opinion, Virginia's beaver-like appearance was karma's way of tempering her extremely selfish personality.

All three girls were shocked, complete with full-on stares and mouths agape toward the sexy Liam Manning (though Virginia's mouth was always ajar). He was tending to his hand, something a quarterback of his potential with college just around the corner should value more than anything. But, as always, he was reckless.

Alyssa saw it every day with him. His hand was reddening, the locker worse for wear. She cared more about the condition of the metal.

That dent could be the side of your face one day Alyssa!

Her sensibilities were beating against the inside of her skull like they knew his fists would be on the outside. But they already had been, hadn't they?

You need to get away from that monster, and soon…

"*You* need to see the nurse," Alyssa said, her words forced and monotone.

"I'll be fine," Liam grunted dismissively. "Unlike that little prick later…"

"Stop it, Liam; why can't you just let it go?"

"Say *what?*" Liam cawed. "Are you falling for that beanpole?"

Alyssa hesitated, letting out a short and wispy gasp.

"Of course not; don't be silly," she said with her next breath.

Liam knew better, the look in his eyes telling her that her hesitation spoke louder than the words that followed.

"Uh huh…" he said, degenerating into a series of mumbles as he flexed the fingers of his hands open and closed.

As his droning subsided, Alyssa thought she could hear *cracking*. Liam, whose hand must've been broken after two punches to a locker with that much force, was moving all his digits around as if nothing was wrong. Yet, there it was again: more cracking. The sound was disturbing and if she didn't know better, it sounded like his bones were making the noise, rubbing against each other like teeth stressfully grinding in the night. But bones didn't do that sort of thing. They *couldn't* do that sort of thing.

Could they?

As the bell rang, the trickling laughter from the crowd seemed to get louder to overcome it. Alyssa felt that it was directed at her for thinking such a silly thing, mocking her for staying with such a terrible man like Liam Manning, and laughing at the fact she even had the audacity to acknowledge Cooper Bennett – a lowly guy far beneath her quality. The loudest cackles were hidden in the masses, and Alyssa found that she didn't care one bit.

Cooper Bennett, she thought. *What is it about you that I...*

"Don't you all have classes to get to!" Liam shouted, interrupting her thoughts. Silence cascaded down the hall like a tsunami.

"Liam, you *really* need to see the nurse," she said as people brushed past, streaming into their classrooms.

"If I wanted your input, I would have asked for it. I. Am. Fine. Now don't you make me repeat myself, especially with the mood I'm in..."

Alyssa jerked her head back. Not so much from the words Liam shoved at her (he did it quite frequently and for some reason she still let him), but the look in his eyes as he spoke. They were fierce, intense, animalistic. Maybe she should be the one to see the nurse because at first, she could hear his bones cracking, and now she swore the blue of his eyes flashed for a second. It had to be a flicker from the overhead lamps, due to those budget cuts the new janitor, Mr. Roper, would natter on about as he mopped, waxed, and scrubbed.

"Okay, fine," she snipped, Liam grabbing her uncomfortably by the waist like he did way too often.

He pulled her to him, leaning for a kiss. She turned, his wet lips finding a place on her cheek instead. Grabbing her chin, he forced her head his way and tried again, and this time she was unable to move.

But she wasn't focused on his lips or hot breath, which smelled like Doublemint gum even when he hadn't chewed any for a while. Instead, she noticed that the hand grabbing her chin – the one that had struck the locker twice, now keeping her locked in place – was perfectly fine.

She breathed a personal, silent sigh of relief that perhaps she wasn't crazy after all. At the same time, she was scared, wondering what kind of hell she had gotten herself into with Liam Manning…

2

Monday August 6, 2001

It was an overcast day which started Alyssa's second year at Riverhill and a good eight months until she would see Cooper Bennett for the first time across the street at Monument Park.

As she closed the car door, her mother Amanda bid her a good day, telling her that their housekeeper Marilyn would be picking her up since students were normally let out early on their first day and she couldn't make it back from work to Goodman in time.

The two exchanged a couple of brief and proper smiles, Amanda watching as her daughter entered the school yard and climbed the steps to the entrance. Each of her little white patent dress shoes seemed to skip up the stairs, her purple pastel dress bouncing like bell-shaped petals. Once she was safe inside, Amanda drove on to Clayton where she worked as part of a team of realtors selling luxury lake and mountain homes in the area.

The school day began and would end without much learning. It was just a run of the mill administrative day, filled with things like the main assembly and greeting of students. The Principal, Mrs. Glenn, stood at the front, explaining the litany of school rules, the purpose of fire drills, and a host of other topics that were drier than a popcorn fart. Not that any part of school – other than recess, lunch, and especially the last bell – was fun for anyone.

The teachers performed their duties in class like well-oiled machines, Alyssa watching from her desk as Mr. Mueller seemed preprogrammed to check the standard clock every ten minutes.

Alyssa silently wished that those minutes were going by as fast as the sweeping red second hand, anxious to get some fresh air. Something had gone wrong with the air conditioning during the assembly and the entire school had become stifling.

Finally recess came, and Alyssa made her way into the playground, letting the breeze caress her. Hunched across the way, beneath a scraggly tree was a little girl, her black hair parted and sweeping over each shoulder. She wore a pretty red dress with a big bow tied around her back. It resembled an apple in a way, fallen from those scary branches that were like a pair of skeletal hands grasping at something just out of reach.

Alyssa made her way over despite those branches.

"Hello," she said, timidly introducing herself. She didn't want to startle the girl.

"Hi," the girl responded without turning.

From here, Alyssa could see that she was crouched, not sitting, her head down toward the flowerbed with her arms wrapped around her knees. It was an odd position to be in to admire flowers, especially ones that were withering and brown.

"Whatcha looking at?" she asked, crouching herself. It was very uncomfortable.

"Just watching the ants," the girl replied and sure enough, Alyssa saw a trail of them marching through the tawny plants like soldiers through a desert. The line meandered for a bit, disappearing beneath the roots of the scary tree. "They help me focus on things."

"Huh," Alyssa said, her mouth crooked from a cramp. *Boys would just burn them with a magnifying lens,* she thought, sliding her behind all the way to the ground. She kicked her feet out a little. It was much better. "That sounds like it'd work pretty good. I normally listen to rain on the roof to do that. It helps me relax."

"Yep!" the girl said, perky. "Only problem is it doesn't rain all the time, does it? These little guys are in a lot of places, rain or sunshine."

Alyssa bobbed her head in that "oh yeah, good point" fashion.

"My name's Alyssa by the way."

"Monica," the girl replied, her timid face lit with the light from the slightest smile.

As the two chatted about their few friends and somehow got on the subject of ponies, Alyssa found Monica to be much like her. Not only in appearance (except for that dark hair) but also personality at that bright age of seven. Where they differed were their parents.

Monica's were kind yet fiercely hard working, both working a lot to ensure their daughter had a good start to her education by going to Riverhill. Alyssa's on the other hand were kind and well meaning, but essentially snobbish social climbers that would look down on a great many things in judgement, even Monica's parents.

"Oh gee, that's great!" Alyssa beamed regardless.

Monica had finished telling a story about her last birthday. Her dad had said to pick any toy she wanted in the department store. Knowing that she'd go for a doll of some kind, he had the store owner, some staff, and of course both Monica's mother and himself waiting with a large sheet cake in the middle of the aisle. It was decorated with chocolate icing, a host of sprinkles, and candles arranged in a loose smiley face (so loose that it appeared to be having a stroke).

Alyssa suspected that had been the first time Monica received something special to that degree, and that warmed her heart more than any of the cold Noble gifts she'd received in spades. A moment later she rolled her shoulders like something cold was poured over them, the feeling of someone watching – stalking – washing over her.

Taking quick glances around, she eventually spied a boy looking at them from across the playground. He was cute, dressed in a crisp plaid button up and black jeans, hanging like a monkey from the appropriately named bars. But as cute as he was, there something sinister about him. She couldn't put her finger on it then (she didn't have the words or references to draw on), but as her eighteen-year-old mind remembered that day, it was like the boy was just shell wrapped around something angry and old.

Alyssa returned her attention to Monica, and from the corner of her eye she saw the boy's ominous smile change like the wind into a scowl. The ringing school bell added to her feeling of dread, but getting up from the ground, she brushed herself off and walked back in to the stagnant, but safe, interior.

After a few more hours inside muggy classrooms, the last bell of the first school day rang out at one o'clock. As students happily filed out of the building onto school buses and into their parent's cars, Alyssa waited patiently on the steps.

Marilyn had texted her, stuck in a line of traffic on West Pine. City officials had finally approved funds to fix the road's ever-growing collection of pot holes, sealing Alyssa's fate.

If only there wasn't construction that day. Alyssa reminisced. *If only Marilyn had been on time…*

Due to the housekeeper's tardiness, Alyssa was left to meet the boy who had been looking at her during recess. He wasn't in her class (thankfully) but was there now (regrettably), standing to her left as she sat on those lonely stairs.

Up close he was even better looking, even at that age; a boy that any mom would have been proud to call her own. What struck Alyssa the most were his blue eyes. They were piercing like daggers, and those blades were cutting through her as she looked up at him.

"Can I help you?" she asked boldly.

"No."

"Then why are you looking at me like that?"

"Because I like what I see..." he said and Alyssa was, for a split second, flattered until he added, "and I always get what I like..."

She looked out. Still no Marilyn. She looked back at the boy. He was closer to her now.

"My name is Liam," he said, reaching out not to shake her hand, but to run a single finger through her hair.

Alyssa shuddered as a seven-year-old would.

"Mine's... Alyssa..."

It was almost automatic, the words spilling out of her mouth before she'd even thought to seal them up.

"Alyssa," he repeated slowly, and suddenly he was smiling. "I like that, too."

What is this feeling? Alyssa wondered. She was drawn to it like a moth to a flame.

My God you were a stupid little girl! she scolded herself upon reflection.

Her name had become her chain, securing her position as a token piece for Liam to brandish for the next eleven years, and as the lonely girl who filled the role of chipper cheerleader very well. Her heavy eyes would tell anyone that knew where to look a different story.

Liam would be relentless in his possessiveness over the years and Alyssa had nowhere – and no one – to turn to. Even her parents were no help. Being the social climbers that they were, the both of them latched onto the fact that a Manning liked their little girl. A *Manning*! Did you hear *that* neighbors? It was like a gift from the gods.

Thankfully, eight months after she first met Liam, Alyssa caught a glimpse of a scrawny boy riding his bike along the front of Monument Park. His look of such genuine wonder (*it couldn't have been love then, could it?*) carried so much weight that a piece of her latched onto that. It was probably the only thing that kept her from falling into a complete state of depression because as the years went by, Liam became more aroused by the attention he was getting from everyone – seeking more and more. Alyssa became put off by it, yearning for something different, something that befitted her true personality and not the fake one she had to maintain to survive and avoid getting treated like shit from her supposed friends, all of whom would no sooner smile at her before stabbing her in the back.

Monica would never have been that way.

I wonder whatever happened to her? Alyssa thought.

Her thoughts meandered; Monica never did come to Goodman Middle School with the rest of the students. Alyssa knew that had she done so, she would have sought her out and continued their friendship, instead of being around such materialistic girls. Girls with things like three names, royal-sounding surnames, and outrageous braces.

Monica was real and full of positive energy even on the first day they met. It was totally different than what she felt when she was around Liam (*shudder*) and she missed it. Perhaps that's what she also saw in Cooper: a second chance to be true to herself. But of course, she had to overcome the mess that had surrounded her.

Alyssa assumed Monica hadn't left for anything she had done, that she'd instead been whisked away by her family, as often happened in Goodman when people found opportunities in more mainstream places. Monica had mentioned that her dad was looking for a better job in Greenville, so that must've been it. She missed Monica for sure, recalling the days at Goodman Middle School when she would get glimpses of Riverhill on her way in and out. It was nice to see the tree and flowers where they had first met growing nicely over the years, almost an affirmation of the good and genuine times the two girls had.

Little did Alyssa know – and had she known, she would have been driven insane by the thought of something so horrible – but Monica had, in fact, never left Goodman. Her family had done so, in grief and sorrow at the pain of their missing daughter, a fact which was easy to keep out of the *Goodman Courier's* limited reach for reasons of privacy.

As for the little girl with black hair in the red dress, she stayed and forever would remain in Goodman, a victim of the same fate that would nearly befall Billy Arnett four years later on Halloween in 2005. Monica had become the very reason that the scary tree – their tree – was growing so well.

CHAPTER 8: WAKING FROM A BAD DREAM

Monday September 3, 2012

1

Blood flowing like a river from a horribly mangled right leg...

Pain coursing through every single part of a battered and broken body...

Cold wind blowing through moonlit treetops while yellow eyes stared out from the darkness beneath...

Cooper Bennett woke suddenly from a deep, medically-induced sleep. He looked around, terrified that he was still trapped in that nightmare up on the mountain trail, but after seeing he was no longer in any danger, he was able to calm down and take in his surroundings.

A sterile room surrounded him, monochrome and drab, and an array of monitoring equipment, hoses, and wires filled the space with a low hum punctuated by repetitive beeps. He was at Goodman Hospital, an inpatient due to the severity of his wounds.

The room was empty and he was alone, the only personal touches that stood out were bursts of color from modest cards and gifts on a small table near the door. There was also a boxed pecan pie from Mr. and Mrs. Arnett, and a half-eaten box of chocolate chip cookies with a sticky note on top saying "sorry" in Billy's scribbly handwriting. Some of the cards were from his teachers and associates at school, Mr. Schneck sending a huge bag of replacement gum and a six pack of soda, while his dad... well, he had sent nothing at all. Cooper expected he would be getting a gift from him when he got home, in the shape of a familiar fist or a belt. The brown one with the brass buckle was his favorite.

You best get used to it in here, Cooper thought, *because Pops will make sure you're back in no time, eating your dinner through one of these tubes.*

Cooper mulled a little bit on how he got to the hospital, vaguely remembering a wobbling journey to the bright lights of the bus station. The gruff face of a trucker also came to mind, bobtailing along Foothill Road. Cooper tried to remember his name – it might have been Travis or something like that – but he really couldn't recall. Hell, in the state he was in, he might not have asked. Thankfully, whoever he was happened to be passing by the station when a badly bleeding boy stumbled out of the fog, falling to the hard pavement.

Trying to recall more details, the faint sound of water flowing filled his ears. After looking around for a fountain or other source of the noise, Cooper finally glanced along the left edge of the bed. A catheter hose was snaking out from beneath the white and blue-speckled sheets, filling a large bag that was hanging on the side.

Lifting the end of the sheets, he peeked curiously under it and then his gown, somewhat afraid of what he would see down there. He'd heard of these things before but hadn't seen one in real life, never mind had one inserted up inside his urethra. Cringing at the visual, he saw a hose currently occupied with amber piss that strangely resembled lager. One end he'd already noticed – the one that lead to the now-filling bag. The other end plunged down into the tip of his penis like some medieval torture device, continuing all the way to his bladder. However, despite what looked like a painful muddle was quite the opposite. There was little to no discomfort at all. Yes, he had the urge to pee, but not much else. But that wasn't the weirdest thing.

His memory, fragmented as it was, recalled blood. A lot of it, along with his battered and torn skin. However, beneath the sheets and his billowy hospital robe, he only saw a modest collection of scratches across his torso, which also seemed more defined.

How is that possible? Maybe you imagined things far worse than they were, Coop. Yeah, that has to be it. You probably just fell as you were leaving Billy's place.

The marks across his abs were no larger than one would get in such a tumble, or from fingernails scraping bare flesh during a rough night of seraphic intercourse (which he imagined, still being a virgin, but he'd be lying if he said he hadn't watched a lot of porn over the years).

Then something clicked into crystal clear focus.

"MY EYES!" Cooper exclaimed, feeling for his glasses. They weren't on his face, but still somewhere on the forest floor up in the northern mountains.

I can see? he thought apprehensively, holding both of his hands in front of his face. Just like the scratches on his torso, he could see them perfectly, no matter how far he held them – right up to his nose or at the maximum extension his gaunt arms could get, they were crystal clear.

I CAN SEE!

All of this wasn't making any sense, and as he continued examining his arms up close (*are they thicker?*), he saw the most unbelievable thing. Some of the smaller scratches were disappearing like a magic eraser was wiping his skin free of injury. The larger ones still looked unchanged, but those smaller ones... *yes!* They were gone, not a single scar left in their place. In fact, his skin felt smoother, as if lathered in coconut oil.

Oh, my God, he thought. *What the hell is happening? This has to be hallucinations from the rabies that big ass wolf gave you!*

He paused.

The WOLF!

Surely the bite that feral beast gave him would still be there. Cooper flung the sheet off his leg to check, but the bite was practically healed.

"What in the ever-loving fuck?" he said aloud in complete astonishment, poking a finger on his soft and spongy skin.

He wasn't complaining by any means, just weirded out. The wound now looked like a minor bump you'd get from banging a shin on the edge of a nightstand, not bloody strings of lacerated flesh caused by the teeth of a ferocious wolf.

There came a knock on the door, causing Cooper to jump.

"W-Who is it?" he asked, stammering anxiously.

"Alyssa," a soft voice replied and his heart nearly burst out of Cooper's chest like an alien in the titular movie.

His mind was muddled.

"Come on in..." he began, then frantically followed up with, "I... I mean hang on a minute!"

Piss was still flowing out of his limp dick into the bag.

"Shit... shit... shit..." he whispered frantically, but the door was already opening. Alyssa must not have heard his pleas. He wanted to scream.

"It sounds like you're feeling better," Alyssa said as she came in. "Yesterday was quite..."

"GAH!" Cooper shouted, hitching the blanket back over himself.

She let out a scream at his sudden outburst, eyes bulging at the rim of her skull. She glared at him in the hospital bed, peeking out from behind the protection of a shield-blanket. Those only worked when you were in single digits old.

"OH GOD COOPER! You scared the shit out of me!"

Unlike the piss that's still flowing out of me? he thought before they both burst into laughter.

"Well I learned something new today: who needs double shots of espresso to wake your ass up when you know Cooper Bennett!"

Tugging a white string that was floating behind her, a bright red balloon bounced into the room, playing on the air currents. Its mylar face turned, the words GET WELL SOON appearing in block capital letters.

"You know, Cooper, I swear your hair has already grown since yesterday," Alyssa said, tying the string to the back of a chair near the gift table. She sat down.

Tight lipped, Cooper merely bobbed his head while she arched a suspicious eyebrow.

"What's wrong?"

"N-nothing…" Cooper said.

He was still peeing into the bag. She had to have heard something, or at least seen him doing it. I mean it was *right there.*

Then Alyssa giggled, watching Cooper unconsciously dart his eyes between her, the balloon, and the catheter bag. Repeat. Alyssa, balloon, catheter bag. Repeat. His heart rate monitor was beeping a little bit faster.

"I wouldn't worry too much about *that*," she told him reassuringly. "I've seen you doing it several times already."

Oh, okay, if you say so… that's perfectly fine then!

"WHAT?" he snipped.

"Yesterday…" Alyssa clarified, deliberately drawing out the *s* sound. "I came to visit when your friend Billy was here. I managed to wrestle those cookies away from him in the nick of time. Forced the gluttonous bastard to leave you an apology note too. Can you believe he wasn't going to?"

Cooper didn't know what to believe at that moment. He was mortified.

As if things couldn't get any better! he opined. *Both Billy and Alyssa have met, all while watching you pee, Coop. I bet you farted to top it all off like a great big goddamn cherry!*

"Billy's a really nice guy, Cooper," Alyssa said, thinking Cooper's expression might be one of annoyance with Billy, "and he loves you dearly as a friend and a brother. I think that may be partly why Liam…"

Cooper's head dropped in disgust at the mention of his name. Alyssa stopped, hesitating to continue. Ultimately, she went ahead.

"I think that may be partly why Liam bullies you two more than any of the others." She placed her hands in her crossed lap after fixing the hair behind her ears. "It's that bond, you see. Liam will *never* have what you and Billy do with his pack of idiots. He might think he does, but Derek and Mark are only around for the power he grants, and out of fear mixed with generous amounts of stupidity. They will never feel the way Billy does about you. I honestly don't think they're capable."

She paused and Cooper looked up at her. The expression she had was one of poise, but hidden behind it was pain. He shifted his legs over and gently swooped his head back to invite her to sit.

Alyssa got up and relocated to the corner of the hospital bed. Her back was touching Cooper's left leg as she continued.

"Let me put it this way: I've only really gotten to know Billy this weekend but before that I could see it strongly at school. I've known *you* for quite a while and find it..." her voice trailed off, hesitant to continue again. "Cherish that, Cooper. It's a gift that I had once with a girl back in elementary school and she moved away. I miss that kind of genuine friendship and love. It can shape the person you are and can become."

Cooper saw her eyes fall to the floor. He didn't like seeing her unhappy.

I plan to, he thought, *and would not mind being that for you.*

"Thanks for coming and being here, Alyssa," he said, "and for being you."

Her eyes perked back up, sparkling like champagne. She moved a hand from her thigh to his, fingers rubbing the blanket and through it, him. Then Alyssa smiled that gorgeous smile again and Cooper had no choice but to do the same.

Suddenly, he looked spooked.

"Cooper, what's wrong?" Alyssa asked, worry spreading across her face.

He didn't answer, using his tongue to feel around his mouth. Liam had knocked one of his teeth out – a front one – up on the mountain and the thought of him grinning with that embarrassing gap was almost too much to bear. But as he felt around, now with his fingers as well, they were all there.

"What is wrong with you today?" she asked.

This is getting way too crazy! he thought. *First healing up like nothing was wrong, seeing without his glasses, and now this! Next stop for Cooper Bennett: the insane asylum!*

Settling down, he finally answered Alyssa.

"It must just be effects of the medication. I could've sworn I..." He paused, wanting to tell her more but thinking it might be better if he didn't. He'd likely scare her away and that would tear him apart more than that wolf ever could. "It's nothing. Seriously... just hospital heebie-jeebies."

Cooper could tell that Alyssa was still cagey, but that – and the fact her hand hadn't moved from its resting place on his thigh – were clear signs that she hadn't stopped caring.

He knew that going forward was going to be a strange adventure, especially if the revelations in the hospital room were anything to go by, but with Alyssa there and knowing that Billy was also going to be there for him, he was perfectly fine with that.

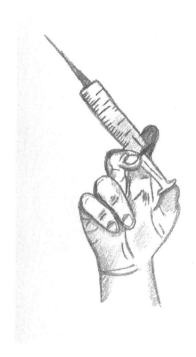

CHAPTER 9: BLOOD TESTS

Tuesday, September 4, 2012

1

Most of the doctors at Goodman Hospital were baffled by the Bennett

boy's astonishing recovery. Someone with that level of injury should have

been hospitalized for weeks, even months, which did not include the litany

of physical therapy sessions that would have followed. Instead, this

eighteen-year-old was practically back to normal in just three days, not even having the decency to take Labor Day off for rest.

The mood was one of overwrought enthusiasm that morning on the third floor. A Committee meeting was underway, most of the doctors and staff present interested in documenting the Bennett case for further study. They cited the potential of something miraculous circulating in Cooper's blood, allowing for such an unheard-of recovery time with little to no scarring.

A dissenting voice rose amongst the excited chatter, asking, "Have we all lost our sanity this morning? Everything you are saying is simply *not possible*: biologically, physically, or otherwise."

"But it *is* possible," another excitable Committee member said. "We've all seen the data. Now, if whatever this is can be identified and then harnessed properly, it could be used to create new treatments and vaccines, possibly even cures for various diseases only dreamed of before!"

The chance of success was promising and the benefits arising from it great, but there were still a few who maintained a healthy dose of level-headed skepticism.

"Marsha, while that would certainly be wonderful *if true*, let's not get ahead of ourselves and dash off into *Wonderland* just yet. This same sort of thing has crept up time after time in these so-called miracle cases. No, no, sometimes the simplest solution is the right one, which is likely the case here. Now, the boy's treating physician is Dr. Ross, am I right?"

There were a few hesitant nods around the room.

"Yes? Okay, so are we all sure he conducted a *proper* examination upon first seeing the patient?"

The man speaking was Hugh Coleman, a long-time Committee member and naysayer. His appearance was like a parched mummy that had come to life, donned a loose suit, and arrived that very morning for a Committee meeting at the hospital.

"I agree with Coleman," said Regina Ruehlman, a hawkish woman whose nose would turn up as if smelling something rank at every mention of Dr. Ross' name. "Is all the paperwork correct? Ross *has* been known to cut corners before."

Marsha shrank back in her ironically uncomfortable ergonomic chair, Regina's head tilted forward just enough so she could look down the bridge of her beak-like nose.

There was a sigh from the back of the conference room. A stout, attractive man was leaning against a wall of regulatory notices and posters. A large, blue one directly behind him said: COUGHING AND SNEEZES SPREAD DISEASES.

"There would be no harm in continuing to examine the boy," he said with a calm, almost dreamy voice. It was Dr. Ross, trying to bring some order to the situation.

"Oh no harm at all," Coleman said, "except for all the expenses. But…"

"But…" Dr. Ross went on, "before anything can happen, the patient must first agree to do it. When I last checked, this was not a prison, nor is Mr. Bennett a lab rat that can be caged and stabbed with needles at our whim. Though admittedly, from what I'm seeing and hearing this morning with all the pitchforks, the two might not be that dissimilar."

"Oh my…" Hugh blustered. "Outrageous!"

"So, you would agree to look at him?" Marsha asked hopefully, leaning forward in her seat again. She was ignoring Hugh's blathering, still going on across the table. Regina's inauspicious stare was also trying to depose her.

"Yes, but again *only* if the patient agrees."

"Well, is there anything we can do to help *encourage* that decision?" Martha asked.

Dr. Ross paused for a moment, pulling out a ballpoint pen from the clipboard held in his right hand. He started to chew on the cap.

"Now that you mention it, as a matter fact, I think there is."

2

Cooper blinked a couple of times while looking at his dad, unkempt and angry as usual, propped up against the wall of the hospital room. Cooper then glanced over to his treating physician in awe. In the doorway was a man whose lab coat and scrubs both strained against the size of his muscles. If the visible part of his veiny forearms and the thickness of his neck were anything to go by, Dr. Ross was built like a tank. Not a dumb one either (*unlike a certain quarterback*).

It was about ten fifteen per the wall clock, and Dr. Ross had been telling Cooper and his dad that the Medical Executive Committee were extending an offer for him to return for weekly checkups.

"They'd be for the next month at least," Dr. Ross said, "possibly two depending on what the results showed."

Dr. Ross had been waiting patiently for an answer. Despite his formidable size, he could not force Cooper to stay if he didn't want to.

"So, all you white-coats think my son is some kind of freak?" Roland Bennett snapped, crossing his arms. He looked ready to spit.

Cooper knew that stance as his dad's hopeful one, wherein the doctor would reply with "indeed I am calling your son a freak, what are you going to do about it?" That'd leave Roland no choice but to start a fight, which could lead to a lawsuit if he were lucky. Or death if he weren't considering the size and obvious strength of his opponent.

"Not at all, Mr. Bennett," Dr. Ross replied, refusing to take the bait. "In fact, we believe Cooper to be quite… special."

"Special's just another of way of saying freak, doc. You know, like those ret…"

"No need to dive into the details of that, Mr. Bennett," Dr. Ross said, his clipboard raised and waving. "*Again,* let me assure you that your son is in no way a freak and we have no ill intent."

"What a load of shit. You have intent," Roland continued, not wanting to let it go. "I want my son to have nothing more to do with you goddamn blood-suckers; worse than vampires when it comes to bleeding me dry of my hard-earned money."

Dr. Ross clarified that there would be no charge for this *voluntary* contribution to the "advancement of medicine" as Marsha put it, and before Roland could spit out another protest, Dr. Ross told them that the hospital would even pay Cooper one hundred dollars per visit for the privilege of taking samples.

Roland opened his mouth anyway…

"Weekends are fine, too," Dr. Ross said, "so as not to interrupt his school any more than already has been. I'll adjust my schedule so I can personally perform the exams."

Roland snapped his mouth shut, then dropped it open again like a broken mailbox door. He wanted nothing to do with these damn tests or the damn hospital, and Cooper realized the reason for all the protesting was because *he* was getting all the attention. Such "easy money" being handed out (to his worthless son no less), while all his (and his alone, goddammit) was "hard-earned."

Good ol' Pops, putting family first as always.

"No offense intended to you, Mr. Bennett," Dr. Ross chimed in, the cords along the side of his neck jutting out as he tried to keep himself professional, "but as your son is eighteen, he is entitled to make this decision *without* your consent."

Roland scoffed as he pushed off the wall, arms plunging to his side. Cooper tensed up, expecting him to start swinging at any moment but there were no punches. Instead, Roland stormed toward the exit, making sure his shoulder struck Dr. Ross' as he passed.

The doctor didn't move, sending Roland flying to the left like he'd hit a brick wall.

Roland muttered "asshole" in a desperate effort to recover his machismo. Then the door slammed so hard something cracked.

"Such a charming man," Dr. Ross said, looking back to Cooper. "I don't see how you've managed for so long."

A look of instant regret popped up on the doctor's face; his professionalism had apparently just left the room with Roland.

"I wonder that myself," Cooper said with a laugh. "All the time."

"Well, please forgive me for my momentary lapse in etiquette, Cooper. As far as these tests go, this is your call. The results could be astonishing, but you're in no way required to do anything. I know you've been through a lot, so just let me know. Either way you go, the paperwork's been done."

There was a knock at the door, too gentle to be Cooper's dad. He would have just barged back in.

"I'll do it," Cooper replied, admittedly more to find things out for himself than to help others.

Dr. Ross smiled and opened the door.

"Thank you, Cooper. I'll plan to see you early this Saturday then." Nodding to someone on the other side of the door, Dr. Ross looked back to Cooper. "You have a new visitor my friend. Quite the popular fellow this weekend."

"Yeah, who'd have thought all it would take was getting attacked up on a mountain to bring out all my fans," Cooper replied.

Dr. Ross left chuckling, swinging his wide frame sideways to let the guest in as he went out.

"Hello," Cooper said pleasantly to the stoic and suited figure. "I'm not sure we've met."

"No, Mr. Bennett, we have not. Not in person at least," the man replied, adjusting his expensive watch then tie somewhat nervously. "But I believe

you *have* met my son. My name is Grayson Manning, and I've come to talk

to you about Liam…"

3

Cooper finally felt his jaw lift off the tiled floor, hinging back into place

with a comedic *creak*. A cold spot still clung to him, cold like snow, snow

as white as Grayson Manning's hair.

Grayson closed the door. Stepped forward. Found a place to rest against

the wall. It was just past the foot of the hospital bed; the same area Cooper's

father had occupied before he left in a rage. A popular spot for fathers, it

seemed.

"Mr. Bennett, I must apologize for my son's actions," Grayson said. It

sounded like a rehearsed line that'd been repeated over and over, a new

name inserted at the front each time. "The injuries he's caused you are a

cause for great concern."

Great concern for me or you? Cooper thought, leaning back on a stack

of pillows. Lacing his fingers behind his head, it wasn't as comfortable as

he'd have liked. He opened his mouth and with newfound confidence spoke

from his gut, his brain having no idea what was about to come out.

"While I appreciate that, Mr. Manning, I have to ask: would your apology be for *all* your son's "actions"? I'm talking about the ones he's performed in the classrooms and down the halls at school, the ones on the sidewalks and streets of town – guaranteed delivery rain, or snow, or shine. The ones last week, last month, last year, and many *years* ago. Or, Mr. Manning, is your apology just for his actions this past Friday night, since they became so public and, as you said, are a cause for concern?"

Grayson stared numbly without a single movement nor blink. His look was one of a man that hadn't realized the breadth of his son's transgressions. Yes, he was aware of most things Liam had done (he literally had to pay for them), but somehow nothing pertaining to the Bennett boy. Liam had hidden that well but now Grayson could see the upset within in the boy's eyes for himself, so deep his soul was hurting.

"Mr. Bennett, my..."

"Cooper's fine."

"Well then, Cooper," Grayson amended, "my apology extends to *all* of those things. Past and present."

"And future, I'll guarantee it," Cooper added, crossing his arms in the hopes that would be more comfortable. It wasn't, the entire conversation with Liam's dad the reason why.

"Let's hope not..."

Cooper didn't reply, not wanting to push the issue even though he knew he was right. Grayson looked as though he knew it too.

"Let's not beat around the bush," Grayson said, placing one hand in his trouser pockets while running the other along the sheets. He was pacing along the edge of the bed. "I will be covering all of your outstanding medical expenses. There's no point in arguing, it's already been taken care of."

Are you nuts, Mr. Manning? Cooper thought, changing positions for a third time. He had no intention of disagreeing, though had his father still been there he would certainly find a reason to.

Grayson continued to talk, mainly about Liam's temper being the cause of all these issues, and as he did, Cooper realized that the two of them had something in common. It was a thin strand tying them both together: while Cooper had a constant and daily struggle with his dad's rage, Grayson was dealing with the same from his son. They both would likely agree, had it come up in conversation, that fixing the problem was far harder than just dealing with the colorful aftermath. Cooper's took on shades of black and blue, Grayson's green wallet turning red.

Then came a fleeting thought: *what if Pops and Liam were father and son...* Cooper sheared it from his mind before the shuddering stopped.

"So, that brings us to the injuries Liam gave you," Grayson said, his mind not wandering though frightening parental combinations but staying focused on Cooper's face and body parts not covered by the gown or bedsheets.

Like anyone else hearing of this attack, Grayson expected to see sutured gashes and stained gauze across heavily damaged skin – the typical hallmarks of a physical assault of this caliber. Yet, there wasn't anything more than a few scratches and some faint blotches of discoloration. That could mean one of several things Grayson was aware of that Cooper was not, but one more than any other stood out in the forefront of Grayson's mind...

"Liam did manage to beat the shit out of me," Cooper said casting his eyes down toward his lap, "and his sidekicks Mark –"

"Brown and Derek Wilder?"

Cooper nodded. Grayson's once gliding fingers dug into the sheets. If had long nails they would have torn the cotton.

"This is going to sound like a very bizarre question, Cooper," Grayson said in a low voice. It was almost too low, as if he didn't want it heard at all.

More bizarre than your son magically turning into a wolf, Mr. Manning?

Cooper wanted to say that very thing but didn't. Something told him not to. Not yet at least.

Grayson cleared his throat and let out a sigh, asking, "Did any of those three boys *bite* you?"

Cooper shook his head this time and watched Mr. Manning's dug-in fingers draw the sheets up into a fist. It was trembling.

"So, none of them bit you?" Grayson asked with a troubling look in his eyes. Their blue sparkle was dying.

"No..." Cooper said, and then came the words Grayson secretly did not want to hear. "I was bitten by a wolf..."

Grayson quickly let go of the sheets, stepping back against the wall as if avoiding something vile and contagious.

"A big, black wolf, in fact," Cooper continued. "It had such fierce yellow eyes. I'll remember them until the day I die."

Had Grayson been brushed by feather, he would've been knocked over. His face grew pale, garish against the whiteness of his hair. Sweat started forming on his face and had he been hooked up to the machines instead of Cooper, they'd have indicated high blood pressure and an escalating heart rate.

"I... must go. I've forgotten about another appointment," Grayson said suddenly, swiping a forearm across his brow. The sweat left a dark stain on the suit fabric.

"Mr. Manning..." Cooper said, knowing no appointment existed.

"What *are you?*"

Grayson stopped just ahead of the door, his arm already outstretched with a hand resting on the handle. Cooper had seen more than he was letting on.

"'What are *we?*' you mean to say, Mr. Bennett," he replied, the door creaking and moaning as it swung open. "*We* are in uncharted territory; dangerous without a map to guide us. Now, please, I must go. Again, don't worry about the expenses, they've been taken care of. I'm sure our paths will cross soon, but until then I bid a good day to you."

CHAPTER 10: TOGETHER

Thursday September 20, 2012

1

Cooper had been back at school for two weeks and due to his lack of gruesome injuries (everyone expecting blood and guts with so many horror movies releasing over the next month), a bunch of students and even faculty – though only within the walls and closed doors of the staff break room –

whispered that the details of Cooper Bennett's injuries had been greatly exaggerated.

Waves of backlash broke against the victim, foaming with accusations that he was just "a lonely nerd making shit up for more attention from Alyssa Noble" and that "a girl like her would never pay a boy like him any attention." Many went so far as to doubt it was a wild animal attack to begin with, suggesting Cooper had been tossed over the handlebars of his bicycle when he hit a pothole ("because, what kind of eighteen-year-old doesn't have a car?) or dared to walk and chew gum at the same time ("because, as we *all* know he's not *that* talented").

Despite all of the hate, or rather because of it, his budding relationship with Alyssa had plenty of fertilizer to grow in. It kept rising and they bonded quickly since her hospital visits. They would steal glances in the halls between classes – long enough at times to be noticed by someone but quick enough to be shrugged off as a figment of their obviously defunct imagination. There was even one time in the Pine Sol scented darkness of the janitor's closet just outside Mr. Whitaker's classroom where Cooper actually *kissed* Alyssa. It was just before lunch and they only had a few minutes away from prying eyes, but the outfit she was wearing (a red knit sweater, trendy corduroy shorts hitched at mid-thigh, and long, black stockings that clung to her shapely legs) drove him to take the chance. They would have gotten away with it unnoticed, too, had Cooper not gotten a little too excited, knocking over a forest of brooms and mops, causing Mr. Roper to jerk the door open, his own broom at the ready to smash against the skull of the giant rats he was sure were plaguing the walls. Instead he found Cooper and Alyssa in there, shooing them off to lunch.

"Horny kids!" he shouted. "Get a room!"

The two decided to move their more physical encounters to after school hours. When Alyssa could evade Liam, she'd often meet Cooper at one of Goodman's many small parks, the two simply passing the time in each other's company while laughing about the day, especially when it came to Billy and his never-ending appetite.

Speaking of him, Billy had found Cooper's backpack (the one he'd thrown into the yard when running for his life) early the morning of September first. The soggy grass and light rain overnight had soaked through the thin exterior, swelling the textbooks inside to double their size. Cooper's relationship with Billy had grown like those books, just as it had for many years before, yet it was becoming more obvious each day (starting as a hunch but manifesting as prolonged stares), that Billy seemed bothered by having to share Cooper's time with Alyssa. Regardless of those kinks, things were good between all three of them.

After all, why wouldn't they be? Cooper thought. *They did bond over your unconscious self peeing into a bag.*

Cooper chuckled at his thoughts that early Thursday morning, making his way across the one and a half eastward miles to Alyssa's house. Feeling more energetic since leaving the hospital and after their janitor closet encounter, Cooper had started jogging every other morning with her. On the alternate days they didn't run, she would help with an early morning yoga class. It was in the field across from Roop's Den, on the south side of town across Beast's Crossing.

Cooper stopped briefly in the parking lot of the East Pine Strip Mall, recalling their last trip along Wolf's Ridge Greenway. It was a little over a week ago, on a morning similar to this one, though it yielded scenery far more appalling than the light fog currently blanketing the streets in a veil of...

2

Wednesday, September 12, 2012

"Gray," Cooper said, panting lightly. "All I'm managing to see right now is gray." He closed his eyes and frowned. "Along with some random flashes of light. Lucky me!"

"Well, that's because you *already* ran nearly two miles here!" Alyssa laughed, stepping up to Cooper's side before doing standing leg stretches. He might have taken a peek while she did them. "I'm surprised you're not seeing the back of your eyelids; I'd have fainted by now!"

"Oh, I like what I'm seeing now," he replied. "I still might faint."

Cooper had hardly broken a sweat. If not for his light breaths, it'd be impossible to tell he'd been running at all.

Alyssa finished stretching and glanced over to him, dressed in plain joggers and a tee-shirt, white like most days (she thought if he had worn his gray one, that would have been hilarious). It was strange, but he seemed to fill out his clothes more these days, notable in the chest, arms, and butt (not that she looked at it more than once… or perhaps *three* times at most).

"You almost ready?" Cooper asked, rolling his eyes as she began yet *another* set of stretches. After a week, his hair had gotten significantly longer, affording him the opportunity for a swift, mocking hair flip. "Geez, woman."

"Better a woman than a diva, Coop."

Alyssa lived in a nice house: three stories and brick, with a stunning wraparound porch on the first and second floors. She and Cooper were standing on the first floor looking north from the back of the house. Situated at the end of leaf-strewn Ridgeline Lane, the home was on the border of Goodman and the Jameson Nature Preserve, nestled amongst dense trees that surrounded the subdivision of Primwood Estates.

While doing her routine, now a set of standing straight leg stretches that arched her back and popped out her behind in sensuous fashion, Alyssa smirked, knowing Cooper didn't mind the view despite his feeble complaining. She was glad they'd decided to go on these morning jogs together, helping to clear her mind and bring them closer. After all, this would be their third run and as the old adage goes: third time's a charm.

"Okay, I'm ready," she said, securing her hair with a lilac tie. "North again?"

"How about we switch it up this time and go south?"

"After you sir." She extended a hand toward the stairs in the center of the porch.

"Oh no, one has to be respectful of their elders. After *you.*"

"I'm only two days older!" Alyssa scoffed, her voice as sharp as her nipples in the cool morning air.

"Key word's right there at the end, milady."

Alyssa rolled her eyes so far back in her head she could see into the kitchen behind her. Eventually sliding her eyes back into place and caving to such incredible amounts of ageist pressure, Alyssa made way for the steps. Cooper followed, and the two of them proceeded to cross the spongy lawn at a light pace, meandering down a misty trail worn between the trees on the west side of the property. It led them to the edge of a babbling stream, the shaded trail of Wolf's Ridge Greenway running alongside for a total of two and a half miles. Based on Cooper's suggestion, the pair turned south and began their run.

"How far do you want to head?" Cooper asked.

"All the way to the highway and back?" Alyssa suggested, her breasts bouncing with each word. "It's about one and a half miles from here, so that'd be a good three-mile haul. Unless you're not up for that since you *did* decide to run to my house first."

"Oh, I'm up for the challenge."

"I bet you're *up* for a lot of things," she replied playfully. "You know you're not going to smell very good when we're done, right?"

"You expect anything else from me?" he said. "Full on B.O. means one thing…"

Cooper's body started responding to all the banter, making it more difficult to run. His foot hit a shallow indention, twisted, and he stumbled forward, managing to right himself before falling completely over.

"A water-conserving shower back at the house before we head to class?" Alyssa said and Cooper had to stop running, an instant splint forming down his right leg.

Not sure what I was thinking but that takes the prize!

Alyssa blushed, noticing Cooper's impediment in his joggers. Since the two of them had only kissed each other up to that point (not counting the janitor's closet where things were getting more physical), they were both more than ready to release essentially years of built up tension.

However, as Cooper's life always seemed to request and cruel fate would deliver, their plans were cut short when passing one of many benches lining the forest side of the trail. This particular one was innocuous enough, the small memorial plaque dedicated to a MR. JOHN GRIMES. The engraved letters were shallow and worn – nearly illegible – but there were flecks of red on it. Those drew Cooper's attention like a fish to a wriggling worm. Below the sign was a dark stain on the mossy wood slats. It was ruddy and fresh. More red splotches were beyond the bench, splashed like a Jackson Pollock painting against a canvas of green and yellow foliage.

"Is that what I think it is?" Alyssa asked, half withdrawing, half leaning forward.

Cooper muttered something that sounded like a "yes" but it could have been a sigh. He moved ahead, wrestling free of Alyssa's hand which was trying, quite unsuccessfully, to keep him from doing so.

"Cooper, wait," she begged. "Let's get a hold of the police to…"

It was no use, Cooper already past the bench and halfway to the tree line. From there, he spotted an object lodged in the middle of a split, lichen-crusted trunk. It was a fitted baseball cap, bright red in color. The woods seemed to darken the longer Cooper stared.

Alyssa looked on from a safe distance as Cooper walked through the overgrowth toward the cap, unable to call his name which was locked in her throat behind a thin wall of dread.

This is a bad idea Coop, he thought, seeing the cap was actually white, the red dripping off it like wax from a guttered candle. Yet this was no wax cast.

As a disgusting (*rather, delicious*) metallic smell swirled in his nostrils, it confirmed what Cooper feared (*rather, loved*). A copious amount of blood was dripping from the cap; fresh as juice from a squeezed grapefruit. He reached out to check if the cap was the only thing lodged in the tree and when he touched it, something slid forward to greet him.

Cooper jerked away, the blank and lifeless eyes of nineteen-year-old Jamie Henderson (missing about the same time Cooper went in hospital) staring skyward, forever unseeing.

Alyssa had stepped up to the overgrown brush, peering through the branches as Cooper circled around the tree. Her eyes widened, hands flying to the sides of her face as Cooper gasped, a little vomit escaping. Half the boy's body was missing, gnawed off grotesquely even through the bones. Uneven spears of rib jutted out from an emptied chest cavity like broken teeth from diseased gums. As Cooper recoiled, a rancid smell grabbed hold, assaulting him where the visuals had not.

The wall of dread Alyssa had constructed collapsed and the scream she had been holding back finally broke through, flooding the peaceful trail with a terrible noise that silenced the birds and sent them scattering from the trees.

The third time was a charm alright. A real doozy.

3

Thursday September 20, 2012

While in math class waiting impatiently for the block to end, Cooper shuddered at the memory of seeing such a mangled body eight days ago. A younger version of himself might have been scared shitless – and rightfully so – but something about seeing it that day seemed... okay.

Cooper shook his head; perhaps okay wasn't the right word for this (seeing corpses brutalized to that extent should never be *okay*). He mulled it over and decided that "desensitized" was a better way of describing how all this made him feel, especially after the bite. He'd never tell anyone, including Billy and Alyssa, but secretly a part of him admired what he saw. Craved it. Wanted to *do* it...

Okay, okay that's enough, Coop!

He tried to take his mind off the blood and gore, fidgeting for a moment with a No. 2 pencil. It was nowhere near as fun, switching his concentration to the jumble of complex equations and numbers Mrs. Kenamer had scrolled all over the whiteboard.

What is that mess? he thought. *Who in their right mind is going to use all this crap in real life?*

Once again, Cooper found himself thinking about the woods as he tried to decipher the mass of equations, and Mrs. Kenamer's liberal use of red ink to underline and circle points all over the board reminded him of all that splattered blood.

Cooper's mind drifted over to his visits with Dr. Ross at Goodman Hospital. He'd been there two Saturdays in a row, earning himself two-hundred dollars so far. His next appointment was on the twenty-second; the day after tomorrow.

For some reason Dr. Ross found himself excitedly telling stories while pulling blood, hair and tissue samples for testing. At least he let Cooper do the urine and stool samples in private. Perhaps Dr. Ross saw something in Cooper that reminded him of someone – a son, a nephew, a friend – Cooper had no idea but he sure welcomed the information.

The doctor would slip into tales of the injuries he'd seen over the years.

Some in the past were quite nasty, making Cooper feel nauseous, but recently the descriptions of the wounds Dr. Ross relayed were all consistent in their gruesome detail.

What the hell is happening in Goodman? Cooper pondered.

It wouldn't surprise him one bit if news broke on TV or even in the *Courier* one day that Liam Manning had been arrested on charges for killing all these people. He was temperamental enough to do it, and probably had done so to all those innocent lives. But what proof was there short of a full confession? Cooper's word? There was more of a chance that Santa Claus would come waltzing into the classroom to rub his belly, farting on the unlucky children that would be receiving coal than Liam stood of getting arrested because poor Cooper Bennett pointed a finger at the mean, rich bully.

If it's not Liam doing the killings, Cooper's mind raced, *then what about that black wolf?*

Cooper's pencil snapped in two, his strength still on the rise.

Never mind what's happening in Goodman... what's happening to you, Coop?

Dr. Ross had said the results from the first set of samples should start coming back for him to do a more detailed analysis within a week, two at the latest. The lab the hospital used normally had a quick turnaround, but had been backlogged with a lot of work out of Alabama's gulf coast. Something was apparently in the water there, causing symptoms akin to food poisoning, but that's all the doctor knew about that situation and thus, all Cooper knew about what happened to him

At last, the bell rang and class was over.

Cooper collected his things and walked the halls looking for Billy. Lunch was right after the next class and he wanted to check if they were going to the cafeteria (serving Asian cuisine that day) or somewhere offsite. He could hear not-so-quiet whispers as he moved down the hall. Some were amazed by the changes in his body. Others aroused by them, wondering if the growth was *everywhere*. Most however were suspicious, apparently thinking he was on steroids since he had put on some weight.

Guess an alleged fall from a bike or chewing gum while walking warrants steroid use, Cooper thought angrily. He tried not to show it in his face. Roid rage and all.

To their defense, Cooper had put on at least twenty pounds in the last two weeks alone, hovering around the one-sixty mark on the scale his last visit to the doctor's office. Dr. Ross assured the school that Cooper was not under the influence of any illegal substances – they took far longer to act than just two weeks to add that much weight – and that it was just a growth spurt alongside ample amounts of good food during recovery. Of course,

Dr. Ross had no idea what the real cause was, at least not yet, but the added muscle growth was obviously triggered by Cooper's injuries up in the mountains. He supposed there had been a chemical shift that caused the muscle fibers to spontaneously generate new myofibrils. It was all just a stab in the dark for now, hopes held high that the incoming test results would shed light on some, if not all, of Cooper's changes.

Another effect that lead people to think Cooper was infusing testosterone through a needle was all that rapid hair growth. It made for a hilarious sight that Billy would point out often: quite a lot of students – girls *and* boys – were jealous of it, some were downright horny, their eyes grabbing what their hands could not. While modest on his arms, chest, and legs (those were covered in a light dusting of fur), it was his head and face where the most dramatic and attractive changes occurred.

Where he'd once been eternally buzzed, making his body resemble a walking cotton swab, his head now flowed with silky, ebony locks that ran down to the tip of his nose when pulled. He'd also grown a thick yet short beard. Using some of the money he'd made from the first rounds of tests, Cooper splurged on a haircut (zero to number two mid-fade, short on the back, long on the top and front). Not only did it look amazing on him, it was like a buy one, get one free offer when it also sent his father (and his fists) reeling into the walls of their house.

That incident underscored a long running sentiment that both men could not wait to part ways at the end of the school year. If they never heard from each other again, it would have been too soon.

4

The same could not be said for Liam Manning, who had been simmering in his own pool of jealous juices all day long. He couldn't *wait* for a chance to see Cooper one on one after school. There was something about seeing him strut about the school with his new hair, build, and clothes – still from the goodwill shop on the corner of Market and Center Streets, but stylish nonetheless – sucking up the attention that should be Liam's. He'd never admit it, but Cooper was a threat to his dominance now. That had to end, for good.

Having extracted details from an unfortunate sophomore (he overhead Cooper and Alyssa talking at lunch about hanging out at Spring Park after school), Liam hopped into his BMW and drove that way, Mark and Derek in tow as always.

This is gonna end now, bitch…

Turning off Hanlon Road a few minutes later – he hit every red light along the way – Liam scanned the park, skidding to a halt when he saw both Alyssa and Cooper sitting on a bench overlooking the small lake.

His arm was around her.

Her head was resting peacefully against his shoulder.

A family of ducks were swimming peacefully in the water.

The afternoon sun peeked in and out of the clouds overhead.

All of it made Liam sick. Resentful. Incensed.

He bolted from his car, no real thoughts on his mind but heat flaming in his eyes. His heart raced and his legs burned as they carried him sprinting toward the couple.

"Bennett!" Liam shouted, immediately swinging down at Cooper's annoying little head.

Cooper was swift, dodging it so quickly that Alyssa slid down the bench, narrowly missing getting struck herself. Liam's hand met the wood, splintering it on impact.

"As a quarterback, you really need to work on your aim," Cooper said as he rose.

Hidden in her flattened position on the bench, Alyssa smiled.

"Come on you FUCK!" Liam shouted. It was almost desperate. "Stop talking and let's get this shit over and done... NOW!"

He didn't give Cooper a chance to reply before swinging again. This one made contact with his chest but was far less effective than up on the mountain. Enraged, Liam struck again and...

Cooper held out his hand, suddenly stopping Liam mid-punch.

Mark and Derek moved to attack.

"No!" Liam shouted with an exasperated breath. He had expended a lot of energy with those swings. "I have to do *this* alone! As for you..." he directed to Alyssa with malice in his words. "You need to choose. Right here, right now!"

She was standing up by the bench now, hands clasped tightly in front of her waist. School-girlish. Proper. Obedient.

He didn't get a reply, instead Alyssa continued standing there defiantly in silence, a breeze stirring her hair like writhing serpents. Her soft eyes were brimming, filled with fear (of what Liam might do), sadness (that it had come to this), and glee (that her sentence may *actually* be over).

Is this bitch forgetting her place? Liam thought, lips quivering. Nobody forgot their place when it came to the Mannings. Not one person, not even for a second, especially some blonde cunt named Alyssa Noble.

"I'm waiting," Liam said. His free hand was down at his side, fingers curled around like the legs of huge, dead spiders. His bones were *cracking* again. It was a terrible sound. "Interest is stacking up high and I don't think you'll have enough to pay for the wrong decision."

Liam waited, but couldn't spot a trace of discomfort or fear in her face. It was gone, replaced by something he never expected to see from her:

confidence.

"It seems like you've made up my mind for me," she replied quietly, walking over to Cooper.

He let go of Liam's fist and the couple joined hands.

Liam staggered back, face twitching between shock and anger. He didn't know how to take this new feeling of rejection. He didn't know or like the feeling of being second to anything. All he *did* know is that she had just made the...

Wrong choice.

"Wilder! Brown! Come on, let's go," he said.

The trio made way for the BMW, speeding west along Market Street once they were all inside.

"Guess that's over," Cooper said, leaning in to kiss Alyssa.

"No," she said afterward. "If the years have taught me anything, it's that Liam won't give up that easily. His approach is going to change, but we're far from done with him yet."

"Oh joy," Cooper replied, spinning at the sound of crunching gravel.

Ready to fight again, Cooper relaxed when he saw that it was Billy walking up behind them, returning from a food run.

"You're always eating," Alyssa said.

"Your point?" Billy replied with a cream-filled, chocolate donut in his mouth.

Alyssa feigned a gasp.

"My point, *William*, is one: you're going to get fat if you aren't careful. But two, and most importantly: where's *my* food?"

Digging around in his pocket with a sour face (nobody called him William without the sour face), he tossed Alyssa her car keys. His other hand was precariously balancing a gigantic box of pizza from Castillo's – edges rimmed in mouth-watering grease. Above that was another sizable box of original glazed donuts from Kimmy's ("Hole foods are part of a balanced diet").

Alyssa tossed her keys into her bag and took the boxes off Billy's hands. They were heavier – and hotter – than they looked.

"So," Billy said, removing the creamy donut. A great, big bite of it was missing and a large blob of filling dropped to the ground as he chewed. "What'd I miss?"

Chapter 11: A Night to Remember

Friday, September 28, 2012

1

It'd been quite the tumultuous week since Alyssa and Cooper had decided to give each other's company an official whirl. As Alyssa predicted, Liam and his bullying all but disappeared from their lives. His presence at school, though still physical, was much less an impact on their daily routine. Alyssa found it a reprieve, though she was still leery of what Liam would try to do as penance for her "wrong decision." Maintaining her guard despite the thin smile she wore and well-manicured appearance she maintained, she was prepared for it to happen at any time.

What she was unprepared for (though it made her feel better to lie that she knew it was coming) was that Liam's absence in her old life added depth to the new one that all the shallow, fair-weather friends could not afford to drown in. So, they gladly turned their backs on her, stepping away from the water's edge.

Earlier in the week on Tuesday, things had gotten bad. A new gang of supposed bullies tried to make up for the lack of Manning-branded thrills and spectacles, their leader – a junior by the name of Ralph Bester – walking around as if he had a pair of pendulous balls stuffed into his Fruit of the Loom tighty-whities. Entering the cafeteria with enough feigned swagger for an entire gang of Wild West outlaws, Ralph strode right up to Cooper Bennett, grabbed his plastic food tray, and pushed it and its contents right into his favorite tee-shirt.

The simple motion of turning up that tray sparked an immense food fight – the largest and messiest the school had ever seen – but Cooper was not using mashed potatoes to deliver his blows by the end.

Ralph was sent to the hospital with a broken nose and Cooper was relegated to detention for God knows how long, the only thing holding off expulsion was Dr. Ross again saving him with the fact he was not under the influence of illegal drugs, and the boy in the hospital had delivered the first blow.

Alyssa was in her room that Friday afternoon. It was a rather charming and beautiful space, the centerpiece an over-sized bed fitted with floral print bedding in differing shades of purple and green. It smelled like fresh linens on clothesline in there, and the walls were painted a vintage blue like an overcast sky. They brimmed with antiqued frames that matched the furniture pieces and robust shelves of all sizes, all overflowing with tasteful and simple trinkets. She was getting ready to take a shower before getting herself lost in a book when her phone's alert chimed pleasantly.

Checking it, she saw that it was a text message from Cooper (he'd bought a cheap smartphone with another batch of earnings from his hospital tests).

WANT 2 GO OUT? the message asked.

The invite, Alyssa would later learn, was for a proper date; their first since she'd officially chosen him to be her boyfriend.

Yes, her fingers tapped anyway, simply wanting to see his face after the crazy week they'd both had. It was becoming like a drug, and being away gave her withdrawals. *PS: no need to yell with all capital letters. LOL.*

I'M SORRY!

Then another reply came through at once, all lower case.

really sorry this time! ps last detention served, so im yours after school again :)

2

Smiling as she speedily typed her reply, Alyssa hit send, forgetting the period.

"Well, I just told my mother I wasn't going to make the dinner she set up with the Cuffles. Oops."

She was wearing a dark blue cotton dress which showed off her sleek legs, capped with a cute pair of peep-toe wedges.

"Who are they?" asked the driver.

"The owners of Cuffle's Barbecue, the joint just down from Goodman Middle School. They also happen to own a couple of large restaurants in Clayton and I *think* even the Crispy Biscuit in town, but don't quote me on that. In short, there's a lot of food service money and an eligible son, so Mom's desperately trying to fill this gaping social hole with it."

"The one that's there because Liam's out of the picture?"

"Bingo," Alyssa replied, her index finger bouncing with the syllables. "Bye, bye, Manning Moolah."

"I have to ask: why do you like me so much then? I'm not made of money…"

Alyssa's smile fractured into a broken one, genuinely caught off-guard.

"Cooper, it's not your money or your looks that caught me," she said, looking over to the driver's seat. Cooper was there, shirt straining against the size of his thickened arms as he steered. "It's your personality more than anything. Who you are versus *what* you are, if that makes sense."

Sinking back in the seat, brown snapback cap turned forward, Cooper looked like a wannabe gangster, driving her Acura RL like it was an eighties Caddy raised up on solid gold twenty-fours. He was bobbing his head in agreement.

"You better calm down *Mister* Bennett," she warned, emphasizing his title with an extra-long *s* as they rode south on Center Street. "You don't want us to get pulled over and *you* a citation for driving without a license."

Alyssa's warning, though crass, was warranted. Goodman's south end was far cleaner and ritzier (by small town standards) than elsewhere within the limits and as such the people who lived there were more prudish if putting it nicely, snobbish assholes if being honest. Alyssa preferred to use the latter all the time while her mother liked the former when in the presence of others, saving the latter for use behind closed doors.

"Fine," Cooper said disappointingly, adding a pout for emphasis.

He twisted the brim toward the back and his hair flopped alluringly through the cap's opening. A skosh more of the good ol' country boy was coming back through. Fitting, since not two minutes later their car was stuck behind a tractor, its wide tires taking up most of the road. Normally the situation would have warranted plenty of road rage, but that night it didn't bother either of them the least bit.

More time together, Alyssa thought, seeing the same sentiment in Cooper's dark and seductive eyes when he occasionally glanced her way.

Alyssa didn't know if it was due to the way light was falling on Cooper's smooth skin, or the fact he smelled incredible (though she knew he didn't have any cologne), but she stirred in her seat, crossing her legs to stop the flow of excitement. That was just from *looking* at him – someone who had everything she desired from Liam and more.

After fifteen minutes for a ride that should have taken five, the two pulled into the parking lot of Wilson's Sports Bar and Grill. It was located on the outer edge of town across the four lanes of U.S. 76. Over time, the highway had become more of a dam than a road, Goodman's social elite stacking up along the town side like deep water, while those businesses and residents on the "other side" found themselves bereft of their pleasantries.

Thank God for that, most of them would think, but not the proprietor of Wilson's, who knew all green bills spent the same.

The parking lot of the restaurant was sparse, most people forgetting their differences while enjoying time under the *Friday Night Lights,* swooning over Liam and his pigskin at Goodman High.

Cooper wheeled into one of the empty spaces along the front of the establishment, one over from a handicapped space occupied by a rusted out '87 Buick Regal. As the Acura came to a stop, Cooper watched the heavily tattooed proprietor – Alyssa mentioned his name was Jake or Jacob, something along those lines – taping a notice up on both double doors.

"I hope they're not closing early," he moaned, some of that pent-up tractor-rage leeching out.

"I don't think so," Alyssa said, noticing a lot written on the letter-sized paper. She squinted, but couldn't make out the text below the large COMING SOON that had been printed across the top.

Cooper tried and found he was able to read the whole thing easily. Apparently, Jacob was working on a deal to get cameras set up at the high school so he could stream the game on one or more of the television screens inside. Cooper thought that would be an expensive and risky thing to do, but given the number of people that could potentially come in on Fridays so long as they had a glimpse of the score and some visuals to go with it, he could very well rise out of the red, break even, and be in the black before long.

Great, was all Alyssa could think about as Cooper relayed what it said line by line, *this will be one less place to escape the mad Manning worshipers.*

Her attention shifted back to better things, Cooper just opening his car door. She couldn't help but notice his strapping forearm again (the right one, closest to her, still up on the steering wheel).

Alyssa had seen him shirtless both before and after the remarkable changes over the last month, and though she already admitted (truthfully) to liking Cooper for who he was, the physical transformation was like icing on a very tasty cake. It led her to wonder where else on his body veins were protruding from tight skin.

Cooper made his way around and opened her side of the car, and the way he looked down as she slid those long legs out and onto the pavement let her know without question that she would be finding out soon enough.

3

The food at Wilson's was inexpensive but satisfying, a good value for the amount and quality received. Cooper took full advantage of it, yet Alyssa found herself more charmed by the little happy dance he would do every time a new dish came out.

Was it childish? *Yes.*

Was it true to who he was? *You bet.*

Cooper had ordered not one, or two, but *three* appetizers (Thai chicken tenders, spicy meatballs, and loaded potatoes wedges), along with a ribeye steak with broccoli and cheddar macaroni. For dessert, he went surprisingly simple: one bowl of plain vanilla ice cream topped with a single cherry.

Though he had ordered that feast for himself, he did offer to share the occasional bite with her. She would wave him off, not wanting to ruin her own appetite, yet despite all the protests Alyssa was still only able to eat half of her Cobb salad; Italian vinaigrette on the side. Cooper gladly took her plate when done and polished it off for her.

"You sure you don't want to ask for dust next time?" Cooper asked her, correcting himself immediately with, "Oh that's right: too many calories."

Kicking him under the table, Alyssa's wedges made a satisfying *thump* against his shin. She beamed, then laughed along with him as the server came over with the bill.

A short time later, Alyssa was breathing in the evening air as they left. It was warmer than earlier, the smell of distant rain on the wind. However, the night was still young and the tension between the two was becoming palpable in ways other than their glances. Alyssa developed a warmth behind her ears that trickled down her neck and a flutter in her chest like the wings of a hundred butterflies beating in unison. Cooper on the other hand looked calm yet carnal; a gentleman ready to pounce like a beast.

"Guess that's it then," he said, baiting the hook. It was his eyes that gave it away – lustful and wanting. He opened her door.

"Well," Alyssa said, slipping into the seat as if sitting upon that fishhook. "It doesn't have to be over. Keller's is just up the street and I'm sure they're showing something decent."

Cooper was seeing something decent alright. Alyssa had left her legs out, crossing them slowly. Her hands slid down the outside of that snug dress, clutching the fabric as if she was going to rip the entire thing off.

"I've never been to a drive-in movie theater before," Cooper said with a smirk, his right arm propped against the door frame, his left dangling while two fingers danced on her thigh.

"Me either..." she panted.

"Guess this is a night of firsts for us then." His eyes narrowed.

"I certainly hope so," she said through a quivering sigh. "Come on, let's go see what's playing."

Keller's was Goodman's only theater, opening fifteen years earlier in 1997. Being within the small-town limits (even on "the other side" of U.S. 76), it also resisted growth into the new century. If anybody in town wanted a selection of movies to see on the big screen, the closest complex was fifteen miles north of town and across the state line, right outside of Franklin.

Like the bar and grill, the theater wasn't busy when the couple arrived.

In fact, after paying for their tickets (which were only five dollars each) and moving the car into place, Alyssa noticed that they were the *only* ones there.

"Quiet night," she said, opening her door and stepping out. She stretched and Cooper watched, opening his door a short time later to do the same.

"Lucky for us," he said, reaching for the rear passenger door. His fingers wrapped around the handle and with a quick jerk he tugged it open. Nodding in its direction he climbed in without a word.

Alyssa tittered and eagerly followed him into the back of the car, her dress riding up along the back of her thighs, the soft and supple leather caressing her skin.

The movie started, light from the opening logos and credits spilling in through the front windshield, now speckled with moisture from a misty rain just starting to fall. The images were obscured, the colors scattered across the interior of the car. It was okay, though, as Cooper had no intention of viewing whatever movie he'd paid for.

Leaning in, his thick lips met Alyssa's neck, beginning what would be the real highlight of the night.

She trembled as he continued, feeling the brush of his palm on the inside of her left thigh as his hand made its way between her legs. They found no panties to halt their journey, Alyssa's groans indicating the gratification of a goal being attained as Cooper's finger did their business. It was joined by another.

Gasping, she turned her head, forcing him to move his lips onto hers. They kissed, each second adding speed to his finger's movements. It was euphoric, sending her rushing toward a cliff upon which she teetered on the edge.

"Take your shirt off," Alyssa muttered, not wishing to go over the brink just yet.

"Yeah?"

"Y-y-yes..."

Cooper pulled out and away, grabbing hold of the tee at the base with both hands. Slowly they rose, pulling the soft shirt along his skin, the deep-cut lines of his muscles revealed in the shifting light of the movie screen. It was a glorious sight and as his back arched – the shirt clearing his shoulders and head – his messy hair fell back over his eyes, one peering out from the forest of black with a golden fire inside.

"Like what you see?" he asked, flinging the shirt into the front seat. His body was heaving, swollen from the exhilaration he saw in her.

She nodded, whimpering as he drew close again. Reaching around, he found the tiny zipper at the base of her neck and slowly peeled her outfit away like the skin of some ripe fruit ready to devour. Cooper's cock grew rigid in his pants; she was completely naked underneath, prepared it seemed for that very moment.

He grinned as the dress slid down to her hips, exposing her buttery skin and breasts. Lifting her with ease, she was able to guide the dress the rest of the way down her legs to the floor, kicking off her shoes at the end.

Cooper began massaging her breasts, finding her nipples firm, teasing each one at a time between his teeth. Moving his hands toward his jeans, his mouth took over at her chest while he unfastened them. Grabbing a condom from his back pocket, he slid the jeans down and over his powerful legs. His cock swung as the jeans came off and it would have easily passed his belly button had he pressed it flat against his torso. The thickness of it rivaled his wrist.

Alyssa settled back on the leather, Cooper looming overhead almost predatorily, that golden sparkle still in his eyes. She grabbed her breasts and pressed them together, Cooper forcing himself through the center of those luscious mounds, silken and delicate skin rubbing against each other an explosion of wonder and light.

He was slick, leaving glistening strands behind as he rocked to and fro. Alyssa's tongue collected what she could on each pass, and each time there was more than the last.

Cooper moaned. It felt brilliant but he wanted more. *Needed* more.

His hips moved south, his lips back to hers, and slipping on the condom somewhere during it all, he rested himself against her, imagining himself fully inside.

That's when he plunged like a cliff diver into the sea, filling her in all directions, sending her eyes rolling back in her head. The subtle pain became a pleasure, and the pleasure was suddenly a pain. Together Cooper and Alyssa writhed, her legs hugging his waist and her arms behind his back.

Cooper bit her ear – not hard enough to draw blood but sufficient to cause to her gasp, quiver, and get wetter. His movements changed from long and slow strokes to a swift thumping. Fingers became entangled in her blonde mane, her head jerked back to expose her graceful neck. He kissed her there, tickled her with soft prickles of beard, tortured her with delirious smells and thrusts so hard that his balls made a loud *slap* every time he dove back in.

Cooper could see himself racing toward the cliff's edge, Alyssa's ecstatic moans fading back and forth to a timid whimper. Again, and again, and again until the two of them rolled like thunder in climax.

In the end, her fingernails had clawed eight deep scratches into his back, Cooper driving into her again as punishment. She rode the edge, unable to spill over as he drew it out as long as he could until that final second where he roared and released himself for the second time.

"That was amazing," Alyssa said after a few minutes, still barely enough breath for words. She did not mention it, but even though it was Cooper's first time, it was far superior to what she'd experienced with Liam.

"It must be the full moon," Cooper joked, the two shifting positions so that he was on the car seat.

Alyssa nestled her head atop Cooper's bare chest. It rose and fell with each of his deep breaths, and he smoothed her hair with the back of his fingers. She watched as he looked up and out of the steamy window, her stare following his. The moon wasn't quite full yet – that would be tomorrow night – wrapped in strands of shadowy clouds that resembled cobwebs dangling at the end of a dark hallway lit by a single flashlight.

His heart was remarkably calm, beating slow and powerfully, but his face was almost like the boy before the transformation. It told on his mind, revealing disquiet on a hundred different things in as many scattered directions.

Alyssa moved a hand up to his cheek, pressed against it, and moved his gaze toward her.

"You seem troubled," she said.

"It's... nothing," he replied delicately before kissing her just as lightly on the forehead. Then he grinned, white teeth gleaming.

"You sure?" she asked, concern not leaving her face.

"I am," Cooper said, and if he didn't mean it, he hid that fact well. "Now, come on, let's not bring down the mood with this sort of thinking. Tonight's been a night to remember!"

"You're right. It has been, Cooper," Alyssa said, her eyes welling as her words began to catch. "Thank you for finally opening my eyes and waking me up."

"To what?"

"To you, Cooper Bennett. To you…"

Chapter 12: A Night to Forget

Saturday, September 29, 2012

1

Cooper sat patiently in one of two padded chairs, the weekend sun shining through venetian blinds covering the windows of a well-ordered doctor's office. Horizontal shadows were cast on the large desk in front of him, paperwork, pens, and yellow Post-it notes scattered over the work surface. A beige folder sat in the center of it all, drawing Cooper's attention. He craned his neck, reading the tiny label affixed to the folder's tab.

BENNETT, COOPER. BATCH ANALYSES 2012-0809, 2012-1509

Cooper was waiting for Dr. Ross to return from the bathroom so they could discuss the results of samples drawn on September eighth and fifteenth in an attempt to figure out what was happening to him. All of the obvious physical and mental changes aside, Cooper needed to hear the potential causes. Up to that point, it had been like driving blindfolded – doable but with no idea where you came from, where you were going, or worse: who or what you were going to crash into along the way. Cooper's luck had been just that: luck, and his gut pestered him in recent days saying that it was about to run out.

As Cooper stared at the wall behind the desk, teeming with framed degrees and awards, the office door opened and Dr. Ross came in wearing a set of navy scrubs with no lab coat over it.

"Sorry about that," he said, taking a seat not behind the desk but in the chair next to Cooper. They'd gotten to know each other quite well over the last month and were on this journey of discovery together. "When nature calls, you listen or get embarrassed."

"No worries," Cooper replied. "I think one of the things I've had to do more than anything since the bite is piss!"

Dr. Ross laughed, grabbing the folder. He then snatched a lollipop from a small vase where they were displayed like a colorful bouquet of flowers.

"Want one?"

"No thanks," Cooper said. "So, is there *anything* at all that sheds some light on things, doc?"

"Oh, there was more than I expected," Dr. Ross replied, unpeeling the wrapper before popping the lollipop in his mouth. "Not that I am any closer to understanding *how*, at least I can hypothesize the *what*."

He started flipping through the folder, but it was more for show than anything. He remembered everything he'd seen from his review.

"Where to begin?"

"Your call," Cooper said, leaning back in his seat in anticipation. "Because I'm still in the dark."

Dr. Ross twirled the lollipop in his mouth, the white stick shifting from the left side to the right and back again. Cooper found it funny to see such a strapping man doing something so inherently childish. It was oddly refreshing.

"Ah, that's as good as place as any," Dr. Ross said, closing the folder as he looked across to Cooper. "This new look of yours. I'm thinking that it's likely caused by high levels of both cortisol and androgens, spurred on by overactive adrenal glands."

Cooper didn't know doc-speak all too well and didn't protest since he figured there would be a lot of it. Pointing to his face and hair, he swept his finger up and down.

"Haha, yes," Ross said, lollipop in hand following the same movement. "It's like you have sudden adrenal hyperplasia, but it came from an external source. I've never seen anything like this."

"So, the bite then?"

"Yes, and it was from a *wolf* as far as you can remember?"

"A lot of it is still foggy, but yes," Cooper replied. "One that was black as the night."

Dr. Ross pondered for a moment, looking over his notes – secured to the inside of the folder with sticky notes. The handwriting on them was barely legible.

"Well then, in a way, all of those accusations by your fellow students are true."

"The accusations?"

"You remember: all those steroid allegations I had to talk to the school about on your behalf."

"Ah... yeah."

"Seeing the data, it *is* like you've taken a ton of them, but your body is actually manufacturing these levels versus you injecting yourself from a vial. With all those increased androgens, it's probably why you've packed on what, thirty or forty pounds?"

"Thirty-eight, according to the nurse."

"Damn, I'll admit to being a little jealous," Dr. Ross said, biting down on the lollipop. "It took me years to put on that much lean mass. If I had to guess, I'd think your gains will taper off soon. It has to or your system will burn out; it's already maxed as it is. Have you been hot?"

"Very, especially at night. It's like I jumped into a swimming pool right before crawling into bed."

"For all the sweating?"

"Yes."

"Yup," Dr. Ross said, "and thinking about it a little more, it would seem your body is making itself more athletic for a reason. Any more mass on your frame would start to inhibit your speed. But honestly Cooper, I'm totally guessing at all of this. I've never seen anything at these levels in someone so young... well, shit, in anyone actually."

"What about all this healing stuff?

"*That's* where I'm at a total loss. It's still unexplainable, at least by my level of medical and biological knowledge. I've sent some info to a colleague out in LA but it may be a while before I hear anything – I think he's on vacation in New Zealand. But back to this, there's just no way your body should be able to heal itself at least, oh, two or three *thousand* times faster than usual. You're still being left with scars, right?"

"Yeah, but just on the really deep ones" Cooper said, rolling up his jeans and pointing to where the bite had occurred. Evidence of it was nearly gone, but a faint trace of it was still there nonetheless.

"What about your level fatigue? Good, bad, gone?"

"Honestly, I rarely feel tired anymore."

"And you can run a fair bit without losing your breath?"

Cooper nodded again.

"I thought so. Something is driving extra blood to the wounds, carrying ample amounts of the stuff they need – oxygen, sugar, platelets, white blood cells, and whatever else in surging through there. I've no idea what can do that, the data isn't telling me, nor how your blood is storing extra oxygen for you to pull from. One thing I can bet on: your appetite is probably through the roof."

"Yeah, I'm craving about three large pizzas right now! But Billy is the same relative to his appetite."

"Billy?"

"A long-time friend from school. I've known him for years."

"It may seem that way, Cooper, but trust me when I say your metabolic rate dwarfs anyone without your... condition."

Cooper thought about what the doctor was saying, speculating that all these wild hormonal changes he described could also be the cause of his heightened sense of awareness and quicker reflexes. There were times, especially when in danger, that he could practically see things before they happened. That happened with Liam and his punches over at Spring Park, and one night on West Pine when he was able to avoid a drunk driver flattening him without so much as a second thought. Since then, Cooper would run along rooftops more than roads, his lungs full of air and heart full of freedom. They were shortcuts, skillfully navigated by leaping from one to another in the shadows at night (though he did risk daylight travel for the thrill). It was all very adrenaline-charged and addicting, but far from normal. Like he had an affliction, or a condition...

"Condition?" Cooper repeated. "Do you think this is some kind of disease?"

Dr. Ross frowned.

"If I had to put a label on it," he said meekly, "and with doctor-patient confidentiality in full, two-way effect, I'd say that you were bitten by a werewolf."

Cooper laughed uneasily, trying to make light of the situation but the thought *had* crossed his mind. Several times since speaking with Grayson, each dismissed as crazy fantasy that had a rational explanation.

"Thankfully I haven't changed into anything drastic," Cooper said, his voice tense. He coughed to clear his throat. It had gotten dry.

"Refreshment's just over there," Dr. Ross said, pointing to a pitcher of ice water with a glass on each side.

"Got anything harder?" Cooper asked, halfway joking.

To his surprise, Dr. Ross stood, making his way for a cabinet tucked away in the far corner. There was a large fern on it, lush and green as if to hide the furniture beneath its broad leaves. Inside was a series of crystal decanters. Dr. Ross plucked the foremost one, along with a tumbler, pouring a single shot into it.

Returning to Cooper, he handed him the glass.

"Whiskey neat," he said. "Since this situation is so strange I don't think it would hurt. Besides, you're not going to get drunk off that amount with the changes in your body."

"Secret's safe with me," Cooper said with a wink, downing the drink. It burned on its way down, but was just what he was looking for.

"Back on the topic of changing into something," Dr. Ross continued glumly. "You were in a medically induced sleep right after you were bitten. There was a full moon that night if memory serves so if there's anything to the werewolf legends at all – assuming the one in a gazillionth chance what we are saying is true – the first full moon since your attack will be tonight..."

Cooper didn't say a word. He couldn't, his insides shivering as if someone was walking over his grave.

2

Cooper tossed and turned on the floor of his simple bedroom, situated in the back corner of the one-story 1950s ranch house. He was adjusting a small pillow Alyssa had bought for him out of compromise. She'd insisted on getting him an air mattress or something similar ("Cooper, I don't know if you realize it but you're sleeping on the damn *floor!*"), but he argued with her for days, telling her that it'd ultimately be a waste of money, money better spent on other things. His dad would have found a way to ruin a gift like that, just like every other happy thing and moment that entered his life.

No matter how much he repositioned himself or stayed still on the bumpy floor, covered himself with or kicked off threadbare sheets, rested with his face buried in the fresh pillow or staring at the water-stained ceiling, Cooper couldn't stop his mind racing on nothing in particular. Annoyed, he was nearly driven to tears for lack of sleep. If he'd known then what was happening, he would also have shed them for the small-town kid who would cease to be, forever locked into the life of a shifter.

A sudden and painful itch spread across his body, light from the full moon cascading into the room like a sickening spotlight as he scratched his skin.

Everything burned mercilessly, his expression decaying from frustration to agony, face undulating – shrinking in places, expanding in others – until it began pulling itself into an inhuman shape. His eyes closed, trying to shut out one of his senses. His ears still heard horrid sounds: cracking, sliding, ripping, sloshing. His cries were the worst.

A flush of crimson suddenly surged over his entire body, in an instant challenging the moon for brightness before dark hairs wriggled like worms from his pores.

"Gah, ugh..." Cooper groaned, trying to speak, to shout for help. He couldn't, his words mangled beneath growls and barks.

He jerked, landing flat on his stomach, limbs flailing like a marionette driven by an epileptic having a seizure. They were changing, bending in places they shouldn't while growing longer than they should be. It was a gruesome, and the odor of damp hair and bloody meat came to underscore it all.

Furniture toppled in a racket: small tables with odd bits of junk broken on the floor. Then, as suddenly as it began and as eerily as it felt up on the mountain, silence fell over the room.

"Cooper!" his dad's voice boomed down the short and sparse corridor.

It rattled the closed bedroom door. "What the fuck are you doing in there? Jerking off? I'm trying to get some goddamn sleep!"

Cooper opened his eyes, their vile, yellow irises gazing at the floor. He couldn't answer, his throat stretched, raw, and irritated.

Heavy footsteps marched toward the room.

"Cooper? Are you ignoring me, boy?"

No! Cooper's mind screamed. *No! Don't come in here!*

Meat...

The doorknob rattled. It was locked, Cooper doing it as a way to feel safe – a childhood habit made permanent in practice. Usually he was up well before the sun and his dad (who never bothered to check on him in the middle of night) with plenty of time to unlock it, but tonight was different, and he was in no position to do so even if he wanted.

"What the?" Roland called, banging loudly on the wood. The sound split Cooper's skull like an axe against firewood. "As long as you're in my fucking house you little shit, you'll keep the damn doors *unlocked*, you hear me? Or is another lesson needed?

Yeah... soften... the... meat... yeah...

There were more banging sounds, his dad beating on the door as if it were Cooper. They seemed louder now, more piercing.

"Open up right now!"

The noises ballooned inside Cooper's skull. It felt ready to burst if he didn't do something; anything at all to –

"Owwwooooo!"

The howled escaped before Cooper realized what he was doing, silencing himself with a quick and low growl. He tried talking and though the words were there in his head, the sounds did not come out.

Meat...

Dammit Cooper get a hold of yourself!

Meat...

"The fuck was that?" Roland snarled, his footprints receding in haste down the hall again. "Oh, I'm gonna take care of this shit right now!"

Not good!

Cooper looked around for a way out. The bedroom door was shut, his crazed father beyond it. There were no other exits from the room except the narrow strip of windows in the corner which –

BOOM!

Cooper shrank away. The sounds were like bombs in his mind.

Why is everything so loud?

But it wasn't just his hearing that was amplified, everything else was, too. Cooper's sight was clear, like everything was lit by the noon sun on a cloudless day. He could smell his father's disgusting, skid-marked underwear each time he raised his leg to kick the door.

BOOM!

BOOM!

BOOM!

On the last strike, the door flung open, swinging in a full arc before striking the wall, the doorknob leaving a large indention in the wall. A large shadow stepped into the room, backlit by the dancing lights of a muted television show playing on the living room set. The shadow was holding a shotgun with both hands.

"How the hell did you get in here, mutt?" Roland hissed, chambering a cartridge. "Did you cause all this mess?"

Cooper was disoriented, half-crazed by the crazy amounts of hormones flooding his system. Yet even then he could still tell his dad was more upset at the property damage than the whereabouts of his own damn son.

Emotions took over and Cooper rushed him, barking like a feral hound. Luckily Roland didn't get a chance to fire before Cooper's head came crashing into his gut. The hit was strong, knocking Roland into the wall.

Cooper collapsed to the floor. Scrambling while he had the chance, he looped around, running toward the windows. Leaping through the sharp glass and splintered wood frame, he emerged on the other side with lacerations and tufts of missing fur, but the night was around him and he was —

BANG!

The blast struck his hindquarters.

"Goddamn animal!" Roland screamed, the gunfire and yelling causing random lights to flick on up and down the street.

Cooper had to get out of there; otherwise he wasn't going to live much longer.

He fled from his own house, hip searing with pain, his dad firing again as he tried to kill the nasty beast he didn't know was his son. Hell, as Cooper raced across Hanscom Road, cutting through yards as he headed toward the back of Goodman Middle School, he thought that even if his dad had known, he would have found it the perfect excuse to unburden himself of the wrinkled pink *thing* he never wanted in the first place.

Cooper should have made a break for the woods while he could, but something urged him to stay. He veered west and barreled toward downtown, weaving through the interconnected alleyways and side streets to avoid being seen.

Before long Cooper was there, bathed in the orange light from the street lamps surrounding the square. He needed to find shelter and find it fast, else be spotted by a passerby or worse, the police, ending up right back in the same mess as before. Scurrying north on Center Street, puffs of steaming breath trailing behind him, Cooper stumbled upon an abandoned clothing store between Hooper Road and Kennedy Street. A hole had been cut into a side entry door, made wider over time by vagrants, allowing him easy access inside.

As he entered, the cool breeze died down and the welcoming sound of nothing but damp paws on rubbish filled the space.

But Cooper was not alone.

A homeless squatter had taken up residence in the dump.

"Git!" the man shouted aggressively, picking up a piece of crumbled brickwork. He hurled it at Cooper, narrowly missing his front paw as it smashed against the floor. "I said GIT!"

Please stop... Cooper said, but it came out as a menacing growl.

"W-why ain't y-ya listenin' to me? GIT!" the man sneered, breaking into a fit of shouting. He was most likely drunk or high, possibly both, and in an instant, he came at Cooper brandishing a broken bottle.

Cooper whined, the sharp glass cutting him across a shoulder and his chest. It burned, his eyes a sinister amber gaze.

The vagabond slashed at Cooper again, cutting him, but this time it was all the yelling, ragged and broken through years of harsh throat, that pierced Cooper's skull just like the banging did back at home.

Cooper... don't do it.

Something in him shattered.

Cooper…

And a part of his humanity slipped away through the cracks.

Kumbaya, my Lord! Kumbay-fucking-ya!

It was too late and there was no turning back.

Cooper… Cooper NO!

The wolf snarled, his white teeth bared like daggers, his growl so appalling it seemed to shake the walls themselves. That's when Cooper lunged at the vagrant, who shrieked then gurgled beneath the sound of a colossal snap.

Then all fell silent.

It was done.

3

Later that same night it began to rain. Not a gentle, misty rain that so often came over Goodman, but one of those heavy thunderstorms with fat raindrops that stung if they hit your skin.

Cooper was outside in it, his naked body pummeled as he sat in the side alley. He was looking at his reflection in a pane of glass across the way, still-yellow eyes diminished to their base human qualities.

Dried blood had caked on his lips, and from each side of his mouth the rain made long, red streaks that flowed down his entire body to the cold stone pavers.

Mixed in with the rain were tears. They happened to sting the most because from then on, Cooper knew his world was changed. Forever.

PART TWO: When the Darkness Falls

CHAPTER 13: A MEETING ON THE MOUNTAIN

Wednesday October 10, 2012

1

Murders were still happening in Goodman, a few within the town limits now, starting with the brutalized body of a homeless man at the former location of the white wolf pack's safe house, an abandoned clothing store between Hooper Road and Kennedy Street. Another body had turned up behind Edwards Floral on the east side of town, a third beside the mailboxes at Camelot Apartments on the north side, and a fourth at Robinson Row

Apartments – in front of a dumpster, on the west side. While the victims outside the town in the mountains and on trails seemed to be indiscriminately targeted, those within the town limits appeared limited to destitute persons over fifty years of age.

Grayson slung his head low before looking up the slope to Toluca Springs National Forest, a large bus pulling away from the station behind him.

Despite his last, best hope that perhaps, somewhere along the way, they'd been wrong and all the surfacing evidence was purely coincidental, it was being quickly proven untrue. The slaughter was notably on the rise, getting more violent as the days wore on. With pressure building from the Order and on himself, Grayson supposed Lance Goddard was using all of this as some sort of psychological tactic to wear them down before attacking outright. It wouldn't be too long before things started to crack on multiple fronts, presenting Lance with the perfect conditions to strike.

Grayson walked forward and started to climb the trail.

He had reached the point of feeling that despite his united pack's best efforts to keep things subdued, word was going to leak out to the town about what was happening. Therefore, despite the pleas of omega and subordinate wolves alike, he made the difficult decision to venture up into the mountains himself to meet Lance face to face.

Accompanying him on the trek was a contingent of guards, along with Liam, who languished behind the group to bring up the rear.

Once the men had passed beneath the cover and secrecy of the trees, Grayson shed his suit, handing it off to one of his protectors before shifting into wolf form. Onward he led, white fur catching flashes of sunlight as they ventured deep into the autumn carpeted forest.

Reaching a familiar spot, one that hadn't been seen by Grayson's eyes in eighteen years, he howled. If Lance was behind any of this and had any semblance of honor still flowing in his veins, he would have no choice but to heed the call.

"Owwwooooo," came another long howl, jarring as usual but nonetheless heralding the arrival of Lance Goddard with his own entourage.

Shifting into human form, Lance looked vastly different than Grayson remembered. His short hair had been replaced with long, flowing strands that ran in curls down his forehead, while geometric black and white tattoos covered a wide swath of his athletic body.

"So, you have finally come to see me?" he asked, arms outstretched as if to say: *Take a good, long look. Here I am!* "I told you that I would return to claim what is mine…"

Grayson scoffed.

"I see you did not bring your teddy bears this time," Lance continued, looking around facetiously for anyone else. "A pity not many of them are around anymore…"

"This is a wolf matter, *Schattenträger*," Grayson replied, still shifted.

"Ah, so we are using *that* title!" Lance said, clapping his hands together with a sharp *slap*. "I've not heard that one said in quite a long a long time!"

"Four hundred years," Grayson added, "but who's counting?"

"So, Light Bearer, I need to know: have you come up here to stop me?" Lance said, counting the number of wolves Grayson had brought with him. "Let me make an amendment to my words. Have you come to *try* and stop me? I'm just going to let you know right up front: that force you have won't make a dent in the army I have built."

Army? Grayson thought worryingly. The hairs on his body began to stand on end; what had sounded like an innocuous idea before became much bleaker.

Lance nodded to his subordinates who all shifted en masse to their wolf forms. The sound was deafening, but quickly faded, though the sea of yellow eyes was certainly intimidating.

Grayson returned the sentiment, howling to signal his pack to transform as well. Everyone other than Liam did so, the Beta remaining standing in his favorite school jacket and jeans. He stared into the penetrating eyes of one of the wolves behind Lance.

"Lance! This is enough!" Grayson roared. "I have not come to stop you on this day at least. Only to treat with you."

"Treat with *me?* What makes you think I want to discuss anything with you, Grayson?" Lance asked callously, and his shadow pack began to advance.

"Because I know how you operate, Lance, and deals are part of the game even if others have to risk making one with a devil dog like yourself."

"Slinging insults while trying to talk?" Lance said. "I'm no hellhound."

"No, they're mindless," Grayson said. "You are devilishly *not.*"

Suddenly Lance held up a hand and his pack halted. There were a few disappointed yelps amongst the group.

"Do we have a problem?" Lance asked to Liam, who had remained transfixed on the one wolf.

"Yeah…" he answered. "If we're going to get skinned alive, I want to give that one the joy of trying."

"Wolfrick here?" Lance asked, hiking a thumb in the wolf's direction.

Liam nodded.

Grayson was very uneasy. He did not like his son being addressed directly by a rival Alpha. Catching the gleam of vengeance in Liam's eyes, along with his heavy breathing, beads of sweat on his brow, and flared nostrils, Grayson saw a beast on the verge of doing something drastically stupid.

"Ah! Yes! I remember now," Lance continued, his fingers snapping with a jovial sound of remembrance. "Wolfrick here was the one you encountered, oh, a month and some change ago when you chased that human boy up here. What was his name?"

"Cooper," Liam answered at once and his face grew even more acrid. "Cooper Bennett."

Both packs growled, all but their Alphas. Grayson saw a triumphant look spreading across Lance's face. It was like he'd just been delivered exactly what he needed.

"Are you done addressing the Beta?" Grayson bellowed.

Liam glowered, and Grayson was able to feel his son's eyes burning into the back of him.

"I have what I need," Lance replied, withholding a smile. "It would seem, Grayson, that you have more problems than just us. Tsk, tsk, tsk. The silver fox is failing."

"What are you implying?"

"Oh, come on. Surely you don't suspect that *I've* sent my pack into Goodman prematurely to prey upon society's rejects? From here, it seems that Mr. Bennett is attempting to harness his emotions from the Change. Perhaps he will succeed, but without guidance from someone with more experience, it's likely he'll just continue to spiral out of control."

Grayson mulled over what Lance was saying, knowing that Cooper was a rogue element at play. The boy would probably be a lone wolf at best, or degrade into a raging Primal at worst. Either way, his fate relative to the white wolves was sealed, yet something delayed Grayson's decision in that matter.

"While what you say is true Lance, I don't consider Cooper a separate problem; his fur is quite *dark* after all," Grayson retorted, returning to his human form. "So please, why don't you call your little subordinate back to the pack, give him a good spanking for the havoc he's caused in Goodman, and then let the big dogs address the real concern: *you*."

"An errant bite has nothing to do with allegiances, Light Bearer. One that would never have happened had your pup not run him up here in the first place!"

"Always one to shirk responsibilities," Grayson replied.

"I could say the same about you," Lance countered, looking toward Liam once again.

The packs grew restless behind both Alphas, tension layering upon itself like snow in the mountains threatening an avalanche. There was intermittent barking and anticipatory whines. It felt like the prelude to 1994 all over again.

"Lance," Grayson said, pleading, "there will be a war if you do not stop! Whatever it is that you are seeking, the Order is aware and…"

"Have done nothing to stop me. There are larger issues on the rise for them: a demon army has surfaced, calling itself the Noctis …"

"I do not care about demons right now, brother! Only you and this madness! What is here, in Goodman, that you are so driven to risk outright exposure of our kind?"

Lance drew back, offended. He might even have been horrified.

"Can you really not feel it?" Lance asked, his voice somber. "Oh, the bittersweet irony! You don't know what your precious Order is keeping hidden in the bowels of their secret place? The very Vault that you have been guarding on their behalf since those Accords you love so much? How well you've performed your duties, Grayson. The most notable being able to stay firmly on their short leash, doing their bidding."

It was then that Tyler Sheridan's words about the Order suddenly rang out in his mind.

Keep them at arm's length…

Pausing, Grayson reached out and tried to sense, feel, or smell whatever Lance was talking about. For the longest he could not. Then, as if there was a chink in a wall surrounding his memories and he saw…

(flash)

An army of armored wolves raced along a desolate hillside. The trampled earth was black, the trees nothing more than dead spires, the sky murky dusk. They clashed like a wave against another force, a…

(flash)

woman standing with her back toward him. Silhouetted hair whipped wildly in the searing light of a burning building. Screams came from inside the fire, the blackened frame toppling with…

(flash)

the sounds of tremendous chains clanging. The clamor filled the air, followed by the thundering noise of stone, like a boulder crashing against…

(flash)

the bodies of countless dead wolves, black and white alike, spread out from one bleak horizon to the other. Something massive and dark was walking overhead. The smell of it all was atrocious and lasting…

Grayson's nose began to bleed. He staggered over to a nearby tree. Overwhelmed by the rush of imagery, he jutted an arm out and rested.

"Ah, so you felt it too…" Lance charged. "It's calling to me, even now with my eyes wide open. *Lichtträger*, I won't hold a grudge for you doing your duty to stop me; time has at least brought me that gift. Yet it changes nothing. I *will* claim that which is mine from the Order, and I won't rest until that happens."

Grayson wiped his nose; the bleeding had subsided. If he had the power – the numbers – he would have ended things right then and there. As it stood, trying would have been suicide for the white wolves.

"I... don't know what it was that I felt." Grayson sniffed, then coughed.

He was unable to pick apart the fragments he saw, nor did he know what Lance was talking about with regards the Order's hidden things. All he knew was a fight was inevitable, but it would not be today unless Lance was truly immoral.

"Pack. Come," Grayson said cautiously, and without another word bowed and turned away.

His pack reluctantly but obediently fell in behind him as they returned to Goodman, all but Liam who lingered behind the group. His cold eyes were still set on Wolfrick, who was licking his jaws.

Slowly, Liam looked across to Lance and shuddered. The Shadow Alpha was glaring back at him, those yellow eyes locking him in place. Then, as the corner of Lance's mouth turned up into a devious smirk, Liam was freed. He stumbled, then fled with the feeling he would be seeing Lance Goddard again – much sooner than he would like.

CHAPTER 14: THANKSGIVING

Thursday, November 22, 2012

1

Cooper was up early, sitting on the floor of his bedroom wrapped in not one or two, but all three of the tattered sheets he had for bedding. It was incredibly cold, the sun yet to rise while a bitter wind wailed through uneven gaps in boards he had nailed over the large hole in his window.

Roland had shown no interest in repairing any of the damage that "savage mongrel caused" back in late September, likely because it wasn't his room that had been affected but it would be his money that would be spent. He even left the door to Cooper's room broken, so he had unfettered access to all areas of the house at all times. All that didn't bother Cooper nearly as much as the fact his dad didn't even ask if his son had been hurt that night by the creature. Not a single peep.

Roland assumed Cooper was fine since he hadn't developed any diseases (*he got those genetics from me, you know?*), and all his limbs were present and accounted for (*I could get a body like that again in no time, if I wanted*). Had either of those things *not* been the case, Roland was certain those oh-so-friendly medics at Goodman Hospital – especially Dr. Righteous Ross – would have stitched his special son right up (*the cocky shithead*).

Cooper looked over at the alarm clock – an old one with two bells on the top – and sighed. He got up, quickly pulling on a pair of torn jeans (more from age than fashion) and a cheap, long sleeved thermal shirt Alyssa had picked up for him. It clung to his body and said WILL HUG FOR COOKIES across the front. Opening the door with just a pull, he walked to the shared bathroom. It sat between both bedrooms at the back of the house. His dad's door was closed.

While brushing his teeth, Cooper stared at his reflection in the dingy mirror as tiny specks of toothpaste flicked onto the glass. He looked like a totally different person from just three months ago and though he liked what he saw, there was a price he was paying for it. The faces of his four victims – innocent victims – rose within the swirls of steam from the stained sink, each one bearing an expression of sheer terror on their aged faces.

What have I become? Cooper asked himself. "A monster" seemed too benign an answer.

Turning off the water, Cooper set both hands on the sides of the basin. He bowed his head, long hair dangling, and wept.

"I'm sorry," he whispered aloud. "I didn't ask for any of this to happen and I am so sorry. I'll try to make up for it... somehow... someway I will make up for it. I'm sorry."

The room was quiet except for the gentle drip of the leaky faucet into the drain. Cooper sniffled and looked back up at his reflection. His hair was like a jungle of dark vines across his face. With a quick swipe, he slicked it back, adjusted a few areas that protruded in awkward directions, and made his way for the kitchen.

The kitchen and living room were the only other rooms in the house, the former on the left when coming out of the bathroom and the latter on the right. Each was thinly decorated (speaking of the 1980s furniture and trimmings) but crammed full of *stuff* that Cooper's dad had collected over the years. Stuff for harebrained ideas that would never see the light of day.

Stuff that was worth spending his "hard-earned" money on that was never actually used. Stuff that he just liked and didn't want to get rid of because "it might be useable one day." None of it was for Cooper.

Not that he wanted any of it. To Cooper it felt more like a junkyard than a home, which was part of the reason he had no problems staying away most of the time.

But today's Thanksgiving! he thought. *A family day where Pop is off work and we can both enjoy each other's company, all while being thankful we have each other in our lives!*

Cooper belched.

Yeah right!

Roland would actually head into work later that morning, the allure of time and a half far too great to pass up.

Cooper trudged over to the fridge, a utilitarian Kenmore, sputtering as he opened the door and looked inside. There wasn't much on the shelves, never mind a good selection for any sort of holiday meal. However, as part of his self-assigned effort to do more good (at least for the day), Cooper wanted to give it a shot. He knew it would be an unappreciated mess before the sun set.

Half an hour or so later, the door to Roland's bedroom opened to the smell of scrambled eggs and the sound of turkey bacon sizzling. Cooper had bought some the other day for the first time and given the day, he thought it was appropriate.

"What the hell are you doing?" Roland groused, approaching the table while picking his tight underwear out of his hungry ass crack. He dug in his nose a second later with the same fingers.

"I'm just cooking a little bit of breakfast," Cooper replied cheerily, but his brows were wrinkled, repulsed by the thought of what his dad was smelling.

Roland pulled out a chair and slumped into it. The chair groaned under his weight. His face was puckered.

"What's that Godawful smell?"

After you just sniffed your shit-scented fingers? Cooper thought.

"Turkey bacon."

"*That's* what we're having for Thanksgiving?" Roland said with an offensive snicker. "You must be fucking joking."

Cooper shook his head as he flipped the bacon, imagining the shaking was from his hands clutching Roland's neck.

Be calm, Coop. Be calm...

Roland propped an arm up on the table, positioning his hand as if he were holding a cup. There was nothing in it, so he snapped his fingers.

"Hey, boyo," he said, ticking his head in the direction of his waiting hand. "Sweet tea. Now."

Cooper's lips grew thin. He set down the spatula and made way for the cupboard. Inside was a faded plastic cup from one of several car races he'd been to in the past; it was Roland's go-to. After cracking a few ice cubes into it from a tray in the freezer, then filling it with syrupy tea, Cooper marched over and handed the cup off to his dad.

Their eyes met briefly, challenging each other.

"Would've been better if you bought an *actual* turkey with all that hospital money you were given, instead of getting queer haircuts and all those faggoty accessories you keep wearing. It's fucking embarrassing," Roland carried on, taking two huge gulps amidst his string of insulting words. Some of it trickled down his neck into the patchy hair on his chest, glistening like blotches of sticky sweat. "It smells like shit. Turkey Bacon. Shit."

Oh! Cooper thought. *Well, it would've been better if you'd gotten the fucking turkey and made some effort to be a halfway decent father, you jerk!*

"Cook something else."

"There isn't anything else."

"Well, sounds like you're going to be shopping today."

"No, it sounds like you're shit out of luck!"

Roland stopped midway through his swig of tea, his eyes wide over the brim of his glass.

"What did you say?" he muttered, sickened by the boy he was looking at.

Cooper saw this same look twice a month when the bills started to roll in. It was nothing new, Roland harboring ill feelings since day one, but God dammit he wasn't about to take this sort of thing under his own roof – leaky and dilapidated as it was.

Roland stood up quickly, knocking the chair over. It made a terrible crashing noise. The house was used to it.

Cooper's instinct was to withdraw. Shrink away and take his beating like a good little boy. Belt or fists, let's get it over with. Yet this morning his mind was saying *NO!* and he stood up straight, chest puffed out in defiance.

"I said that *you're* shit out of luck."

Roland was staring firm at Cooper now, a reedy grin on his face that seemed to welcome the confrontation.

"I'm getting –" Cooper started.

"Big ol' balls!" Roland interjected as he marched over to the stove. "You think you got *cojones* now to go along with all those pretty muscles, boy? From what I hear the juice makes them shrivel up like a couple of raisins."

Cooper said nothing, Roland getting right in his face – his unclean morning breath mingled with the scent of sugar-laced tea. One of Roland's palms struck Cooper in the left shoulder, knocking him backwards. His hand hit the pan, knocking the sizzling meat off the burner. He was slightly burned.

"Come on then, boyo, let's see how tough you really are," Roland said, and he hit Cooper again, this time with a fist to the gut.

But Cooper didn't barrel over, only the smallest amount of air leaking out.

"You done?" he asked, looking impassively into his father's eyes.

"Far from it," Roland said with a sneer and before his next swing could connect, Cooper had grabbed hold of his arm, spinning him around and down against the stove. Roland's face hovered right over the burner, the faint red glow of the coils illuminating his face.

"I wonder if your skin would smell better than my shitty turkey bacon?" Cooper asked, pushing his father closer.

Meat... Cooper thought dimly. *Crispy meat tastes good...*

His father let out an awkward groan, struggling to get free. The burner's heat was becoming unbearable. His hands were pressing back against the edge of the stove.

Cooper... said a voice that wasn't his own. It was Alyssa's, soft and

252

gentle.

Cooper trembled, torn between planting the asshole's face right against the red-hot coils and hearing him scream, or just letting him go.

Don't do this, Cooper, her voice continued hopefully. *You're better than that. Better than him.*

Cooper didn't know if that was true, the faces of his other victims coming back to mind. His heart started beating like a hammer against his ribs, and his eyes were agleam with gold.

Trembling and sobbing, Cooper at last opened his mouth, his next words so short yet difficult to say.

"I'm sorry…"

2

Billy was lying face down on his bed, arms crossed beneath his fuzzed-covered chin. *A Charlie Brown Thanksgiving* was on TV, Billy watching as the cartoon played out on his fifteen-inch screen.

Suddenly, his ring tone drowned everything out, and Billy rolled onto his back with a sulking moan. He reached out to the nightstand, somewhere beneath the clutter of empty soda cans and assorted junk food wrappers. Searching through it all (and sending some of the trash to join another pile that had started to form on the floor), he eventually found his phone, picked it up, wiped it free of crumbs, and answered.

"Hello buddy!" Billy said happily, recognizing that it was Cooper. As the voice on the other end of the line mumbled and muttered, Billy's face began to sag.

"Where are you right now?" he asked hurriedly. "Uh huh. The *whole time?* Well, you made the right choice. Jesus. Now I don't want to stick my nose in where it doesn't belong... I know, I know... but *you* know that you're welcome to come over here."

Billy flopped back over, using the remote to turn off the television. *Charlie Brown* faded, collapsed into a thin line of light, then was swallowed by darkness.

"I don't care that it's a holiday, Coop. That's what I meant by 'anytime'. Mom and Dad won't care either, trust me. Now, we've already had our big Thanksgiving lunch, but you're more than welcome to hang out and eat on some of the leftovers." There was a long pause as Billy waited for Cooper to answer. A point came where he thought Cooper was going to hang up and run off, never to be seen again. It was the frantic tone in his voice that–

Cooper finally answered.

"You know I'm always there for you buddy," Billy concluded. "See you soon. Love you."

Hanging up the phone, Billy tapped its corner against his mouth.

Coop, what's going on in that head of yours? he thought anxiously, having seen bits of Liam Manning surfacing in him over the last month.

He'd never say a word about it to Cooper himself, but Alyssa was a different matter. She had been thinking the same thing herself, the two of them talking about it in the hall just after Halloween. At the time, Cooper had literally stolen candy from a baby, threatening to beat up a couple of kids from Riverhill on Halloween night if they didn't give him their spoils of chocolate and sweet tarts.

It's all so out of character... Billy continued to think as he swung his legs off the side of the bed. Standing, he shoved the phone in his pocket, pulling on what was still a clean wife beater (by his standards, not his mother's) that he'd thrown casually into his beanbag chair after lunch.

About an hour later – Billy figuring Cooper was thinking about a lot of things during his walk across town – Cooper arrived at the trailer. Mrs. Arnett promptly rushed him into the kitchen and sat him down at the table, her mothering instincts piling a plate high with leftover turkey, ham, green beans, mashed potatoes, and a delicious casserole of her own creation.

Cooper was ravenous, even rivaling Billy as he shoved food in his mouth seemingly without the need to breathe. Along the way, he alluded to his dad not being able to afford much food these days.

Mr. Arnett, who had been observing and listening the entire time, didn't buy it. A more selfish answer likely being the true one, he thought Roland bought plenty of it, but made sure that Cooper didn't get much.

About an hour after he arrived Cooper had finished his second piece of pecan pie and leaning back on the dining room chair, he linked his hands and rested them on his pregnant food belly.

"That was delicious, Mrs. Arnett," he said appreciatively. "Thank you so much."

"Of course," she replied, and with a tender smile swept his plate off the table and into the sink for cleaning. "Billy, can you put the ice cream back in the freezer dear?"

"Sure thing," he replied, springing to the fridge with the container. As he opened the freezer door on top, he saw Cooper eyeing the wall clock. A thought popped into his head. "Hey, we still have tomorrow off, right?"

"Yeah."

"In that case, why don't you stay over for the night? We could play some video games and *finally* get you caught up on some TV episodes."

"Well, I –"

"I agree," said Mrs. Arnett on his behalf, just before Cooper had a chance to say no. "It's probably best you don't go back to that house tonight any way."

She was sure to place extra emphasis on *that* house versus *your* house, as she thought about *that bastard Roland Bennett* owning it and Cooper being more of a prisoner in its walls. Again, that was something she would often think, but never say aloud. Her eyes did a pretty good job of convincing Cooper to stay this time. It's not like his dad knew *where* he'd stormed off to after leaving him with a bruised arm and face dangling mere inches from a stove burner.

"Hey boys," Mr. Arnett said from his armchair in the living room, "why don't you come out onto the porch with me for a little bit."

He was already up, snatching one of his cigars off the end table before heading to the front door. Once outside, he popped the cigar in his mouth and after scratching his beard, he reached for the matches kept in the front left pocket of his coveralls.

Billy and Cooper popped through the door a few seconds later, sitting on the old couch while Mr. Arnett stayed standing. He struck the match, its orange flame bright before guttering to a small orb of fading blue. After a few puffs, the cigar was lit and he was ready to talk.

"Cooper, I told you before that you were welcome here, that statement hasn't changed nor will it, lest you run off and become some kind of drug addict or cold-blooded killer."

Cooper laughed halfheartedly, watching as the light from the cigar caught in Mr. Arnett's eyes.

"That said, I know how hard it's been since you're over there on Hanscom with your dad, so if you'd rather wait until *after* graduation, the same offer stands."

Cooper perked up in his seat, a hand swiping away a wayward section of hair that had fallen in his face.

"There'd be no rent, other than helping Brenda with chores, or if you need the work, you could help me out over at Rabun Paving for some cash." He hiked a thumb to his left and down the street, the business within view at the end of it. "It's hard work and decent money, and it'd be something at least. Again, no pressure, it's only if you need it."

Billy noticed that Cooper was looking around the porch and became a little embarrassed.

If it were decent money Dad we'd be living in a far more decent house. One that people didn't turn their noses up at or whisper insults in the halls at school ("Billy Arnett's so poor he can't even pay attention" and "Billy's so poor his mom cuts out the pockets of his jeans so he can have something to play with" being the two most recent ones making rounds).

Cooper stood and approached Mr. Arnett, extending his hand.

"Thank you, sir, I may just take you up on that offer."

That was when Billy saw his dad reach into his coveralls and pull something else out of his pocket – a simple black ring that hung on a long black chain. Billy had a similar one he would wear from time to time, and he watched as his dad handed it over to Cooper.

"Here," Mr. Arnett said.

"What's this?" Cooper asked, taking the chain and looking at the ring dangling from it.

"That is the second of two rings my own father had given to me years ago; a few after Billy was born. The first one was white and symbolized purity and hope. With Billy arriving in our lives first, I gave it to him when I thought he would be old enough to understand its meaning. I still wonder if that day will ever come."

Everyone chuckled, though Billy did the least.

"This one," Mr. Arnett continued, "is jet black, symbolizing life's challenges and struggles to overcome. We went through a ton of those – financial, emotional, biological – when trying to grow our family. To give Billy a little brother or sister. Now, Billy's mother considers herself a failure in that, but I don't. I see it as the way life works."

Cooper nodded.

"You son, are in a very similar situation at your place. We've seen the bruises, and heard the excuses Cooper, and trust me when I say: we know. In my eyes – and I spoke to Brenda earlier and it's in hers too – since Billy considers you a brother and because you're more than welcome here at our place as one of our own... I would like you to have it."

Cooper was speechless. This was the first family gift he'd been given in, well, ever.

The metal of the ring was cold against his palm as he closed his hand around it, though there was certainly an absence of that same feeling in his chest, which swelled with comforting warmth.

3

The clock on the wall of the bedroom struck ten o'clock, Billy holding onto his game controller firmly with a piece of red licorice candy flopping out of his mouth like a shoot of grass from a farmworker's.

Cooper was in the same position, but chewing so much that it ballooned his cheeks out like a chipmunk. Both were sitting next to each other – the beanbag supporting the both of them – engrossed in Mission Three of *Double Dragon*. The blocky eight-bit heroes were beating the crap out of a trio of thugs Billy had so cleverly named after Manning, Wilder, and Brown.

Cooper had been telling Billy how far along he and Alyssa had grown in their relationship and while Billy was fundamentally happy for Cooper, a part of him didn't want to talk about that anymore.

Ugh, I can see how well that relationship is going every day at school, he thought bitterly. *Maybe we can talk about my new photography hobby for a bit, or that awesome upper sleeve tattoo Dad said I could get for Christmas. Anything other than the Cooper and Alyssa show...*

Close to the end of the mission, Billy glanced over to Cooper to give him an eye roll, but instead got stuck in an ill-timed stare. He hadn't realized how handsome his friend had gotten until they were this close. Billy was partly jealous and mostly –

"Billy, what's up?" Cooper said after swallowing all the candy. He noticed Billy's character had stopped moving on screen. "Did your lazy-ass fall asleep or something?"

Billy didn't reply. There was something about Cooper that was preventing him from doing so. Perhaps it was the placidity in his eyes, or the warmth of his skin when it accidently brushed against his arm as they played. Billy didn't know for sure, only that he'd been caught by the mystery.

Don't you do it Billy!

"Hey, you sure you haven't keeled over from all that food?" Cooper asked and once turned, he caught Billy staring at him. His cheeks were blushed and his eyes were large in wonder. "Billy, what's –"

Cooper didn't get a chance to finish his sentence before Billy acted. He leaned in and kissed Cooper right on the lips.

What are you doing Billy? He's going to kill you! Jesus shit!

Billy didn't listen to himself. He didn't stop. How could he now that he was committed? Either way he would be screwed.

Expecting Cooper to pull away at any second, thrashing him like Liam used to, Billy closed his mouth and the hairs of Cooper's beard nudged his skin playfully. Then, unexpectedly, Cooper's tongue was pushing Billy's lips apart. It wasn't doing so to stop him, rather it was encouraging him to continue.

After a few impassioned exchanges, Billy shifted, gently setting down the controller and replacing it with a handful of Cooper's thigh. It was thick and muscular, straining against his jeans. Billy rubbed his hand up and down, slipping his fingers into one of the holes that had been worn into the denim. Cooper's cock had started to inch its way out, causing a tent to form in Billy's own pants.

Cooper dropped his controller, grabbing Billy on both sides of his face. He kissed him some more before pushing his head back, gnawing at Billy's neck teasingly.

"Coop... I..." Billy said, but his trembling breath cut him off.

They felt each other for a little while longer. Their hands knew no boundaries. Heat was building, and desires mounted to the point their shirts had to come off...

But that's where it ended, the two suddenly pulling away from each other. Neither was sure who did first, but now that they had the passionate moment receded to a distance where it could not be recovered.

"Coop... I... I'm sorry," Billy said, ashamed. He reached for his shirt and started to put it on. "I don't know what came over me."

"I do," Cooper replied, stopping him. "Missed time... I'd be lying if I denied I felt it too."

Billy nodded, dipping his head low on the last movement.

"You... probably hate me now, don't you?"

Cooper didn't reply.

"Want to leave, don't you?" Billy asked, his voice shaking.

There was still no reply other than Cooper shushing him.

"Don't be so silly," Cooper said at last. "I could never hate you, man. We've known each other for years and you're like a brother to me. Shit, I think we just confirmed that you're a lot more. I... I just don't want to give you false hope, buddy."

Billy sobbed, but it wasn't full of sadness. It was a mix of happiness and relief that sprung out of him.

You best be thankful he didn't kill you! Billy screamed at himself.

"In a different time, that would probably have continued all the way," Cooper said, his eyes checking if those words hurt more than just punching

Billy in the face. "Just... not this time. Hell, who knows, down the road it..."

Cooper's words trailed off; he'd almost added to the false hope again.

"So, you'll still be my friend?" Billy asked with all the innocence of boy ten years younger.

"Always Billy. I think you're stuck with me," Cooper replied with a laugh-filled smile. "Now come on, let's get back to this game and kick some ass."

Billy's smile was bigger than a kid's first Christmas. He grabbed his controller off the floor.

Cooper picked up his, too, still shirtless as he watched Billy reset the game, its flashy logos fading on then off the screen. Cooper didn't say it right then – it wasn't the appropriate time – but he had no idea where he'd be or what he'd be doing had Billy (and by extension the Arnetts) not come into his life. He could have easily turned into a bully like Liam, or worse: ended as worm food, face down in a ditch off U.S. 441.

No, he didn't tell Billy Arnett at the time, but Cooper was incredibly thankful for his friendship and a part of him (not a small one by any means) wished that he'd known how Billy felt all along.

CHAPTER 15: A NOBLE CHRISTMAS

Tuesday December 25, 2012

1

Cooper hurried up the steps to Alyssa's house, motes of snow falling in gentle curtains behind him. He was wearing a pair of thick woolen socks – shoved tightly into his boots – along with jeans and a white tee-shirt, as always. A long-sleeved, hooded sweater was over it all. It was unzipped and the ring Billy's dad had given him bounced around as it dangled on its chain in the middle of his chest.

Once settled on the lower wraparound porch, stomping excess snow off his feet, Cooper looked around at the peaceful scene. The snow was building up on the ground and in the branches of the trees, a winter wonderland slowly forming before his eyes. It was magical, the first time that Christmas felt more than just any other day. Overhead, the porch fans were quietly turning in the cool wind while the normal cushions of the wicker furniture had been replaced with rather gaudy holiday prints. It seemed that every year people would buy them, regardless of how hideous they looked. The same could be said of the wrapping paper Cooper used to cover the three small boxes in his hands. It was some of the ugliest stuff that had ever been manufactured, but it was also the only thing he could afford (from the dollar store off Sixth Street) after spending most of his remaining money on the gifts themselves. There was one each for Alyssa and her parents.

The boxes were bulky enough to occupy both hands, forcing him to use a straining pinky to ring the doorbell – a marbled button inset amongst a lavish gold fixture. It chimed to the sound of Beethoven's *Symphony No. 5* and hearing it for the first time (since Cooper normally met Alyssa around the back of the house for their jogs), he thought it was an ominous melody to announce someone's arrival and then welcome them into a home. He wasn't learned in classical music but if one of Beethoven's' tunes were to be used, he'd have expected *Für Elise* or something like that. Cooper had listened to Alyssa play it from time to time on the grand piano in the parlor.

That's just a pretentious way of saying living room, Cooper thought as he waited in front of the large, decorative front door, its stained glass face a portal into a richer world that he wasn't all too familiar with, but wouldn't mind getting to know. After all, the girl that he had come to love was a part of that world and therefore *he* – even indirectly – was part of it as well.

A second later, a familiar shape appeared in the glass. As the door unlocked and swung inward, Cooper prepared himself to see the gorgeous face of his girlfriend. He brought out his best smile and his eyes began sparkling with delight. However, once the door was fully open and he got a clear look at the person on the other side, he realized it was not Alyssa, but a version of her to come in the years ahead.

"May I help you?" Mrs. Amanda Noble asked. She looked him up and down – puzzled, curious, and even the slightest bit afraid.

He looks like a ruffian, her stern countenance stated, giving little else away.

Cooper didn't expect that (though listening to the doorbell jingle, he should have), and he had to look away.

"Mom?" said a happy voice from inside. "Is that Cooper?"

She didn't answer, instead looking at this *boy* on her steps with an arched eyebrow.

Did he walk *here?* the eyebrow asked. There wasn't a car in the driveway, only fast filling footsteps from a pair of boots, the most expensive thing this *boy* was wearing.

"Good evening, Mrs. Noble," Cooper said in a forced, uncomfortable voice. "My name is..."

"Cooper Bennett, yes I know," she snipped. "My daughter said you would be coming for dinner."

She didn't say anymore, standing like a stone guardian in a designer dress blocking the entrance to a room filled with treasure. Unsympathetic and unmoving.

"Might I come in?" Cooper asked, his arms starting to shiver slightly. "It's starting to get a little cold out here."

Not as cold as this bitch's heart, he thought, then told himself off. No matter how much of an icy shoulder he was being given, this woman was still Alyssa's mother (as much of a social climber as she was) and if she wasn't going to give him any respect, he would make up for it in spades. Well, visually and verbally at least. It sounded like a grandiose gesture, for the time being at least. He might struggle with that as the evening wore on.

Suddenly, like the key to a vault in an action-adventure movie, Alyssa's hands appeared at her mother's side, ushering her out of the way.

"Hey there!" she said immediately, and Cooper's face seemed to brighten and warm up several degrees. "Come on Coop... get in out of the cold and, um, what are *those* in your hands? I told you not to buy anything, silly!"

"Well, I couldn't show up empty-handed," he replied happily, giving her a quick kiss before she took his gray sweater and placed it on a free coat hook.

Neither could see it, but Mrs. Noble's eyes were rolling as her Stuart Weitzmans clicked across the tile floor towards the dining room. *Worthless trash,* that eye roll said about this poor boy and his gifts. Her eyes didn't even need to see what was inside of those repugnant boxes to know it. She could just tell, you see.

Mrs. Noble neared the dining room – at the back of the house along a long line of tall windows – with her hands drawn up reservedly in front of her. Her posture reminded Cooper of those cotillion and etiquette lessons some girls had to take. He could even imagine her with a stick up her...

"Alyssa, dear," Mrs. Noble called, "come along."

Alyssa looked to Cooper, taking one of the boxes (it just so happened to be her gift) so she could hold his hand. Grabbing him and breathing deeply, she led him into the dining room. The place had a different atmosphere than he was used to, classical music playing on a hidden radio elevating the quality of the air to a haughty, humid soup.

Cooper hadn't been in the dining room before, only catching quick glimpses of it when passing through the kitchen or walking by on the back patio heading toward Wolf's Ridge Greenway for their jogs. It was a fancy room, an archway leading into it from the entry hall and another from the kitchen. Striped maroon curtains were drawn back to show off the snowy forest view and along the walls, still life paintings mounted in thick, wooden frames added an opulent flair. The room was lit by an elaborate chandelier above the mahogany and granite table, and four stylish wall sconces provided each corner with a sophisticated up-light. There were six chairs around the rectangular table, set with the clean plates on shining chargers and gleaming silverware that had likely been polished, then polished again for good measure.

Forks were on the left side of the plates, with the salad forks first, and then the dinner forks beside the plates. On the right side were the knives and spoons. All the blades were turned with their cutting sides towards the plates.

Oh, great, Cooper thought fearfully upon seeing the table, missing the relaxed nature of dinner at the Arnetts. *Not only do I have to decide which parent I'm going to get to sit closer to, I'm not going to have a clue how to use the fifty pieces of silverware on the table.*

Seated at the end closest to the window was Mr. Noble. A distinguished man with astute features, he was dressed in a fetching gray suit with red tie. He was reading a copy of the *Courier,* flared out in front of him while the top of his salt and pepper hair bobbed or shook as he read. A brandy was to his right, the only thing missing was a cigar which Cooper was sure he'd break out later.

Mrs. Noble didn't seem like the kind of person that wanted her home smelling of anything other than potpourri. She had perched herself on the opposite end of the table, scrutinizing Alyssa and Cooper as they entered.

"Alyssa," her mother said, "please have a seat."

You know, I'm here, too. Cooper thought, setting his boxes down beside Mr. Noble and sitting in the chair immediately to his right. Alyssa sat across from Cooper on her father's left. She looked excited to have him there, but for some reason he didn't feel the same way.

Dinner commenced when Isabella, their new housekeeper and chef, brought out three bowls of gazpacho, first serving Mr. and Mrs. Noble, then Alyssa. Cooper coughed to get her attention and she apologized, having the gall to say she didn't even see him there.

Alyssa sunk embarrassingly into her seat as she waited for Cooper to get his bowl. Her parents were already slurping, but at the proper volume.

Cold soup for cold hearts, he thought, and when his eyes met Alyssa's he could tell she was thinking the same thing. He winked and let out a smile to let her know he was doing okay. *We can save the heat for later.* Had they known how dinner was going to end, Cooper might have gone ahead and left at that point.

In addition to the holiday gazpacho, the rest of the meal consisted of a green salad with marinated lobster and avocado (*first time with avocados – not too bad*), roasted lemon turkey with pan seared grapes and mashed potatoes with port jus (*the best and most delicious part of the meal*), and spiced red wine-poached pears (*very weird to look at, but tasty nonetheless*).

For those in the know, it was generally understood that you followed the order of utensils from the farthest and worked your way in. Cooper was *not* in the know, and as dinner progressed through its courses he managed to show off that lacking skill set by doing more wrong than right.

Overall, it amounted to good times for Alyssa and good food for Cooper, but the improper etiquette stoked the ire of the Nobles. They didn't say a word *during* dinner, since calling people out would have shown worse manners than simply using the wrong fork, yet afterward, things took a different twist.

"So, Cooper, is it?" Mr. Noble asked, setting his dessert spoon right on top of Cooper's gift boxes. It wobbled as he let go, leaving a little smear of wine sauce on the wrapping paper.

He then leaned forward, and with his elbows barely resting on the edge of the table, strummed the tips of his fingers. With the lights glinting off his expensive cufflinks – probably worth more than Cooper had in his entire closet over the eighteen years of his life – it felt like an interrogation.

"Yes sir," Cooper answered politely.

"Indeed." There was a sharp sound – the intake of breath through gritted teeth. "Well, before we conclude this family occasion I wanted to ask you, Cooper, about *your own* family."

Cooper's heart grabbed hold of his ribs and started shaking them like a prisoner would the bars of a cell.

"What of it, sir?"

Mr. Noble made that sound again. It might as well have been nails on a chalkboard.

"I understand your home life is… less than stable."

"Daddy!" Alyssa snapped at the inappropriateness of the statement.

"Shhh," her mother scolded. "Not while Father is speaking, dear."

Cooper's eyes jumped to Alyssa. He wanted to bolt, but with the topic of his dad laid out he wanted to hear what such a *Nobleman* would say.

"It might be," Cooper replied, "but I fail to see how that applies to me and –"

"Unstable households lead to unstable individuals. That's a plain and simple *fact*, Mr. Bennett. I won't apologize for my tone of voice as I'm just looking out for my daughter's best interests. Surely even you can understand that I want a stable future for her, just like her present is now."

Alyssa was now crying on the inside; tears literally streaming along the shell that her parents were hollowing out. Her eyes begged Cooper not to leave – screaming, *I don't think of you like this at all!*

"I *can* provide that life for her," Cooper said, smiling her way.

It's okay... I'm still here.

"Really now?" Mr. Noble asked, his voice shaking as if he were trying not to laugh. "With what exactly are you going to provide that life with? Dreams? Come now Cooper, the apple doesn't fall far from the tree, and your father is hardly the best society has to offer. Am I right?"

Cooper dropped his eyes. The slivers of pear that were left on his plate reminded him of cuts on his skin from the odd belt snap.

"A thirteen dollar an hour job at Preston's Building Supply or even Rabun Paving? As if that can even begin provide a thing for my baby girl..."

"Dad! Stop!"

He didn't, and Mrs. Noble just sat there reveling in it.

"Not to mention all those upsetting… *instances* you've had at home. I can only imagine how horrific those are, but things like that can only lead a boy such as yourself into the same kind of despicable life. Like breeds like, after all."

"Not true!" Cooper retorted. "Situations like that can drive you… push you to rise above and be a better you!"

"Is that what you told your father after you nearly scalded his face. Pushing *it* toward the stove?"

Alyssa recoiled, not at the fact Cooper had done it (she knew because he told her the day after Thanksgiving) but the fact her own father was twisting his intel to suit his desired endgame. Twisting Christmas into a nightmare.

Shooting to her feet, she cried: "That was when Cooper finally stood up for himself!"

"So, when he stands up in the same way to *you*, Alyssa, you'll be fine with the outcome?"

She collapsed back into her seat, tears starting to stream down her face. Her insides were flooded.

"Mr. Bennett, I honestly don't think you're a very good fit for my girl at all. I can see you are trying, but I know people like you, and they will *always* be society's riffraff."

Cooper pushed his chair away from the table. He stood up slowly.

Mr. Noble was holding out his gifts, unopened, for Cooper to retrieve.

"You'll need these more than we will," he said coldly.

Cooper started to reach for them, and stopped.

"No sir, you keep them. It's the thought that counts after all."

Mr. Noble set the boxes back on the tabletop, tossing his dirty napkin over them.

"That is, if the thoughts matter in the first place, son."

Cooper held his head high, walking out of the dining room without another word.

Alyssa clutched at her gift box, still sitting on the table beside her. She wanted to chase after him but her parent's gaze kept her frozen.

Cooper neared the door, snatching his hooded sweater off the hook. He heard a slight rip (*great, fucking great*) and as he put it on its cheap material brushed against his skin. It might as well be burlap for all he'd been told after dinner. He grasped the door handle and pulled it open, met by the the small blizzard falling down on Goodman. Looking back over his shoulder a last time, the archway into the dining room was empty.

Cooper really didn't know if he'd expected to see Alyssa there, ready to charge into his waiting arms. Since there was nobody there, it felt like a kick to the balls that even his dad hadn't managed to get in.

In protest, he left the door wide open; one of those snooty assholes could close it behind him. He pulled up his hood and then thrust his hands deep into his pockets. It wasn't much warmer there at all and the snow was coming down in great sheets. The wind whipped his already untamable hair all over the place.

Cooper!

Oh, here we go, he thought. *More imaginary voices to remind myself of how shitty my life is.*

"Cooper wait!"

He stopped at the end of the driveway, turning around in what seemed like slow motion. Alyssa was standing outside her front door, her clothes and hair fluttering wildly.

"Baby, get back inside before you get sick!" Cooper shouted at her, but she wasn't listening. Instead, she was running *toward* him – no jacket and a thin pair of shoes over her feet.

"Stubborn!" he yelled as she barreled into his arms. "You really are going to catch your death out here, Alyssa…"

He steered her back toward the house but she resisted.

"I'm so sorry," she said. "I didn't mean things to happen that way at all. I knew they wouldn't take it well, but I figured it being Christmas would soften the blow."

"You've nothing to be sorry about," he said, the bitter wind trying to change his mind.

He looked over to her left hand; she was carrying her gift box. The wind had caught in his poor taping job, trying to rip the paper completely away.

"You might as well help it out," Cooper said, observing Alyssa work her fingers down the ugly wrapping paper. A mammoth gust tore it out of her grip and it disappeared behind a thick sheet of falling snow. Opening the box, she saw a large scarf, handmade and purple.

"Oh my God... is this the one from A Stitch in Time?"

"Better than that," Cooper replied, reaching in to pull it out. He wrapped its warm folds around her neck and shoulders, adjusting it as he went. "I had the owner knit this one just for you. It's one of a kind, so there isn't another like it anywhere."

Alyssa turned up the end and instead of a store tag, there was a small, embroidered one. On it a little message was stitched. It said: WITH LOVE ALWAYS, YOUR COOP.

Alyssa was positively speechless, Cooper guiding her back to the house. They were arm in arm, his head pressed against hers gently, each other's hair whipping their faces.

"So, what did you end up getting them?" Alyssa asked, her curiosity about what was in the boxes for her parents getting the better of her.

"I..." Cooper began, then stopped. He smiled her way, bearing a devious one. "You know what: who cares?" I have all that I need right here, and I plan on keeping it that way."

He pulled her in closer as they walked up the steps, never wanting to let her go.

Chapter 16: Happy Birthday to You (II)

Monday January 7, 2013

1

Every single birthday that came and went in Cooper's tumultuous life turned into a mess. Not the kind that was easy to clean either, but full on explosive diarrhea that coated everything with a thick sludge that would, without fail, leave something stinking behind. His nineteenth birthday – which fell on a Monday that January in 2013 – started out wonderful enough, but by the end would be no different than history intended.

Liam Manning had all but faded to obscurity, the process beginning in early October the year before. Some attributed it to graduation, which was fast approaching. The oceans of college were vast, and even a fish like Liam, who was big in a pond like Goodman, would be small, insignificant, and easily overlooked if he didn't have something to show for himself. Yet after turning nineteen himself, Liam resumed causing misery again, especially for Cooper and his friends.

Loose Cannon Manning, making up for lost time!

Thankfully, Cooper had grown over that same time, channeling his anger and newfound abilities into effective counters not only against Liam, but his pack and life in general.

The last bell of the day rang out through Goodman High, the halls filling with the weary chatter of students still wishing it was Christmas Break, realizing another mundane Monday had come to an end.

Unlike the rest, Cooper was jubilant, sprinting down the halls, weaving amongst the masses as fast as a sewing machine needle through fabric. Reaching the front doors, he burst through with the cheesiest grin on his face, hopping down the stairs and across the lawn toward Hanlon Road.

Alyssa and Billy would catch up with him later. They had to make a couple of stops, the first being Olsen's Pharmacy where Billy was picking up some cold medicine for Mrs. Arnett. She'd gotten sick a few days earlier and in stubborn mom fashion refused to see the doctor herself (not wanting to skip out on any of her duties). From there, the two planned to head over to Simpson's, a new bakery that opened on the second, for Cooper's birthday cake.

I hope they're nabbing me something good! Cooper thought hungrily as he sprinted across East Broadway and past Goodman Police Department.

The wind felt great as it rushed over his face, almost like he was flying.

Flying would *be nice,* he thought, and as he looked down the street at the roof of the First Baptist Church, then up at the three o'clock sun, a preposterous idea came to mind. *You're crazy, Coop, doing this during the day, but it is your birthday after all. So be sure to have...*

Running up to the side of red-bricked building, Cooper leaped against the side, pushing up and off with his foot while twisting in midair.

a...

He grabbed hold of an overhang that jutted out over the daycare drop-off area, lifting himself on it before vaulting up another story to the roof.

"Blast!" he said loudly, followed by a hearty laugh.

A woman in the playground below looked around for the source of the noise, huddling protectively around the few kids that were there. She couldn't see anything, and the last place she would have expected to look was up.

Cooper kneeled just in case.

Although he was only two stories up – three just a little bit down along the church's roof – he might as well have been a mile in the sky for all the joy coursing through his veins. Cooper wondered what he'd done to deserve such amazing gifts, but as time went on he would also begin to wonder if they were really gifts at all.

Standing again, Cooper looked west toward the dense array of downtown rooftops.

"Let's get a move on," he said, and with a deep breath and thumping heart, he ran along the church at breakneck speed, springing to the third floor then up and over Sullivan Street to the neighboring buildings lining the opposite side. Repeating the process several times, the sensation of flying became addictive, along with the passing smell of food and garbage, and the potential of being seen.

Since October, Cooper had refined the process (those first few attempts embarrassingly bad), and was now able to anticipate where inquisitive eyes would be before they discovered him. Undeniably, it was risky to do something that bold in broad daylight, but the adrenaline rush was great and by the time someone would look, the spot he'd occupied was empty (although every now and then, Cooper would dawdle and let a child see him, hopefully sparking their imaginations and desires to create wonderful things… or more likely, committing them to a life behind the walls of a mental institution).

A few seconds later, Cooper landed on the roofs above Center Street, glancing down to a central alcove which connected to a narrow alleyway. Checking it for clearance, he dropped to the pavement a moment later. The landing wasn't superb.

"Whew!" Cooper said, cracking his neck before leaning against a wall to come down off the high. "Best jaunt yet."

Once sufficiently composed, Cooper walked calmly into the alley, appearing on Center Street. A bench, one of many that lined both sides of the street, was a few steps away. Sitting on the back rest, he fiddled with the zipper on the side of his new boots while waiting for Alyssa and Billy to meet him. The plan was to get a quick bite at Castillo's, followed by some birthday cake at the park.

It all sounded amazing, but the hunger that panged in his gut didn't call out for pizza, or for donuts, or for cake. No matter how tasty they were, it called out for meat – sinewy, red, and raw.

2

After unashamedly eating all the confetti cake Alyssa and Billy had picked up from Simpson's (triple layered with nineteen red candles burning brightly in the center), Cooper bid his friends a good night. They'd been hanging out at the small park across from Goodman Elementary; Cooper and Alyssa sitting on the edge of an almost-too-old platform whirl, Billy on a nearby swing. They didn't even know if the place had a proper name, everyone just called it the Kinder Garden.

"You sure you're going to be okay, Cooper?" Alyssa asked, giving him a kiss on the forehead. She fixed his hair for him; it always seemed to have a mind of its own.

"You bet," Cooper replied, waving at Billy who'd already taken shotgun position in her car. His hair fell right back out of place again. "I've walked this path many times."

"I know you have. That's not what I meant. It's just that I wish I could do it with you, especially today being your birthday."

"Ah, well we'll have plenty of opportunities for that later, along new paths of our own."

You're so poetic, Coop, he thought while she nodded, giving him one more kiss. This time it was on the lips, and he could tell that she didn't want to leave.

"Go on now," he said sadly. "Billy needs one of us around to keep him out of trouble."

"I'll call you later," she said along with a light laugh. "I may even stop by, if you'd like."

Cooper smiled. *I hope you do both*, the smile said.

He watched as Alyssa turned and walked toward her car. She got inside, fastened her seatbelt (ordering Billy to do the same), then drove down Second Avenue before turning left to take Billy home.

It was about five o'clock when Cooper started back for his house. For *Roland's* house. Most of Goodman's traffic was flowing out from the downtown area into the surrounding residential zones like a great heart pumping blood to its extremities. Eventually, Cooper was passing by the vacant clothing store where his first... incident... occurred. He paused, again examining his reflection in detail. What he saw was much better than before – no tears nor rain dampening the mood – but he knew that there was still a lot of work to be –

Cooper...

He jerked his head around. It was like someone had whispered in his ear. There was nobody there but a voice... yes, a voice and not the wind like he first thought, had said his name. Cooper couldn't tell if he was imagining things but regardless he looked around some more (even to the rooftops). There was nothing that could have made –

Cooper...

He shivered. There it was again. Eerie and ominous, something was drawing his attention to the north…

Cooper…

Something past Foothill Road and the bus station…

Cooper…

Something up the slopes towards the walking trails…

Cooper…

Something in the spot where he was first bitten those four months ago.

Cooper, come speak to me…

He did his best to ignore what he was hearing. Imaginary voices in one's head was a good reason to get locked up. Listening and doing what those voices said a good reason for the keys to get conveniently "lost". Cooper trudged south on Center Street and despite his best efforts, each step was like wading through molasses. Turning to head back north, he felt unrestrained, even pushed in that direction.

Before he knew it (and much faster than he would have liked), Cooper was back on the trails of Toluca Springs National Forest. The ground was mucky and the air cool. It would be refreshing if not for the trees that were all around, smelling like rotting leaves and reminding him of the bars of a cage. Down the trail about twenty feet away, Cooper could see the gap in the overgrowth that he scurried down to escape Liam, Derek, and Mark that ill-fated August night. It had filled in over the last four months, but there was still a definite space one could fit through to access the embankment.

Nope. Nope. Nope, he thought, but his feet seemed to think the opposite. They were already carrying him toward it, then through.

Cooper skidded down the slope. He looked like he was surfing – hardly skillfully – but maintaining himself upright past mounds of forest litter and over downed trees. He nearly made it all the way down without falling, but the thought of success triggered his failure, and Cooper toppled, yelling as he crashed into the spongy soil right at the bottom.

This is familiar, he recalled, looking around for any yellow eyes. None were there, and neither was the voice in his head. Pushing himself up and onto his knees, Cooper sighed, looking at the smattering of dirt, leaves, and shit (*why is there always shit?*) he was wearing.

"Why'd you come up here, Coop?" he asked himself, looking around as the evening started to grow darker. Surprisingly, the forest looked beautiful from where he was kneeling in the clearing, the caged feeling gone and replaced by –

"You came because I asked you to," said a mysterious voice.

Cooper leaped to his feet, fists closed, eyes alert.

"Who's there?" he asked crossly.

"There's no need to be so tense, Cooper," the voice replied, and from behind a distant tree a figure emerged. It was shrouded in white, a large furry hood draped over its head.

"That's easy for you to say. Seems like you know who I am. I don't have that luxury."

There was a chortle as the figure approached. It sounded friendly, but Cooper remained guarded.

"Well then, let's amend that. My name is Lance Goddard, and I'm the Alpha of the shadow wolves. I'm sure you are... familiar with our kind by now?"

The name didn't strike a bell, but Cooper watched cautiously as Lance removed the hood. A dark-haired man was underneath, attractive with piercing eyes. At times, they seemed yellow, staring at Cooper like a father would a wayward son. It didn't make him feel all too comfortable.

"Yeah, you could say that," Cooper replied. Relaxing his fists, he didn't take his eyes off Lance. He noticed hints of a tattoo peeking out from beneath the cloak and something else, difficult to make out from there. It looked dark.

"Good! Let's have a chat then. To give you some perspective on the current situation."

What situation? Cooper wondered. He felt uneasy.

"You see, there is a little squabble going on between my pack and the white wolves. They live in Goodman, and are led by the Mannings who –"

"I know quite well," Cooper said, a look of disgust briefly flaring across his face. "More Liam than his father, though."

"As the adage goes: father, like son," Lance replied. "There's truth to such sayings, which is why they last. You probably know Grayson better than you think. He is their pack's Alpha, Liam the Beta who will assume control once Grayson dies or is…"

"Otherwise removed?" Cooper said, thinking he knew exactly what the "squabble" was about. It sounded like a typical power play, made by many over the years and many more in years to come.

"Indeed," Lance confirmed, walking by. He was heading deeper into the woods.

Cooper followed, keeping his distance while looking around with each step. He felt like there was an audience for this private chat.

"Despite my assertions to Grayson," Lance continued, "I would rather avoid outright war between our kind. Every drop of blood spilled is a part of something special that would be lost forever. That is something we cannot afford, considering other beast shifters are moving against us; bears and boars mainly, but even darker forces are on the horizon. Demons threaten to wipe everything away…"

"*Woah!*" Cooper exclaimed, stopping mid stride with his arms up.

"Beast shifters? *Demons?* What the hell is this stuff your talking about?"

"It's the true face of the world, Cooper, not the thin veneer of normalcy that covers the planet in ignorance. It's what lies beneath."

Cooper needed time to process all this new information, but wasn't given that luxury.

So, there's more out there than just werewolves? was the only thing he could muster – as if that weren't enough – before Lance began speaking again.

"All that I want is access to what is rightfully mine. Grayson is keeping it from me, like Liam keeps things from you, I'm sure."

Alyssa...

"I see you understand," Lance observed. He had stopped, the forest ahead growing thick with trees and vegetation. The base of his long, white cloak had been scraping the ground, now blackened with grime. "It's one of the worst feelings in the world, isn't it? To be kept from the things you love..."

Cooper looked down, the seeds of doubt planted against the white wolves starting to peek out of the ground. He didn't know if he should let them grow, or use his gloppy boots to squash them flat. Peripherally aware that eyes were sparking like dew in the darkness of the dense foliage, he replied, "Yes, it is."

Cooper took his time looking back up at Lance, feeling like he was being led down a path he couldn't escape; a leash dragging him by the neck to a place he didn't want to go.

That had been the story of his life, and it was about damn time he stood up and said "no."

There was no way he was going deeper into the forest, where branches and thorny vines would snag his clothes and tear his skin, where the smell of hidden, rotting things would be amplified tenfold. But instead of asking Cooper to follow, or summoning forces to drag him wailing into the darkness, Lance asked something unexpected.

"How have you been holding off on the hunger?"

"The hunger?" Cooper repeated in his confusion.

"The desire to eat."

"Oh that. I've been eating quite a lot of..."

"No, I mean meat. Blood."

Cooper looked repulsed.

Lance could see it, and even if he couldn't, he could *smell* it, wafting off Cooper like a stench. It was shame.

"I realize it is difficult to understand morally, but it's in our nature to consume those things."

But it's murder... Cooper thought angrily.

"I've been eating my burgers and steaks rare, if that's what you mean. Sometimes I don't even cook the meat before…"

Lance curled his lips back over his teeth in a sheer look of horror. Cooper fell silent.

"I was not originally planning to do this," Lance said with no indication of his original intent, "but as a gesture of goodwill towards you, I am going to offer you a place in the pack."

There were mixed noises from the woods. Some growls and some howls. Everything was rusty and hoarse. Cooper didn't know if that was good or bad.

Lance didn't seem bothered either way.

"You would be a subordinate, of course, etiquette and all. But should you show fine strength of character I can easily see you rising in the ranks quickly, possibly becoming an omega in five or ten years."

Omega? Cooper pondered. *That doesn't sound anywhere near as great as Alpha. In fact, isn't that the complete opposite?*

Cooper *was* interested though, knowing that if he joined he could learn to harness all these new powers even more. The faces of Alyssa and Billy drifted by in thought, and Cooper sighed. He couldn't do any of it without them.

"So, do we have an agreement?" Lance asked, extending an arm. The cloak shimmered in the evening light as something *dripped* off the sleeve.

"I... uh," Cooper said, still focused on the sleeve, which was dripping yet again. "I would love to, but only if I can still be friends with..."

Lance sighed.

"Friends? Really? Cooper, should you join there would be no time for such frivolous and trivial things. The pack... I... would be your priority."

Cooper shrugged nonchalantly.

"Then there's no deal."

Lance's eyes flickered; the shadows of his expression darkened.

"No matter. The offer was just a nicety. Ultimately, Cooper you will either join this pack at the very bottom or be labeled a lone wolf, which makes you open sport for those of us that like to hunt. As for your *friends*, especially the one I know your heart belongs to..."

"It belongs to *both* of them."

"How quaint," Lance muttered, trying not to laugh. "You would not be allowed to have a mate. Only an Alpha is allowed to..."

"Where's yours then?"

"I beg your pardon?"

"Your mate?"

"That is none of your concern!" Lance roared, and the forest behind him did so too. "You will leave those humans behind or, if they already know about any of *this*, they will be killed!"

Cooper's jovial attitude erupted into hatred.

"Mark my words: if you come anywhere within a mile of either of them, I will do everything in my power to protect them. I'm their shield against all threats, even if one of those is you."

"Oh really?" Lance said, and with a snap of his fingers scores of black wolves emerged from the forest. "Do you *really* think you can overcome me?"

Cooper started to reply, but stopped short when he realized what was beneath the cloak. He had gotten close enough during the exchange to see that it was *blood* under there. A lot of it. The cloak made entirely out of preserved wolf hides; Cooper guessing at least two, maybe three.

"I don't just think I can," Cooper replied. "I know it."

The Shadow Alpha stepped back, something in Cooper's eyes shaking him. They were different, the yellow somehow less intense. After a moment, Lance recovered his stature.

"Mr. Bennett, that's exactly the kind of thinking that can get you killed..."

Chapter 17: A Deal with a Devil Dog

Wednesday, February 27, 2013

1

In the early afternoon of a late February day, Wolfrick, the werewolf who had bitten Cooper and that Liam Manning wanted to kill so badly for it, arrived on the narrow banks of the Chattooga River. He was a big man (not at all fat, just big from years of farm work), wearing a Rabun County Sheriff's uniform.

Lance Goddard was crouched along the water's edge, barefoot and shirtless in a pair of black dress pants. The rest of his suit was draped over a large rock about ten feet away. Passing his hands through the gentle flow, cool water glided over and between his fingers, recalling memories of a sight from long ago. The river Rhine was laden with blood, so much it ran red, while its banks were a stinking sludge.

"A-alpha," Wolfrick said cautiously. He removed his hat, fully aware of how much his master did not like to be disturbed, and what happened should you do so at the wrong time. "Y-you suh-summoned me?"

"Yes," Lance replied, cupping his hands to scoop up some water. He drank, the memory of the Rhine still burning but yielding to the present, then stood. "I believe that we are finally ready to launch an attack against Goodman."

Wolfrick's chest pounded and his ears were red with nervousness. He was aware of the months of preparation and planning – he had been a part of it – but wondered why the Alpha would be telling a lowly subordinate this kind of information. Wolfrick's job was to follow commands, nothing more and certainly nothing less.

"I have a task for you," Lance said, walking along the bank toward a copse of trees standing off from the rest of the surrounding woods. His bare feet left large footprints behind, Lance liking the way the mud squelched between his toes. "Should you succeed, I might have a place for you as an omega. Should you succeed *swiftly*, I will have a place for you as Beta..."

Wolfrick forgot how to speak, his eyes growing large and blank.

Lance smirked, taking that expression as a confirmation. Walking around the thicket, a large trunk came into view. It had been snapped by the wind or some other powerful force about a dozen feet off the ground. In the rooted portion, a seat had been hewn into the wood, its edges detailed with intricate patterns of leaves and vines. The whole thing resembled a throne, and Lance sat upon it, staring out over the west. He couldn't see Goodman from that vantage point (they were lower than the surrounding land), but he knew the town and his prize were out there, waiting.

A majority of the shadow pack had been stationed to the north of town in Toluca Springs National Forest (occupying the woods just across the North Carolina border). They were also east in Jameson Preserve, where they were now along the Chattooga River. Overall Lance's numbers had swelled into an ample attack force, poised to sweep into town and keep any interference from the Order and Manning's pack at bay.

Lance had also spent a significant amount time – the bulk of why they weren't ready sooner – eliminating potential aid from other shifters in the surrounding area. They'd cleared a radius of fifty miles around Goodman.

The Alpha rubbed his fingers along the wooden throne. It was smooth despite its weathered appearance. One of his claws was extended, scraping the letter G in one of the arm rests. He had already placed an L in the other.

Poor Åsbjörn, he thought while leaving his latest mark, *sorry to have decimated your great kingdom.*

Out of his surprised stupor, Wolfrick made his way around to the front of the throne.

"What is it that you need done, my Alpha?" he asked, kneeling.

"I need the final piece that will set everything in motion. Our target is the Order's Vault, located deep beneath that wretched town. In order to enter that place, we will need a key."

"And you wish for me to retrieve this key for you?" Wolfrick asked, staring up at Lance intently.

"No," Lance replied with a dismissive wave of his hand. "I need *you* to retrieve the arrogant shit who can tell me where it is."

2

That afternoon, Liam Manning was basking in the sun as he laid in the prickly grass at the center of a football field. Stealing a private moment for himself that didn't come all too often, Liam had just chased away the trifecta of mean girls – Mary Sue Ellen, Becky Prince, and Virginia Crawford – whose horrid cackles, jarring "high fashion" outfits, and annoying shucking and jiving all gave him a headache, even in memory.

He'd sent Derek and Mark away with them, too, under the auspices of keeping those annoying bitches away. Mark didn't mind at all; he wanted to fuck Mary's brains out (or maybe it was motorboat her tits, Liam couldn't remember or care), while Derek, Liam suspected, just wanted to eat all three of them.

Not even Liam knew, but Derek had gotten very close to succeeding with Virginia once. It was a time long ago when both were twelve; Derek had been stalking her for some time late one afternoon. Ready to pounce, a large group of people rounded a corner, suddenly forcing him to stop. Upset, Derek retreated but soon stumbled upon easier prey. Monica Evans was all alone in the cul-de-sac at the east end of Hooper Road. She had been relaxing like she always did: by watching ants, these marching out of a big mound on the edge of the sidewalk. Derek descended ravenously upon her, giving the girl no time to comprehend what was happening. Otherwise she would have screamed, and surely then someone would have helped her, unlike the ants which continued with their business, unbothered by the horrendous sight and sounds unfolding so close by…

Meat… Derek had said, something crunching right after. *All the meat…*

Back in the present and despite all the hullabaloo, Liam just wanted to be alone, if only until the next bell. Finally, he was… until his father's words came shouting at him from the night before.

Liam, what are you going to do when you're no longer roosting and crowing from the top of the Goodman totem pole?

"Of course, *you* would find a way to bother me now," Liam replied with a spiteful whisper, but deep down he knew that his father was right in this case.

Even though Liam was set to assume the role of the White Alpha, barring Grayson's premature death that wouldn't be for some untold number of long years. He would need to blend in, have a career, or barring that any kind of job. With zero interest in his father's fields of stock market trading and real estate investing, the most promising thing Liam had going for him was football. He had great potential for the college level, and possibly even national level, but only if he battened down the hatches and focused, living up to that tattoo and the type of life it implied. Of course, this all assumed Liam hadn't pissed all the time he had away by asserting himself just to ride a wave of popularity from a bunch of assholes that wouldn't even remember who Liam Manning was past the graduation of the Class of 2013.

"Fuck!" he shouted, kicking out a leg and slamming his fists on the ground.

Above, the clouds drifted in front of the sun, casting Liam under an appropriate swath of shadow. The temperature dropped a few notable degrees, and he found himself happy to have his Wolverines jacket on. A few seconds later, the sun broke free.

You've got to see what you can do, he thought, mainly in the interest of self-preservation. Closing his eyes, he continued mulling. *Fuck Cooper Bennett, what does he have going for himself? Fuck everyone else but you, Liam. You need to refocus on yourself, otherwise you'll be back in this shitty town before you know it, working as the next school custodian, primed and ready for a new generation of kids to point their fingers at and laugh.*

The clouds had rolled back over the sun, the dingy red inside Liam's eyelids becoming darker. Off in the distance, the school bell was ringing, signaling the start of the last class of the day. He could smell something vaguely familiar.

"Wow, that was way too short," he said, stretching one last time. His eyes were still closed, focused on trying to make the relaxation last just a little bit longer. Then the bell stopped ringing as if to spite him. "Fine! Guess I better go find Wilder and –"

"No... I don't think you're going anywhere," said a gruff voice.

Liam's eyes flung open and his face went from shock to anger to confusion in less than a second. The sun was still out and very bright, the shadow across him caused by a county sheriff who was bent over in such a way that he looked upside down. There was no name badge on his uniform, and two other men were positioned on either side of Liam.

"Hello there, Mr. Manning," the sheriff said, a wild gleam of gold flickering in his eyes.

"Wolfrick!" Liam growled, finally connecting the dots and the smell.

The sheriff laughed, rumbling his chest before dropping a huge, oyster-sized blob of phlegm on Liam's face. It pooled in the indention beside his left eye, stinging and oozing down his cheek.

"Come on! Get him up! The Shadow Alpha is waiting."

The other men promptly grabbed hold of Liam's jacket and yanked the jock to his feet. The phlegm slid off in one glopping swoop before a fist came to replace it. Everything suddenly went black, Liam finally able to relax.

3

Darkness all around…

The smell of something decomposing and fetid…

The feel of water splashing into new Converse shoes…

Liam Manning experienced all those things and more as he came to. The side of his face was stinging from where the punch landed, and he had no idea where he was being led other than through the woods. Staying calm, he used what little light was filtering in through the bag on his head to determine their direction.

That asshole Wolfrick had been heading east for some time, the brightest light coming from the sun setting behind them. Then they turned north, traveling along – and Liam *in* –a creek or river. No sooner than he'd figured this out, his hosts lead him onto dry land (a misnomer, since most of what he was forced to walk through was sopping mud up to his shins. It tried to claim Liam's shoes with each humiliating step, sucking and grasping while he tried to stay vertical).

"We're here," Wolfrick grunted to the others, and with a swift kick to the back of Liam's knee, the Manning boy fell to the ground.

Liam could hear light laughter dancing behind him, but it was quickly silenced. He could sense someone else had arrived and above the filthy odor, could smell...

"My Alpha," Wolfrick said reverently, "I have brought what you were looking for."

"Well done," Lance said, "and in record time too. If only the others were half as efficient."

Liam felt a set of large hands grab his shoulders. They held them firm as the bag was taken off his head. As soon as he could see (the Shadow Alpha was seated on some kind of throne in the forest wearing a dirty white cloak), the vile and rotten stench faded.

Plop.

Something dropped on Liam's forehead. It was cold and ran thick like syrup down the bridge of his nose. At first, he thought Wolfrick had spit on him again – wanting to twist that prick's head off his neck – but Liam could see him kneeling immediately to Lance's right.

Wrestling an arm free, he used a hand up to wipe the stuff away, then looked...

What the hell?

There was blood, so aged it was nearly black. Craning his eyes upward, Liam saw what looked like a Halloween mask, but as another drop splattered on his forehead, he trembled, knowing that it was no wolf-man costume.

It was a head.

"I'm sure your father was wondering what happened to Ranger Smith and the others," Lance said a bit too casually.

Liam's eyes had locked on the blackened goop smeared across his palm. Smith had gone missing a couple of months earlier while on patrol, along with two other park rangers. Now his fluids were staining his hand and jacket sleeve. Liam looked past his fingers, focusing on the white cloak Lance was wearing. A shuddering gasp escaped.

"Are... those..."

Lance smirked. It was prideful and full of malice.

"How?"

"Well, skinning them was easy, as you know," Lance replied, slipping out of the cloak. It flopped down across the back of the throne with a wet *thud*.

Liam did not have a clue about skinning things (Derek was more the type for that), but he nodded anyway.

"As for preserving the hides," Lance continued, "we extracted the information from someone I suspect did the same thing to one of my pack a year ago this past January. What was left behind was... disturbing to say the least. I think he was part of the Order, but he might have been a rogue. Such a lonely existence, rogues and lone wolves alike. I actually pitied him."

"Who was he?"

"Strangely enough, he didn't say. That information stayed locked up tighter than all of his other secrets."

"So, you ended up killing him?"

Lance's grin became a grimace. He avoided the question.

Liam stole some of Lance's vanished expression, breaking into the smallest smile, but his elation was short-lived.

Lance pitched his head and the two guards lifted their hostage to his feet. The one on the left grabbed his jacket at the shoulder, dug his long claws in, and tore it. The entire sleeve ripped away. He flung it, drifting somberly through the air like a banner falling from a castle under siege.

"We learned a few other things from the man before he..." Lance stopped, digging into his pocket instead. He pulled out two small items: one was a decorated switchblade, the other a vial of clear liquid.

Liam was afraid. He tried to free one of his arms again, but the guards were ready, overpowering him this time.

Lance admired the knife – *click* – and its blade of cold silver shot out like a bullet. He walked up to Liam, whose exposed arm was covered with gooseflesh.

"As you know, solid silver and werewolves have never been happy bedfellows."

Placing the blade against Liam's bicep, Lance slashed quickly, leaving a thin streak of red along his suntanned skin. Screams roses with the curls of smoke coming from the bleeding laceration.

"Now, silver in other forms has always been *ineffective*," Lance continued, shaking the vial between his thumb and index finger. "Recognize this?"

Liam said nothing, only shivering.

"It's lunar caustic, otherwise known as silver nitrate."

Removing the dropper, Lance placed a single bead of liquid further down on Liam's arm.

He winced, but there was no pain; just a slight effervescent tingle like sticking a finger into a glass of Alka-Seltzer.

"Stop..." Liam begged softly.

"Hmm? Stop? I understood you to do this sort of thing all the time, Liam. Surely a man such as yourself can handle what he dishes out? It's only a few little scrapes after all."

Liam said something indecipherable, then chuckled hysterically.

"Now, where was I? Oh yes, we already knew that solutions in high enough concentrations were more effective against us, but thankfully nothing has ever proven fatal. So, imagine our utter surprise when we learned what happened if we splashed some of *this* onto some of *that*.

Lance pointed to the fresh silver wound across Liam's upper arm.

"No..." Liam begged, still delirious. Lance did not care. "No!"

Another slash! This one went from Liam's elbow down to the wrist. The long cut smoked intensely, blood trickling down both sides from the center like a single rail ladder. Immediately Lance poured half the solution over the wound. It hissed and popped violently. It smelled of anchovy paste and strands of red writhed across Liam's skin, scabbing quickly. The edges of the cut became plump and raw.

Liam screamed, breathed a deep and croaky breath, then screamed again. His throat gurgled; he was choking.

Lance looked admirably over his handiwork, immune to the cries that echoed through the woods.

"More tingle for the mingle," he said as a happy rhyming jingle.

The guards dropped Liam and he fell back to his knees, vomiting. Even that was steaming.

"Don't worry Liam," Lance said reassuringly. "I won't be putting a silver bullet between your eyes today."

"What do you want with me, insane fucker?"

"Such language," Lance derided. "Grayson's raised such a rebellious son of a *bitch*."

"Fuck you."

The guards pummeled Liam from behind. The larger sentry punched him in the back of the head, the other twice in the side.

"Speak with respect!" he growled.

"I would if he had any."

The process repeated, harder and faster this time. After six more bouts Lance finally stopped them.

"Okay that's enough! Liam, I'm not asking for much. I know you would love to get your hands on Wolfrick here, but he's proven himself one of my most loyal subordinates. I have other plans for him, so let me make you another offer. Since Cooper Bennett *is* a shadow wolf, I will make sure the boy is reined in and personally delivered to you."

Liam stopped struggling.

"You'd like that, wouldn't you? You could do *whatever* you want to the boy: beat him, gut him, hell fuck him with that big ol' jock cock if that floats your boat."

Liam stared out through his swollen eyes, a smirk flapping on his busted lips.

"Surely getting your hands on him would garner some favor with the other white wolves. I know your pack is under a lot of strain with everything going on – I don't need to delve into the details you see every day. But, you know," Lance tapped a finger on his mouth, "this *might* even allow you to gain enough support to displace a certain silver fox that's lost his focus and his way. Two wolves felled with a single, subversive bullet."

From what Lance could see, that was enough of a match to ignite Liam's fire, its smoke clouding his common sense. Where he should have questioned why a rival pack's Alpha would be remotely interested in helping him become one himself, Liam simply agreed.

"Yet as nice as I am, I'm not a charity Liam. I will need something in return for all of this."

"What is it?" he asked obediently.

The blue light of his eyes was intense, hands shaking as they raked in handfuls of dirt. It collected under his otherwise pristine nails.

"I will need the key to the Order's Vault."

Liam eyes dropped. Checked his arm. It had stopped bleeding; the edges still irritated but the spidery lines starting to recede.

"I'll find it for you," he answered.

"And then retrieve it and bring it to me."

"Of course."

"Good. It sounds like we have a deal." Lance turned and walked back to his throne. He sat in it and proudly stuck out his tattooed chest. "Now, feel free to shift and heal up, my men will not stop you. I'll have them escort you back to Goodman later tonight."

A delightful vision of Cooper's battered and broken body swam in dim lights across Liam's mind. It drowned out the same common sense that the searing wound had.

"Thank... you... Alpha," he said, spell-bound.

His dream and Cooper's fate would soon be a reality, once the key was safely in the *Schattenträger's* grasp.

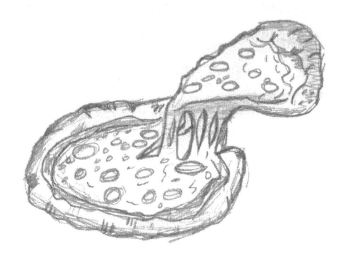

CHAPTER 18: PLANS FOR THE FUTURE

Wednesday, February 27, 2013

1

Alyssa, Billy, and Cooper had made Castillo's their hangout of choice

over the last year. It opened back when they were still in middle school, but

it wasn't until other stores opened around it that they took notice. Alyssa

would often shop at a few boutique stores along Market Street. Her favorite

was the consignment store called A Stitch in Time, where Cooper had gotten her Christmas scarf. Inside were great deals on unique shoes, dresses, and accessories – all stylish and all *not* from the places in the mall the mean girls frequented.

Cooper and Billy were a little different. They liked food a lot (not to the level of being foodies, they just liked to eat), so Castillo's had always been somewhat on their radar. But it was when Kimmy's Donuts opened less than a block away on Center Street that the true love affair began. After all, dessert was – as any sensible person knew – the most important course of any meal.

Therefore, it was no surprise that the trio decided to meet at the Italian joint again.

Cooper dropped down from the rooftops, the walls of the secluded alleyway springing up around him like a security blanket. His landings had greatly improved over the last month, boots making a soft *thump* on the pavement rather than his legs tangling over each other and spilling him onto his ass. (The landing on his birthday was apparently a lucky one.)

Rising from a squatting position, Cooper adjusted the strap of his backpack – a few extra books inside for finals. Striding out from the alley, he walked over to the closest bench, *his* bench now that he used it so frequently. There, he waited for Alyssa and Billy to arrive.

Castillo's beckoned him to come in from across the way, but Cooper sat patiently. Alyssa or Billy always had a quick errand or two to run for their parents after school these days. As annoying as those errands might be, and though it gave Cooper time to improve his parkour, he found himself wishing he had someone along those lines to do things for – a parent worth caring about. Yet his dad was Roland Bennett (*that bastard*, as Mrs. Arnett would think), more deserving of side glances and whispered gossip than gifts and true love.

Three more months, Coop. Just three more months until...

His mind started to drift. It would be three more months until Cooper would be out of that infernal house. He knew that he could have left much sooner, but now it was more of a personal challenge to overcome than plain fear. What made him more upset was the fact it was also three more months until graduation, and therefore separation from those he'd come to care about.

Before those depressing thoughts spiraled too far out of control, Cooper spotted a large man coming out of the eatery. His brows furrowed since the man looked somewhat familiar. Abnormally tall, muscles straining against a black tank top, a burly beard.

It's him! Cooper thought, mulling quickly. It was the guy who rivaled Mark Brown for the title of tallest man in Goodman. *Gosh, haven't seen him in ages!*

Cooper knew that the town gym rats liked to congregate down south, across the highway on the aptly named Beast Crossing. Perhaps that's where *this* guy had disappeared for the last year, feeding on properly portioned protein from the FitPrep store (adjacent to the large steel warehouse housing Roop's Den).

Cooper continued staring.

On second thought, the man looked large enough to have eaten several cows. He let the door close behind him, heading south on Center Street, reminding Cooper of a werewolf now that he was intimately familiar with them. At first it was the beard and furry body that screamed those facts, but in the end, it was the intensity of his eyes, carrying an otherworldly light that made him feel that way. Yet his presence felt different; more substantial than the Shadow Alpha intimidating Cooper back in early January, and certainly more than Liam Manning could ever hope to do.

Cooper sensed the man was aware of him watching, even though he never took his eyes off the pavement. Approaching Market Street, the man suddenly disappeared in a crowd waiting to cross, no easy feat for someone at *least* six-five, and even more so that the group was so small. It shouldn't have been possible and it made Cooper shudder. While he hunted for the man he'd just lost sight of, Alyssa and Billy emerged from another group crossing northbound.

The warm, evening sun lit Alyssa's hair, those golden swirls frolicking like dandelion seeds on a fresh spring wind. Cooper's worries were immediately swept away.

Billy looked far less elegant. He was chewing loudly as always, hand buried in the crackling plastic of a fifty-count bag of Haribo gummy bears.

So much for those being an after-dinner snack, Cooper thought, but he didn't really mind. These two people were his friends, best friends if the term was ever so fitting. He couldn't have been happier.

However, the conversations that were about to happen inside Castillo's would bring a damper to that feeling in record time.

2

The inside of Castillo's was charming, and thankfully not too crowded (lunch time and the weekends being packed). The color of the walls evoked Parmigiano-Reggiano and Bolognese, while the smells wafting out of the kitchen brought piping hot plates of veal parmigiana, bowls of spaghetti with giant meatballs, and, of course, hand-tossed pizza to mind.

Seated in one of the cushy booths lining the spotless windows – square tables with four chairs filling the center of the restaurant – the trio placed their orders with Adriana Castillo, wife of the owner Piero Castillo. Long black hair wrapped around her motherly face, her brown eyes beaming through a pair of black-framed glasses. Cooper was reminded of his old pair; the only thing missing was the tape that held it all together.

"What would you three like today?" she asked in a heartwarming voice, her accent adding layers like a hearty lasagna. "Same as usual?"

They all smiled, memorizing their orders. Each could recite the whole thing without looking at the menu once: two waters, one Pepsi with extra ice, mozzarella sticks and jalapeño poppers for appetizers, cannoli for dessert, and one large Sicilian deluxe pie in between.

"Only *one* today? "Adriana asked.

Billy and Cooper blushed; often ordering two.

"Just the one," Cooper replied tepidly, holding up a single finger. His hair flopped down to block his face.

Adriana smiled then brought them their drinks saying, "*Gli antipasti* will be ready shortly." Then she glided over to the next table to tend to their needs.

Alyssa suddenly scoffed at Billy, resuming an earlier conversation.

"They're both *good* technical colleges."

"What's this about?" Cooper asked.

"It's in reference to Georgia Tech and Logan University, my top two choices."

"Mhmm, if you say so," Billy replied, rather unconvinced – his deadpan expression unblinking.

"Um, I *do* say so," Alyssa said, her eyes proudly adding *thank you very much.*

"Well, nothing against LU, but isn't that in South Carolina?" Billy seemed convinced that the location was a deal-breaker.

"Yeah, it's about… four, five, six hours from here," Alyssa answered, counting on her fingers. "Honestly, I'd love to try the beach life for a little while. Anything but these *endless* mountains."

"You do know that pines are abundant out that way too," Billy prodded.

"I said mountains… trees are trees, *William,*" she replied, breaking out the W-word again to get Billy back in check. "But, the ocean is right there. Imagine: dipping your toes in, letting the sand and water rise to swallow them. It's one of the best feelings in the world."

"*You're* one of the best feelings in *my* world," Cooper interjected, causing Alyssa to inhale the tiniest puff of breath. "Besides, if we're talking beaches I like the Gulf Coast better myself. Especially with all that pure white sand around…"

"But you've never been there," Billy replied presently. His fingers had started to strum on the tabletop like a giant keyboard. *Where's the food?* they typed.

"Hey, I've seen enough pictures to *know* it makes me want to visit,"

Cooper replied. He dipped his head when he remembered agreeing to work some with the Arnett's after graduation. "Eventually... that is."

"In that case, why don't we all plan to go there?" Alyssa suggested, trying to perk them back up.

Billy's eyes dropped to the tabletop like Cooper's.

"I wish that I could..." Billy replied somberly. Unlike Cooper, he didn't have a choice in planning to stay local. It was more like he *had to,* helping his dad with the family business while taking classes at Goodman State University.

As much as Billy'd like to get away, he'd probably be prepped for burial in one of the town's four funeral homes, *A Good Ol' Goodman Boy* engraved on a meager headstone.

"It was just a thought," Alyssa snipped before casting it away with a shrug.

Adriana emerged from the kitchen with the appetizers in hand, Billy snatching a jalapeño popper before the plate was even on the table, then a massive mozzarella stick after Adriana left.

Alyssa wasn't looking at the food but across the table at Cooper.

"So, what about you then?" she asked, knowing his commitment to the Arnetts wouldn't last forever. Her elbows were on the table's edge, arms up, fingers interlaced in waiting.

Cooper remained quiet. He had no idea what to do that far down the road. The werewolf bite was front and center in his thoughts (*what fresh hell is going to rise out of that pit of Alphas, and Betas, and Subs? Oh my.*) Alyssa's planned departure also weighed heavily on his mind.

She noticed his face becoming a pained grimace whenever he flipped between the two thoughts.

"Baby, we won't be ending anytime soon," she said comfortingly, "and no matter where I end up, it won't be far away."

"It'll be far enough..." Cooper said, clearing his throat. There were tears in that coarse sound; she'd never called him "baby" until now.

"I'll just have to drag you along with me then," she said.

A cold chill washed down Billy's back and he dropped the monster mozzarella stick on the tabletop with an abrupt *splat*.

"S-sorry..." he muttered. "Big stick with a lotta grease."

Alyssa chuckled, a cupped hand over her mouth muffling the sound. Everything fell back into a clumsy silence moments later.

Cooper watched as his friends struggled to continue talking about the future. In that passing moment, the two didn't look eighteen anymore; they were their respective ages when he'd first met them so many years ago. Their childhood was on the brink of closure, like a good book whose last chapter drew near. Part of Cooper wanted to slow down, even stop reading altogether, fighting against the part craving to know what happens to them all in the end.

He exhaled a shallow breath, then asked the first question that popped across his mind.

"So did you all notice Liam left early from school today?"

Alyssa and Billy both looked puzzled, and Cooper kicked himself as soon as the words left his mouth. How and why was *Liam Manning* of all things the first topic to come to mind, when that bullying prick should have been the absolute last.

CHAPTER 19: JOURNEYMEN

Friday March 8, 2013

1

It was getting late, the sun sinking fast, the evening sky changing from orange to purple to ultramarine.

Dax Wallace walked up to the doors of Wilson's Sports Bar and Grill. It was busy inside, loud and general bar chatter – along with Kenny Chesney's vocals – making their way outside.

He peered through the dirty glass, checking for anything unusual. Being a large man, Dax looked like he could hold his own in a fight, but the big-ass sledgehammer held tight in his right hand helped where all those muscles alone could not.

Seeing nothing of immediate concern, Dax pushed his way into the vestibule, a pair of naked yellow bulbs creating harsh shadows on his outfit. Tight Wranglers kept his stride short while heavy work boots thumped in sync with the hammer's head on the wood floor and the music playing on the jukebox. A black tank top coddled his skin beneath the faded denim of a ripped-sleeve vest.

On entering the main room, Dax was struck with the smell of stout buffalo wing sauce and even stouter beer. He started coughing and a few men near the bar looked up, derogatory comments at the ready.

That hammer was obviously compensating for the size of his roided-out dick, their lips were ready to say.

They stopped as soon as Dax's own expression warned that he'd shove that dick so far down their throats they'd choke if they didn't piss off. Size matters after all.

Behind the jerks, leaning against the other side of the bar, a huge man loomed. He was in black jeans – torn – and a clingy gray shirt – also torn in random places, especially along his wide shoulders. His hair was an unruly mess, his beard equally shaggy.

Dax gripped the handle of his sledgehammer as he looked the mammoth man over.

Now there's something you don't see every day.

Glancing up from a tall, sweating glass of Budweiser, the big man saw Dax approaching. His lips curled, green eyes flickering with fire.

"What're you looking at, short stuff?" he said as Dax stepped up beside him. His five-foot-six frame looked like a child next to the other man's reversed stats.

"Some big son of a bitch that's about to have a dozen pounds of silver up his ass."

"Sure you can reach?"

"Wanna try me?"

The large man's eyes narrowed into slits.

Dax's too.

They stared each other down until... both burst into friendly rounds of laughter.

"It's really nice to see you again," Dax said, extending a hand. "Ozzy, wasn't it?"

The big bear shifter ignored Dax's hand, going right in for a namesake hug. Dax wrestled himself free – it wasn't easy by any means – and Ásbjörn hesitated for the briefest moment before laughing again.

"You know how much I despise that name," he said. "At least call me Osborne if you're going to fuck up my heritage."

Dax only grinned, wide like a Cheshire cat. Little did he know Ásbjörn didn't mind punching little kittens in the face.

"Pull up a chair, munchkin," Ásbjörn said, yanking out one of the bar stools. It scraped along the floor, leaving scuff marks. "We've got a little catching up to do."

Dax propped his sledgehammer against the bar and sat. The stool wobbled under his weight, threatening to collapse, but in the end stayed balanced.

"Hey Wilson," Ásbjörn called down the bar. "Whatever my tiny buddy here wants, add it to my tab."

"What'll it be?" the owner asked, hunting for something below the bar. His tattooed shoulders looked like painted boulders in the low light. Chesney had stepped off the jukebox stage, replaced by Aldean singing about taking a little ride in a Chevy. Wilson found what he was looking for and pitched a clean napkin on the bar.

"Something stronger than this pussy's drinking," Dax said jokingly, pointing one of his stubby fingers toward the big shifter. "Owner's choice."

Wilson grinned while Ásbjörn knocked Dax with his elbow. Grabbing a tumbler, Wilson set it on the napkin then filled it with Johnnie Walker Black, neat. He brought it over to Dax.

Dax lifted it, sniffed it, sipped it, and was happy.

"Perfect," he whispered, and Wilson nodded his bald head before heading to the far end of the bar. "So what's the situation here, Ozzy?"

"Skirmishes on the fringes – lots of dead humans. Since late September there's also been four murders within the town limits."

"If this were a regular town, I'd think that was alarming, but considering werewolves are involved…" Dax gave his sledgehammer a quick and proud glance "…those numbers actually sound pretty tame. Field operatives have seen much worse than that – not counting 2010."

Ásbjörn took a long gulp of his beer, setting the glass down hard. A little over half of it was gone, the beads of condensation flowing down the sides like tears.

"Haven't we all," he said, using two fingers to wipe away some excess that his beard had caught. "But… it must be bad if the Order's called you in, and brought me out of retirement."

Retirement?

Dax thought he misheard and was about to ask Ásbjörn for clarification, but he'd already picked up his glass and downed the other half of his beer.

"Wilson!" he shouted. "One more when you get the chance."

"Is that gonna be your last one?" Wilson asked. "You're drinking me dry."

Ásbjörn nodded toward the clock, telling him: "Have you seen the time? Answer to that's a resounding 'fuck no'. Besides, why the bitching if I'm still paying your ass?"

"Paying me with a hefty discount…"

"Aw, would you feel better if you blew me?"

"Ladies first…" Wilson answered, pointing below his belt.

Dax sipped his scotch during the continuing exchange, only widening his eyes once at something Wilson said back to the big bear.

"See the kind of shit I get?" Ásbjörn grunted, knuckles knocking on the bar like an impatient kid waiting on his overdue chicken tenders.

"I see that it's deserved," Dax replied lightheartedly.

He'd been brought in from the field due to his experience in handling werewolves, and Goodman was running amok with them. Having been on his way to Ireland for an assignment with a quirky operative named Brandon Byrne, Dax was redirected at the last minute and told to rendezvous with Ásbjörn. The two had met briefly during an Order briefing in 2011, he couldn't remember the location other than it was some Podunk town in the Midwest. Utterly forgetful like he hoped Goodman would be once it was cleaned up and he was back on the road to the coast before heading across the Atlantic Ocean.

Since they'd be working directly with each other, the two relatively private individuals decided to take the opportunity to get to know each other, falling into some reflective conversations.

"Before the Incursion in 2010," Dax said, eyes whirling in his scotch, "I was wading through werewolf shit on the daily. That dated all the way back to ninety-nine."

"That's a lot of shit," Ásbjörn said, sipping out of his new glass of beer. "Imagine if it were bear shifters you were after."

"Haha," Dax laughed. "If they're anything like you then yes: thank God it was just werewolves. But yeah, it was like I was cursed. No matter where I turned after my wife died, I would find them."

"How'd you get by?"

"Used silver bullets for a time, but those would always run out fast, and getting them on the road isn't cheap by any means. So, as any desperate man would do, I tried my bare hands for a while..."

"Those'll be my favorite," Ásbjörn added. His were massive compared to Dax's, easily twice the size.

"Well, with hands like *that*, Ozzy, I'm sure they'd be my favorite too," Hammer chuckled, finishing off his drink. "One's that size are probably good for just about anything."

"When those things fit, brother," Ásbjörn added, slamming his glass down on the table. The rest of his beer was already gone.

"Never had any complaints," Dax said, "and no, that was not an offer. Though I will buy the next round."

Ásbjörn didn't argue.

Dax got up and went to the far end of the bar where Wilson was. He delivered their empty glasses.

"You getting this next one?" Wilson asked.

Dax glanced over his wide shoulder toward Ásbjörn. Due to the shifter's sheer size, the bar looked like a miniature table and that he was ready for a tea party.

"Yeah, and you might as well open a tab for me, too. There's going to be some long nights ahead, so we best kick it off right."

"What kind of work is it that you two do?" Wilson asked.

"Let's just say we work nights, handling things that others can't, or won't."

Wilson didn't ask anything more, unsure that he wanted to know exactly what that meant.

Dax returned with two huge and overflowing steins.

"Why that thing?" Ásbjörn asked, pointing to the sledgehammer propped up on the bar's edge. Its wooden handle peeked up and over the side. Along it were hatch marks. Ásbjörn guessed it was a kill count.

"Because my fists were getting tired and I can swing that and swing it well," Dax said with an arm flex. "I've even thrown it a time or two. That silver head does a lot of damage against werewolves; even a modest blow can cripple. I'm thinking about replacing the wooden handle with an iron one, though."

"Why would you do that, Hammer?"

"'Hammer'..." Dax chuckled as he considered Ásbjörn's latest nickname for him. "I actually like the sound of that one. Now, you've heard about the Noctis, right?"

"That demon army that's been on the move? Yeah, isn't *that* the stuff nightmares are made of?"

"Bingo. Since they're demons and iron is effective against them, I figured I might as well give it a try. It'd be a double whammy, without the need for a single reload."

Ásbjörn grunted in agreement.

"Yeah, that makes sense to me. Iron works against ghosts too, at least that's what I hear from you Order guys. I admit that I don't know much about those kinds of things. Brute force is my game. Always has been since day one."

Dax raised his glass and said: "I can relate to that."

After a few moments of silence, the two looking around the bar for anything suspicious, Dax coughed – another whiff of wing sauce invading his nose.

"Ozzy," he said, "so what's your deal? I mean you're *massive* and I know you're some kind of beast shifter, but there's something about you I can't put my finger on."

"Probably that I'm a hybrid," he replied without a second thought. Dax nearly choked on his beer.

"I'd never in a million years would I have guessed that part. I didn't even know that was possible…"

"Lots of things are possible," Ásbjörn said, "but that doesn't mean *good* things will come from it."

There was a weight in Ásbjörn eyes, a sadness that pulled them down into the beer bubbles to drown.

"Like… what?" Dax asked slowly.

"Like mommy werewolves mating with daddy bear shifters for one. But, here I am! A product of that unholy union… and here my brother is not."

Dax now knew what he meant, Ásbjörn looking at an empty bar stool nearby.

"So, he…"

"Yes, he died when he was born. He had already shifted in the womb, and that was way too early in his development. Hammer, it was a mess: no eyes, melted face and limbs, and... God... those cries out of that deformed mouth. They were the kind that reached into your head and clawed themselves into your memories. Thank goodness they only lasted a few minutes, otherwise I don't know if I..."

"I'm so sorry," Dax said somberly.

"Don't be," Ásbjörn said. "Some of us are born to take more shit than others and destined to be alone."

"True, but at least you have a pack to lead as Alpha."

Ásbjörn shook his head.

"But your dossier says..."

"Paperwork's wrong. I'm alone there, too, Hammer. Lots of factors went into that but the top two are one: werewolves and two: black fur. Those bastards came during the night this past October – out near the Chattooga River. Killed everyone in the den but me and vandalized the throne. Every single one, Hammer, including the cubs. Shifters tend to mate for life, you see, so she was my entire existence. There was a time I wanted to crawl into a hole and simply end... but no kingdom, no subject, and no mate leaves a man filled with all the rage in the world. I won't stop until the one that did this is gone himself. It all went down a little while after Grayson – the White

Wolf Alpha we are seeing tomorrow – sent word to me that the shadow

pack had returned. I guess the Shadow Alpha didn't want to risk my

interference like what happened back in 1994. He's going to get it anyway."

"My God..." Dax whispered thinly. "How many wolves would it have

taken to..."

"A lot of them," Ásbjörn cut in. "Far more than should be out there in

this part of the world for sure."

"So, this is the same pack that didn't comply with the Accords?"

Ásbjörn nodded, his words having to build back up.

"Who is their Alpha, by the way?"

"Goes by the name Goddard. Son of a bitch can suck a horse cock

dipped in horse shit while it's pissing."

Dax recoiled in shock, nearly falling out of his seat. Righting himself,

he began to stroke his scruffy chin. His eyes were huge and hurt. His brow

was wrinkled and skin so pallid that he looked at least decade older.

"L-lance Goddard?" he stammered, an angry redness returning to his

cheeks.

"Yes," Ásbjörn said. "Why? What's the matter? You look like you've

seen a ghost."

"Not so much a ghost," Dax said, "but Lance Goddard was the name of

the Alpha that took my wife away and set me on this shitty, werewolf-filled path."

CHAPTER 20: HAS IT BEEN FOR NOTHING?

Saturday March 9, 2013

1

The large home sat tranquilly on its neatly manicured lawn in the center of Grayson Loop, the pretentiousness of it all echoing through Ásbjörn's mind as he waited rather impatiently with Dax Wallace for the front door to open.

Hi, my name is Grayson Manning and I live at Grayson Estate which is located at Grayson Loop...

Ásbjörn rolled his eyes so far back they became white slits.

Jesus Christ, Snowy, what the hell's happening to us shifters?

"We should have gone for pancakes, Hammer," the bear muttered, trying to take his mind off things.

"We *could* have," Dax said, "but *someone* decided they needed the extra beauty sleep. A real shame it didn't work."

Ásbjörn grumbled. It sounded a lot like "fuck off."

"Pancakes would have been amazing though, but we would have missed this meeting if we hadn't hauled ass when we did. One thing I've learned about the civil shifters is they value their time, and being late would have started the day off on the wrong foot with Mr. Manning."

"Yet here we are," Ásbjörn replied, "kept waiting on *Mr. Manning's* schedule."

"Actually Ozzy, we're a little early. It's not quite time for..."

The fussy sounds of way-too-many locks unlatching cut through the conversation. The ornate doors pulled back from them, revealing Fridolf standing there in the center. He was dressed in another custom-made black suit with patterned lapels.

Grayson had warned the young wolf about their guests, but upon actually *seeing* them his eyes had trouble taking in the true scale of what was there.

Two equally enormous men at two vastly different heights were waiting to enter. Was Grayson absolutely sure that both weren't bear shifters? They looked it, the shorter one far friendlier in appearance except for that massive sledgehammer.

Fridolf leaned a little closer in order to get a better look, taking a couple of hurried steps back when he noticed that it was made of silver.

He couldn't even look at the taller one for very long – he just looked hungry, which was the only thing Fridolf could deduce in the few seconds without having to turn away.

While Ásbjörn continued staring hungrily at Fridolf, Dax noticed that the pattern on his lapels were small words that had been imprinted on the fabric. He was trying to make them out when Ásbjörn suddenly let out a sound akin to a half laugh-half growl.

"What's wrong with your hair?" he asked Fridolf, noticing the excessive amounts of sheen in the slicked back hairstyle. Ásbjörn reached out to touch it, then decided against it, shielding his beard instead. "Are greasy wolf glands contagious? Something even the Change can't cure?"

"I beg your pardon?" Fridolf snapped, pointing to his suit while breathing erratically. (Grayson had been helping him with different means of channeling recent, rage-filled outbursts.)

Ásbjörn squinted to get a better view, the pattern spelling out the words PISS OFF and FUCK YOU in series.

"Well ain't that the shit?" Ásbjörn said with a smile. "I want a suit like this when we're done, Hammer."

Dax tried to remain serious, asking if they could come in. Fridolf stepped to the side to let them. Entering the foyer, Ásbjörn walked up and rested on the central table while Dax used his hammer like a walking stick.

"Can I, um, *hang* that up for you?" Fridolf asked, afraid to get too close to the thing.

"Well, if you don't mind, I'd rather keep hold of it," Dax replied.

Fridolf nodded politely, having just noticed the tally marks on the handle. Once again, he backed away slowly, eyes unblinking.

"Gentlemen," came a robust voice from down the hall. It was Grayson, who'd arrived right on time just as the clock struck eight. "If you'd like to follow me, we can get this meeting underway."

He led them down the short hallway, the others following close behind. Upon entering his office, the smell of wood panels and citrus oil didn't bother anyone but Ásbjörn. His nose was running into his beard, and his eyes started to feel puffy.

"Are you alright Ásbjörn?" Grayson asked, handing him a small square of thin tissue paper. There wasn't even enough to *start* dabbing the mess.

"What am I supposed to do with *this?*" Ásbjörn asked, snatching it out of Grayson's hand.

"Clean yourself up *and...*" Grayson was quick to cut off the bear shifter before he started ranting, "you can take up the recent budgetary considerations with Fridolf."

Dax and Ásbjörn took seats on a sofa in front of the large fireplace on the left. Grayson remained standing while Fridolf sat in an armchair facing him.

Dax looked at the paintings hanging on the walls, Fridolf and Ásbjörn exchanging indistinct words back and forth. In spite of its size, the large landscape painting above the fireplace caught his attention more than any of the others. A small brass plate on the bottom of the rugged frame read COLONGNE, GERMANY, depicting the foreign landscape in subdued shades of blue and green. Coupled with the sight of forests filled with blackened, dead trees, the mood was cold and unsettling to say the least. As Dax looked, he felt pulled toward the oil on canvas.

Wait, what's that?

His gaze was drawn to the shapes within some of the branches. There were two in particular – one of the left side of the painting and one on the right – that seemed to form intricate symbols where their branches overlapped. They almost looked like sigils of some kind, reminiscent of the

Solomon seals he'd learned about when he first joined the Order ranks.

But why are they here?

The left one he couldn't make out – the details were too intricate – but the right one resembled the twelfth seal (the Fifth Pentacle of Mars) which, in short terms, protected against negative energies by transmuting them into positive ones. It was often used by the Journeymen as a boosting seal to amplify others paired with it, meaning Dax needed to figure out what the *other* symbol was.

Dammit, that's the one I'm having trouble with.

He got ready to tell the others what he'd noticed, pretty sure that the shifters had no idea about magical seals or what they did, especially in some of the artwork around the place. However, Grayson was about to begin speaking on the more urgent matter at hand.

Dax looked at the painting one more time, desperately trying to decipher that left symbol.

Dammit, nothing.

He stowed his thoughts for now.

"As you all know," Grayson began, leaning against the side of the stone mantel. He was nervous, fidgeting with his shirt sleeves and buttons as he talked. "Lance Goddard has returned to Goodman and is poised to launch an attack against the town. He tried this once in 1994, thwarted by the combined forces of the White Wolves and the Blue Ridge Bears."

"You make it sound like some kind of football team," Ásbjörn said with a tinge of antipathy – having no interest in human sports nor the fact Liam played them. Nonetheless, he bowed his head. "It was an honor for my crew to aid you against that dark tide, Ursa rest their souls."

"What is he after?" Dax asked. "I mean, attacking the town for food or people to turn is one thing, but he could have done that with any of the other communities in the surrounding area."

"It's the Order's Vault," Grayson said, shaking his head in that way which asked: *how has it come to this?* "He claims there is something inside of it, and that thing is rightfully *his.* Apparently the Order has been keeping it from him. Mr. Wallace, if you could let me know what exactly the Order has in there?"

Grayson knew that the bear was clueless, but Dax had very limited knowledge himself.

"There are so many things they have shoved in there. It could literally be anything," Dax said, Grayson visibly upset. "Another grimoire like the one that started the Incursion, an amulet, a ..."

"A big-ass weapon?" Ásbjörn added, and Dax nodded.

"But why now Mr. Manning..." Dax asked.

"Please, call me Grayson. We are all friends here."

"Will do, if you call me Dax…"

"Hammer is better," Ásbjörn mumbled.

"Fine, *Ozzy*," Dax replied in jest. "But in all seriousness, why now, or even back in, what, ninety-four you said? The Vault's been here since 1967. It would have been easier to take what he needed back then. I assume he is older than that."

"We both are," Grayson said, his eyes flicking briefly to the large painting above the fireplace. He started to pace.

"Maybe something new was moved in that caught his attention back in 1994?" Ásbjörn proposed. "I know that it doesn't happen too often these days, but it's a possibility, right?"

Grayson appeared distracted, but his head was bobbing.

"So, we could be sitting atop another Incursion?" he asked. "Blissfully unaware that such power and destruction lies right under our feet?"

"Yes, but maybe that's how things *should* be," Dax suggested, playing with the handle of his sledgehammer. It had been resting on the side of the sumptuous couch. "Otherwise there would be panic in the streets, far more than the layperson would be able to handle."

"Agreed." Grayson said. "But Mr. Wallace… I mean Hammer, should such things be kept from the very people who are supposed to protect the world against them?"

Dax opened his mouth, about to say, "Yes, of course!" Yet, as he thought about what Grayson was saying, he wasn't so sure.

"See, that is exactly my point," Grayson murmured, letting out a sigh which changed into a frustrated cry. "Sadly, it's not a black and white issue. I am sure the Incursion was the product of a similar level of arrogance on the Order's part. My gosh, how did I not question this before?"

"We were swayed by the promises and potential of the Accords," Ásbjörn said. "They sounded good."

"By no means am I agreeing with Lance and his methods but we may have been swayed so much so that we rushed into this decision," Grayson responded. "To your prior question, I'm starting to think the Accords were part of something bigger... especially if something new did go into that Vault eighteen, no, nineteen years ago now. Back in January last year, I encountered a man who told me to keep them at arm's length. When he told me that, I thought he might have been exaggerating. Now, I think he may have been on to something."

"Do you remember his name?" Dax inquired, curious as to the Journeyman who would have said it. He was starting to feel the same way.

Grayson hesitated, then replied, "No, unfortunately he never gave me a name, just the preliminary notice that Lance had returned."

They both looked over to Ásbjörn – all of them having been hurt in some way by the Shadow Alpha – and the room became quiet. Only the wood in the fireplace made any noise, crackling and spitting, completely unaware of the heavy weight bearing down on those in the room with it.

Dax reflected: *The numbers we lost during the Incursion were tremendous, but it seems the foundation of the Order itself has fractured.*

If that was true, even remotely, it was not a good thing in light of the growing demon army.

"I have to be completely honest gentlemen," Grayson continued, "I'm concerned and frightened that I've been helping guard something beneath Goodman – the key *here* in my very own house – without knowing if what's inside *deserves* to be guarded. Has it all been for nothing?"

Glancing at the painting, there was another flash of memory in Grayson's mind: green eyes that pierced his soul, then a growl which rose up from deep within the Earth.

A loud *thud* jolted Grayson back to reality; Ásbjörn's palm had smacked the tabletop.

"Can I go just back to drinking and fucking now?" he asked, getting up from the couch. He swaggered over to the bar without a single issue in taking the top shelf whiskey and guzzling it right out of the bottle. "Life was much simpler before you werewolves and Journeymen came gallivanting through bear country."

"Simpler and less sophisticated," Dax said jokingly, "but don't forget you're *half* werewolf, too."

Grayson grinned. Fridolf looked mortified.

"The *lesser* half, true. No offense intended to you, Snowy, but maybe a little for you, Slick."

Fridolf huffed and crossed his arms, middle fingers casually raised like pistols in his hands.

"None taken," Grayson replied, grabbing an empty glass from his desk. There was a thin layer of evaporated alcohol residue across the base, its appearance like crystallized honey.

The night before happened to be a rough one. Liam sparked yet another argument after a long period of good behavior.

Grayson waved the glass toward the beastly man to fill. Ásbjörn walked over and started to.

"You're one to talk," he said to Dax, "A brute that smashes things with an oversized hammer. Please don't proceed to lecture me on sophistication, tool-man."

"I wasn't lecturing anyone but you know, one more notch would make forty, Ozzy," Dax replied. "Just give me a reason, or better yet a goddamn drink, either one of you. You're both making me thirsty."

The three broke out in mild laughter, Fridolf joining them a moment later.

Unbeknownst to the group, Liam had been standing outside listening in. He looked longingly toward the large painting which hung above the fireplace.

"Gotcha," he whispered, the distant firelight catching in his eyes.

2

Friday March 15, 2013

Liam trudged east through the woods of the Preserve, using his memory to recall the long walk he was forced to take just over two weeks earlier. There were faint, familiar smells and sounds to guide him, useful since it was already getting dark when he left.

He would have departed the estate much sooner, but his father had called another meeting – this one unexpected – with the human werewolf killer and that repugnant hybrid shifter. Liam disliked him more than the human; the mere thought of mixing different species of shifter blood was vile (*might as well be fucking animals*, he thought, and it made him sick to his stomach). The group seemed on edge as they talked, like something was about to happen, before finally leaving hours later for a quick dinner. That was around half past six, and once they were gone Liam entered his father's office to retrieve his prize.

As he pushed his way through jutting branches and vines teeming with sharp thorns, Liam recalled himself approaching the large painting above the fireplace. Behind it in a hidden alcove was a small safe, the combination a very simple six-digit code.

0-5-0-1-9-4

Liam guessed it on his third try, the order being the day, month, and year of his birth in European order, opposed to the American way he was used to.

Unsurprisingly, his father still held out hope that his son would one day make him proud. This day would not rank highly on that scale. As Liam opened the safe and peered inside, he saw many things that didn't belong to him. There was a large folder with an elegant label – LAST WILL & TESTAMENT FOR GRAYSON MANNING, PREPARED BY MACK & MONTGOMERY – situated at the very front. If he had rummaged through that stack of papers, he would have been stunned by how little his father had allocated for him (Grayson realizing the difference between holding out hope and being blinded by it).

Paperwork was the last thing on Liam's mind that evening; the one item that he desired most being the key to the Order Vault. The ordinary looking thing just so happened to be standing upright, waiting patiently for him in the corner of the lock box. Using a couple of dirty hand towels that he'd collected from the laundry room, Liam wrapped it up to avoid caustic burns as it transformed into a silver cylinder six-inches in length, decorated with a raised pattern across its entire outer surface. He shoved it into the front pocket of his pants.

Suddenly he felt something wet, not caused by the considerable bulge the key caused in his jeans. He looked down, seeing his foot sloshing around in the waters of the Chattooga. A half-eaten fish listed on the trivial waves, its eyeless head pointing northward. The smell of its rotting flesh urged Liam in that direction.

It would have been the perfect night as Liam continued through the woods – a comfy sixty-eight degrees moderated by a crisp breeze, gaps in the clouds letting a smattering of starlight shine down, and no rain to put a damper on the whole thing – had he not felt eyes on him each step of the way, watching with ill intent from the darkness beyond.

If this had been any other night (in the unlikely event he'd be walking in the mountains by himself), Liam would have been anxious, possibly even afraid. However, on *this* night the precious item he carried in his jeans pocket bestowed something vitalizing – a feeling that filled him with the same gratification kid's faces would when they oozed snot and tears just before his fist came in to clean up the mess. It was power. He had it and those in the darkness did not – for now.

With conviction Liam continued. After half an hour, he could tell a clearing was approaching; the trees along the bank started to thin, the river itself babbling louder. Rounding a sharp bend, Liam paused. There were figures upstream, lingering between the trunks beyond. Their yellowed eyes glared like fireflies against the gloom.

Undeterred, Liam marched right up to them. The sentries remained unmoving.

"I'm here to see Lance," Liam said cockily to the closest one. His breathing was labored, holding back some anger.

Without warning the guard's arm lashed out, hand striking Liam in the chest. He stumbled; it nearly knocked him to his ass.

"*Who* are you here to see?" the sentry asked gruffly.

"I'm here to see your Alpha, you idiot," Liam scoffed.

There was no reply. Liam's blue eyes engaged with the yellow in a fight for dominance.

"Don't you know who I am?"

There was still no reply. The sentries either didn't know or didn't care. Chances were greater for the second.

"Goddamn subs," Liam scowled, attempting to force his way through. Another strike led to another tumble. This time Liam was on his ass, filth covering his back pockets.

"That's enough!" Lance's voice decreed. "Allow him through,"

The men parted and Liam stepped through the gap. He gave each of them each a brutal stare, murderous in its severity.

Lance was perched on top of the tree-throne, this time dressed in a full suit except for his feet, still bare. His thick toes wriggled on the ground like impatient worms.

"I was beginning to think you had forgotten about our little bargain," Lance said, looking down from the high seat.

"It's only been a couple of weeks," Liam said indifferently.

"I'm used to my requests seeing faster action, Mr. Manning."

"Well, did you want this key or not?" Liam asked reproachfully, producing the towel-wrapped package from his pocket. He flipped it like a baton three times in a row.

Lance didn't reply right away, unimpressed with Liam's antics. Eventually he stopped, and there was a revealing tremble in his grip as he tried to hold the key steady.

"Give it to me," Lance demanded, holding out an expectant hand. "Now."

"I..." Liam hesitated. "I want to see Cooper first."

Lance chuckled. It sounded weary and ominous at the same time.

"You're not in a position to be making demands of me, child."

Liam glanced around; the sentries had encircled them, the ring drawing tighter with each passing moment. His heart was beating much faster than he showed, though his sweltering forehead might give away his apprehension.

"We had a deal!" he howled. "Tell them to stop or I'll smash it."

Lance raised a hand. His guards halted their advance.

"See how fast that action was? Now, I know that you wouldn't break that key, Liam…"

"Try me," he snarled, holding his arm and the key aloft.

"That trinket is the only thing keeping you away from sudden death. I think even you realize that, despite the grand levels of stupidity you're choosing to show."

Liam looked around. Yellow eyes were everywhere. What was he thinking?

"As for our bargain, I seem to recall that it required that *you* give *me* that thing in your hand before I even consider delivering your reward."

Liam shuddered, then lowered his arm. Stepping up the small incline to the base of the throne, he held out the key.

"Thank you, Liam," said Lance, a wicked gleam his eyes as he grabbed hold of it. Removing the towels, he checked the item for authenticity. It was genuine. "Thank you indeed. Now! Let us discuss your reward."

Liam raised his head, ready to discuss delivery of that prick Cooper as

soon as –

From out of nowhere a cloud of maroon dust floated across Liam's face.

It had been tossed by one of the guards. Shimmering as he breathed in swirls

of the stuff, it smelled something like cherries soaked in strong liquor. Then

it began to burn mercilessly, causing Liam to hack and wheeze. The back

of this throat was aflame.

One of the guards closest to Liam seized his forearm while he was

distracted. He was wearing a bandana across his nose and mouth.

"What are you doing?" Liam roared, struggling to pull away. They both

fell to the ground fighting, Liam's punches hard and swift. The shadow

guard then shifted into his wolf form, latching onto Liam's arm before

giving it a tremendous tug.

Screaming in pain, Liam tried to change. He couldn't.

"What was that? What have you done to me?"

Lance didn't answer, he only watched as another guard swooped in,

clothes flying away in tatters, canine jaws clamping down on one of Liam's

bucking legs.

"Stop!"

Liam's eyes welled up as he was bitten in his free arm by a third wolf.

354

Then he bit his lip as a fourth descended on him, the last set of slobbering jaws now locked in to the bone.

"Let this be a lesson to you, young one. I am rewarding you as a betrayer should be rewarded," Lance said.

The four wolves backed away from each other, pulling on Liam – still centered – as hard as they could. His limbs were splayed and he hovered mere inches off the ground. The pain was intolerable. He thought he was being quartered.

"C-Cooper's n-not h-here, is h-he?" Liam struggled to speak. He was on the verge of blacking out.

Lance chuckled with an infernal laugh that soon became a howl.

"Did you really think I could trust having you *and* Cooper Bennett together? Especially since you just betrayed your own pack *and* blood to get me what I wanted?"

The quartet of wolves began to move slowly across the clearing, towards the deepening woods. They were carrying Liam with them, still outstretched in their jaws.

"You asked me to!" Liam screeched, using the last of his strength. He could see the stars above, and treetops as more started to come into view. "You asked me!"

"Yes, I did ask you Mr. Manning, but you managed to do *all* the rest.

And so it begins…"

Liam could hear Lance howling over his panicked breaths, feel his own warm tears and piss running in thin streams off his body. The Shadow Alpha's cry was joined by many more, unseen sources just like that fateful night in early January nineteen years ago. The air was filled with a storm of caterwauls, and somehow only then did Liam realize he'd made a terribly stupid mistake.

He should have done so much earlier, because this time there would be no way to charm nor buy his way out of the stinking pile of shit he'd fallen into.

CHAPTER 21: SHADOWS FALL

Saturday March 16, 2013

1

The twenty-eighth annual St. Paddy's Day Festival ("Wishing you a pot of gold and all the joy your heart can hold!") was supposed to be a memorable occasion like it had been every year since 1985. The current festival would, in the end, serve up memories galore, but they wouldn't be joyful. Instead, they would be corrupted by pain and death, Goodman about to learn that childhood nightmares were indeed very real.

Since the big day fell on a Sunday in 2013, and respectable citizens would never drink on the same day as they went to church, the celebration was set for the day before, which held no such restrictions on getting (respectably) wasted.

The town wasn't Irish in the slightest – unless you counted Police Chief John O'Carroll and his working-class Dublin dialect – yet the downtown area had been transformed into a tacky, commercialized version of the island. Green was everywhere, as if the surrounding forests had sprouted plastic seedlings in the urban center, bearing glossy fruit in the shape of leprechauns, rainbows, and shamrocks. Had there been a fountain outside the town hall, it would resemble a stagnant pond spurting its moldy water in uneven arcs back into the reservoir.

At least that's what Cooper imagined the fountain to look like as he gazed across Market Street to one of the four large clocks mounted on the exterior of town hall.

Nine o'clock.

"Where was Billy again?" Alyssa asked as they walked. Her arm was locked with Cooper's, tugging ever so slightly while another couple came toward them. They were sharing a bottle of liquor, passing the half empty bottle of Wild Turkey between themselves.

"I guess it is five o'clock somewhere," Cooper whispered, leaning his head closer to her.

"Yeah," she muttered, "like Moscow."

They giggled softly as the couple passed, continuing to sway and shake their way down the street. The man stumbled off the sidewalk, nearly taking his lady friend with him.

"I don't think they're going to get very far," Cooper said, Alyssa nodding with her gaze still across her shoulder. "As for Billy, he's supposed to be meeting us at Panda Studios, but I think he may be sneaking a bite to eat somewhere along here. We should find him after a stop at Nicholson's."

Alyssa turned her attention back to Cooper's face. There was something different about him this morning – something greater. His smooth skin and jet-black hair seemed almost ethereal that morning in the brightening light. Her heart skipped a beat or two. She wondered what he had in mind, appreciating Cooper was a beautiful soul both inside and out.

Nicholson's was a jewelry store, located a block up the street on the corner of Market and Center Streets. They sold higher end items (things Cooper could not afford), but often had special offers and sales. She hoped Cooper wasn't planning on getting her something – she wasn't about flashy status symbols – but thinking on it further, there wouldn't be any harm in looking. Especially with him.

Legs knotting as her foot met an uneven portion of sidewalk, Alyssa nearly spilled herself on the pavement but Cooper managed to stop her mid-fall. She wondered if karma was getting back at her for making fun of the drunk couple.

"Wow. Sorry. I don't know what happened there," she apologized.

Cooper passed a thumb over her lower lip. It was soothing as he wiped away a small, rosy streak. She must have bitten her lip when she stumbled.

"There's no need to apologize," he said softly, wiping the blood on his jeans. He then held Alyssa's shoulders, staring into her eyes.

"Your eyes are amazing," she said, grinning and spellbound.

His brown eyes normally had a yellowish gleam to them – like a distant candle burning in a far-off window – but for an instant, as the wind caught in his hair, billowing it like folds of midnight silk, they seemed more like sparkling emeralds.

"Thank you," he gently said. "I'm still getting used to the beauty they're blessed to see..."

Distracted by something from the north, he paused. There was a low rumble that he couldn't so much hear but *feel* in the sidewalk. The windows nearby trembled, sensation subtle. He didn't think Alyssa or anyone else could feel it, yet, but something large was coming.

"Come on, we need to find Billy," he said, his voice the definition of urgency. The photography studio was two blocks to the north, Cooper now charging up Center Street unable to restrain his concern for Billy.

"Cooper? What's the matter?" Alyssa asked. "Cooper!"

Frantically Alyssa tried to keep up with him, her arm extended and grasping his hand. It was hot and sweaty, itself attached to his veiny, trailing arm as he walked briskly with purpose.

"Cooper, what's wrong?" she pressed, but by the time he turned his head to her, she already knew.

The ground was shaking beneath her feet, the vibrations in her legs like those from the cheap, coin-operated massage chairs in the mall.

Cooper halted beside the brick wall of Kimmy's Donuts, frozen by what he saw. He stood there like a child having an innocent daydream, but the darkness rushing toward them was more the stuff of nightmares.

"The shadow wolves..." he muttered, his words drowned out by the sound of Alyssa's scream – herself weighed down so heavily with fear that she could not move.

"Alyssa, you need to get inside!" Cooper shouted. His voice managed to knock some of that weight off her, his strength crumbling the rest as he urged her toward the side entrance. "Go, NOW!"

Without delay, she dashed for the door. Kimmy herself opened it, holding out a hand. Glancing left, Alyssa saw a black tide filled with the undulating bodies of wolves. They were flooding the streets like a wave, and any people that were in the way – be they man, woman, or child – stood no chance, pulled under the onslaught of black fur, pointed claws, and razor-sharp teeth. There were screams, the sounds of things tearing, and sloshing.

"Come on, honey!" Kimmy yelled, refusing to look down the street. She shook her hand in the hopes it would speed Alyssa up.

Alyssa was running fast as she could, the door close. Her left foot rose, met the curb, then slipped. She tumbled forward, her knees taking the brunt of the fall. Pain shot into her hips.

Other patrons stared in disbelief and terror. Some of them were slapping their hands against the glass trying to rouse her to her feet. There was no time. The wolves were nearly there.

"Cooper!" she cried, high pitched and full of despair. A sallow mix of sniffling and tears followed.

Cooper rushed to her aide, standing ahead of her like a guardian. A squad of the attacking wolves broke off, coming right for him with near mindless ferocity. He removed his shirt – still a favorite – and flung it to the side as he let out a mighty roar.

Alyssa covered her ears, rolling onto her back. It was deafening, drowning out the rumble of the oncoming beasts, and then she watched with amazed horror as Cooper's body jerked and twisted like a doll in the hands of a careless child.

"I love you," he said, glancing down at her with a distorted smile. "No matter what happens baby… I will always love you."

What developed in front of her was gruesome; the stuff of horror movies and books, though sickeningly real. Yet despite the sounds, visuals, and smells, there was something in Coop's – no, this *thing's* – eyes that told her not to be afraid. It told her that she could trust it, and against all her better judgement and common sense, she did.

With heart thumping in anger and aegis, hair erupted from Cooper's mangled body. It wasn't black as it had been for the prior transformations, nor white like the Mannings. It was a salt and peppered mix of gray, like snow falling upon scorched earth. In the final moments of transition, the gold in his eyes became a sunrise, changing to the color of green grass on the first day of spring. They were shiny like dew on those fresh blades of grass.

"Owwwooooo!" Cooper howled. "Owwwooooo!"

Faced with this new sound, the shadow wolves stopped dead in their tracks – hackles raised, jowls drooling.

They paced, scurried about for a few moments, then lunged at Cooper all at once.

He reared up on his hind legs, forelimb swiping, and with a tremendous *snap* it lengthened into something more like an arm, a clawed hand snatching the foremost wolf by the neck.

It whined, then fell silent when its windpipe was crushed like an empty soda can.

Cooper's other limb did the same thing, knocking away two more of the attacking wolves with the effort of swatting a pesky fly. He howled again, and the squad fled toward the west of town.

Alyssa was in shock, looking from the monstrous thing in front of her to Cooper's shirt, laying like a piece of the innocent past in the middle of the street.

"Oh my God," she muttered, still processing everything. Somehow it all made sense, even though she didn't have a clue what was happening. *"Cooper?"*

The monster spun around, its face a menacing snarl. Drool dropped from its fangs – *splat* – as it strode forward – *splat*. Its footfalls were huge and they shook the ground.

Alyssa gasped. She knew this creature was Cooper but her reflexes did not. She scrambled away, unable to get far. The brick wall of the donut shop stopped her.

The beast reached out with its bloodied hand. Its claws were shining while its hair was matted with shadow wolf blood. It bent those long fingers, the sharp points of its nails hovering just inches above Alyssa's stomach, then her breasts – heaving for air – and finally, her tense face.

"Cooper... it's me... Alyssa."

The beast looked at her, its green eyes sparkling. Her name was like a spell that summoned tears and they flowed down Cooper's mottled fur. The outer curve of a single claw pressed itself gently against Alyssa's forehead like a kiss.

Then, in a deep voice that croaked with each word, the monster said, "I... love... you..." and began to transform again, jerking and shrinking into the much lesser, and at the same time greater, Cooper Bennett.

Alyssa could not believe what she'd seen, and had she heard it from anyone else she would have been angry they'd wasted her time with ridiculous fairytales. Yet wrapping her arms around Cooper's familiar but shivering shoulders made this real. All too real, and Cooper Bennett's secret life was not so secret anymore.

"You have a *lot* of explaining to do," she said quietly. Her smile was huge. Her hug tight.

Cooper responded with a laugh, shaking from the coldness that always rushed his body after the Change.

"Yeah, I definitely will once I figure this all out myself."

There was a sudden noise, one of something collapsing. Both Cooper and Alyssa turned to look back north.

The sun was bright, hiding nothing in shadow. Shining down on a broken street sign which had just toppled, a single person was standing beyond amidst the grizzly backdrop of blood and death.

"Billy?" Cooper asked, squinting his eyes to reduce some of the glare coming off the windows of parked cars. "Billy, is that you?"

It certainly was Billy Arnett, splattered from head to toe in red, along with chunks of what looked like overcooked hamburger. His right hand was clamped tightly as he held something.

"Are you okay?" Alyssa asked, letting go of Cooper.

"Yeah," he replied soberly. The answer was obviously forced. Plunging his head, he saw paw prints made of mud and blood marring the roadway. "I'm okay… but…"

Alyssa stood up, the silence around them overbearing. She checked Cooper one more time, then marched over to Billy.

"What is it?" she asked, placing a gentle hand on his shoulder. "What's happened?"

He made a face so sad it broke her heart. Wincing, his voice was full of pain. It took forever to form the words.

"M…mom… and dad," he said. "They're dead."

Alyssa's mouth fell open but she didn't say anything else. Instead, she hugged him tightly.

"Happy Saint Patrick's Day," Billy said, his fist opening. A four-leaf clover fell out of it, fluttering like a dying butterfly until it hit the sullied ground.

2

Billy was having a rough week, which started back on the ninth after he'd gotten hold of a bad sandwich from the Royal Burger off Highway 76. Even though the bread, meat, *and* cheese was ice cold (the latter not in a state of melty heaven, but rather akin to an orange brick that could have been taken right off the walls of Goodman High itself), he woofed the whole thing down like a ravenous dog. Within an hour, he was starting the regret that decision – his stomach objecting to every bite his brain told him not to take.

Making matters worse, and against the advice of both Cooper *and* Alyssa, Billy insisted that a banana smoothie from Sir Mixalot was all it would take to remedy his aching belly. Of course, it didn't help, and he spent the rest of the night into the early hours of the morning with his insides churning like the blenders used to make the godforsaken drink. To top it all off, his body reached the point of purging and he spent another half an hour playing see-saw between the sink (spewing a ton of acrid fluid from his mouth) and the toilet (dropping pungent loads into it).

He felt better by the morning of the eleventh, a healthy dose of motherly love from Mrs. Arnett helping things along. That was when his newly acquired camera – a vintage Pentax with chrome finish and a thirty-five-millimeter lens – ended up taking a nose dive into the floor. Its strap had caught on one of the knobs of a dresser drawer. With the lens shattered, Billy dropped it off at Panda Studios. They ordered a replacement for him, the whole unexpected operation due to be completed by the sixteenth, which brought Billy to that very morning before Saint Patrick's Day.

He was excited for the festival, excited about getting his camera back, and excited about spending time with Cooper and Alyssa, who he'd grown to know and like more as their after-school errands led to more personal discussions – mainly about Cooper himself. It was their little secret. Surely Cooper had a few of his own.

Billy woofed down breakfast, kissing his mother on the cheek after he'd placed the dirty dishes in the sink. To this day, she insisted upon doing them herself, even though the dishwasher was in perfect working order.

"I'll see you later mom!" he said jovially, grabbing a plastic bag from under the sink and stuffing it full of snacks.

"It's a miracle you aren't fat, Billy," she said.

"Would you love me less if I was?" he snickered, and she shook her head.

"Of course not. There'd just be more of you for me to love."

Billy laughed, then shoved his index finger down his throat to feign throwing up.

"Very funny," Mrs. Arnett replied, starting to clean the dishes. "I'd have thought you'd be sick of vomiting by now."

With a smile Billy bounded for the front door.

His dad was seated on the couch in the living room, wearing a plaid shirt instead of his typical coveralls. Its sleeves were rolled up and there were a couple of fresh bruises on his forearms from an argument with a plate compactor. Apparently, it won.

"Hey son," Mr. Arnett called just as Billy grabbed the doorknob. It was cool to the touch. "Before you go, I wanted you to have something. Hopefully it'll bring you a bit of good luck today."

"What is it?"

Mr. Arnett held out his hand and Billy did the same, a perfect four-leaf clover dropping from one to the other.

Billy's eyes would always open wide with childlike wonder, and his dad loved seeing it, since he'd not had many opportunities to do so growing up himself. In a way, he was living vicariously through his son. He hoped Billy never changed his outlook on life.

Maybe he'll remember all this before pawning me off for senior care when my beard goes gray, Mr. Arnett would think.

"Thanks!" Billy said, closing his fist around the clover. He gave his dad a quick hug, then opened the door. "I'll see you guys tonight!"

"See you later," Mrs. Arnett called lovingly from the kitchen, his dad just smiling as the door closed.

Moving over to one of the small front windows, Mr. Arnett hitched back the curtain and watched his son head down Cherry Lane, disappearing behind the large privacy fence across the street.

Little did he know that would be the last time they would ever be together. Just moments later he saw something that terrified him.

"Brenda!" Branson Arnett shouted – his loud, panic-driven tone booming through their home. "Jesus Christ! Wolves! There are wolves everywhere!"

3

The trio marched west along Hanlon Road, deciding at Cooper's request to head toward Grayson Estate for help, answers, or fight – he really had no idea. From where they were, the area ahead was inundated with smoke, its source hard to make out due to the gray veil that hung over the west like a thick fog. It didn't even seem like morning anymore.

"Guys, not to be a bother, but I really need to get out of these clothes," Billy said, the small flecks of flesh starting to nauseate him with their foul odor.

"There's a clothing store up ahead, I'm sure the owners won't mind us... borrowing something, given the situation."

Cooper agreed, not wanting to walk around too much longer in nothing but his skin.

They stopped at the quaint boutique shop. Billy changed out of his soiled attire into something clean, while Cooper donned a pair of sweatpants.

"So... was it bad?" Cooper asked as he pulled his shirt over himself, adjusting the base. "What you went through?"

Billy was quiet, like someone who had seen a lot of nasty things far too quickly.

"I..." he said quietly.

"It's okay," said Alyssa. "We'll be here for you when you're ready."

"Thanks," he said, standing a little taller. He puffed his chest out a slight bit.

"Come on," Cooper said, "The Manning place isn't too far ahead."

Carrying on in silence, they passed by masses of mangled bodies littering the streets and yards. It was ghastly, some of the bodies – store owners they had seen every day, patrons at places like Castillo's, and even fellow students (including Mark Brown and Derek Wilder) – were still moving, whether consciously or not. Others were crying in half-dead wails that begged for the rest to take over.

"I can't..." Alyssa started to say, but her emotions got the better of her. She placed a hand over her mouth, but a sigh still escaped, new tears making their way down dried tracks on her cheeks.

Cooper quieted her, placing an arm around her waist. After a few steps, he also grabbed Billy by the shoulder and yanked him over.

"You know, with the three of us together we *will* get through this," he said. "We've been through a lot over the years."

"Nothing like *this*," Alyssa said.

Billy mumbled in agreement, one of his hands fiddling with the white ring chained around his neck.

"You know, I've been thinking about that time we first met," Billy said. "Do you think that Derek Wilder is... *was*... one of these things?"

Cooper nodded, then Billy did too – reluctantly.

"So that must mean..."

"That Liam is one as well," Cooper added, "and his father."

Alyssa let out a laugh that made her sound like a mad woman.

"Special report: werewolves are real! Story tonight at nine," she said with a mock news anchor accent.

"Were *you* one back then?" Billy asked, his voice so timid it was like he didn't want Cooper to hear he'd asked.

"If I was, do you think I would have looked like the poster boy for Q-tips?" Cooper laughed.

"I guess not," Billy answered, smiling. "The new version of you is much better anyway."

"But the qualities of the *old* you are what made us both like you," Alyssa added. "I think you've always been a kind person, Cooper. I used to see how angry you'd get at Liam and the others when they'd bully people. Even more when they got away with it. Now, you can act on those desires to do good."

"Huh, I guess you're right," he said. "I hope that counts for something."

"It counts for everything in my book," Billy said.

"Mine too," Alyssa replied.

"It's good to have you two here," Cooper said, "despite the situation."

Making their way onto Grayson Loop, it became apparent that the birthplace of all the smoke was their destination. Thick clouds rose from the skeletal remains of the burnt-out home while the base was awash in an eerie red glow. Scores of shadowy figures milled around, Cooper preparing for the worst before realizing they were not poised for attack. They were responding to the devastation.

"I really do hate this town," Billy said as he watched several silhouetted shapes transform from wolves into men. "Why can't we live somewhere normal?"

"Seems this is 'normal' now," Alyssa replied, her hand holding Cooper's firmly.

Suddenly, an incredibly tall man emerged from the crowd. He seemed to grow larger than life as he approached.

"Stop!" he shouted and once he was flanked by two others, the trio complied. "Who are you? Another one of *his* emissaries?"

"No..." the leftmost shape said. "This, my friend, is Mr. Cooper Bennett."

As the three veiled shapes got closer, their features emerged from the smoke. The one that had spoken was Grayson Manning. To his left stood the huge man Cooper had seen from time to time outside Castillo's. On the far end was another man, short but powerfully built. He reminded Cooper a lot of Dr. Ross but was even more muscular. There was a large sledgehammer slung across his upper back.

After a fleeting round of introductions, Grayson could sense there was something *unusual* about Cooper. He had not been able to smell him as he approached, only recognizing the boy once he saw him up close. This was something the White Wolf Alpha had not felt in a long time, yet despite his qualms – not believing it, or thinking that perhaps he was wrong – with one look toward Ásbjörn, it was confirmed.

Cooper Bennett, a nineteen-year-old that had been turned by the errant bite of a shadow wolf, had gained the status of an Alpha. He was one in the purest sense of the word, and unbeknownst to any of them at the time, his resolve made him one of the most powerful.

Chapter 22: A Gray Day

1

"So... do you like pizza?" Cooper asked casually, trying to lure the atmosphere off the brink of misery.

The bear shifter next to him half smiled, half contorting his face into a puzzled looked of *Why the hell are you asking me that now?* He couldn't deny it, though, even if Cooper hadn't seen him coming out of Castillo's so many (or rather too many) times before.

"Yes, I do," Ásbjörn said proudly, both men laughing as they sat on one of several picnic tables placed in the front lawn of Grayson's house. "But, I suppose we may have to find a new place to go after all this is said and done. My understanding is that the shadow wolves did quite a number downtown."

"From what I saw yeah, they did. Well, wherever that new place is, the first pie is on me," Cooper said, suddenly and strangely caring about the whereabouts of his father. "Do you happen to know where else they struck?"

"No, not fully yet," Ásbjörn replied, standing from the seat. Climbing onto the tabletop, he plopped back down on it. There was more room there for someone his size. He stretched out his arms, the span incredibly wide. "From what I've been told and what you know first-hand, they sent a wave in from the north out of Toluca Springs. That one cut a large path of death from Foothill Road all the way down to West Pine Street. For some reason, they didn't seem too interested in venturing beyond it that much. Obviously, their fire rune stones did a number on Grayson's place out here to the west." He kicked a thumb over toward the smoldering ruins. "I heard that another force came out of Jameson Preserve to the east of town. Those wolves crashed all the way to Jackson Street where…"

"Riverhill School is," Cooper said.

"Indeed," Ásbjörn replied, nodding. "Ol' Snowy thinks Goddard is heading for the Vault around Monument Park to retrieve whatever it is he's after. I for one hope he finds my fist in his skull for all the shit he's caused. Hopefully before he does much more to this poor town."

Cooper drifted off in thought. The town was suffering under the onslaught of something they had no idea was coming, and he wondered if Mr. Reid would dryly recount the day the town's population dropped by the thousands to future history classes at Goodman High. That is, if the school was even there anymore. Then he wondered if his dad was affected in any way, or if he had... perished. Vowing to check and see after they dealt with the immediate problem of Lance Goddard, Cooper's brain then snared itself on what Ásbjörn had said.

Wait... a vault?

"I'm sorry, Osborne, was it? What is this Vault that you're talking about?"

"Oh, my apologies," Ásbjörn said, explaining all that he knew.

Cooper was astonished by these significant things happening in the background of the town. He would have asked more questions, but Ásbjörn became distracted.

"Stay here," he said, leaping off the table. His landing made a loud *thud*. "Another one of his messengers is here."

"Who? Lance?"

"Indeed. Now please, do as I say and stay put."

Ásbjörn then walked off toward the northern section of the Loop, Cooper disobediently sliding off his seat to follow. Grayson joined them while Dax brought up the rear. He stood next to Cooper, the four of them watching the Shadow Alpha's herald advance.

He was wearing a county sheriff's uniform, yellow eyes glowing beneath the brim of his hat. In his hands was something large and wadded, the colors gold and black.

"My name is Wolfrick, liaison to the great…"

"We are aware of his titles," Ásbjörn growled. "Now get on with it, *sub*."

"Beta, actually," Wolfrick snapped.

"Is that supposed to *impress* me?" Ásbjörn retorted (and Cooper smirked behind him; he liked this guy a lot).

"Anyway, I haven't come to talk to the rabble, especially the likes of an abomination whose crown has lost its majesty," Wolfrick said, glaring at Ásbjörn with derision. He laughed, softly at first, then louder as he looked them all up and down.

"It's alright Ásbjörn, I know that he is here to see me."

"Ah, Grayson Manning. I come bearing a gift for you…"

Wolfrick didn't need to be within twenty feet for Grayson to know what the thing in his hands was. Nor did he need to see him unfurl the coat, then fling it disrespectfully at his feet. Bending down on one knee, Grayson picked up the school jacket, the Goodman High School Wolverines logo emblazoned across its back. A darkness fell across his eyes like a blue sky chased away by dusk. One of the jacket's sleeves had been torn off. It was rife with Liam's scent.

"What have you done with him?" Grayson asked, his heart wanting to hear that...

"He is safe, for now."

Thank goodness.

"How can I be sure you aren't lying?"

"You can't. Surety is something that the Shadow Alpha does not provide. However, he is not without generosity. Consider this as a second gift: your son's fate will ultimately be decided *by you,* old wolf."

"You know, it's not often that ambassadors are such assholes," Ásbjörn cut in, his large arms folded over his chest. "Your *own* fate might be in the hand of others, too, wolf. I think that becoming a Beta has gone straight to your head. It's hardly becoming."

"Neither is your stench."

"Enough! Both of you," Grayson barked.

He stood, his son's jacket dangling limp like a skinned hide from his right hand. Handing it off to Fridolf, who had walked over from what remained of the house, Grayson lifted his eyes toward Wolfrick.

"What must I do?"

"The Shadow Alpha kindly requests your presence in the Vault."

"*In* the Vault? To what end?"

"That I don't know," Wolfrick answered, though a dim smirk across his thin lips betrayed his words.

Grayson looked up, billowing smoke blocking the view of the late morning sky. However, a single pinprick of light managed to break through from the sun. It gave him a small bit of comfort knowing that light still existed in full brightness up there.

There is still hope? he questioned, trying desperately to think of an alternative, but there seemed to be little choice but to go.

"You know, your Alpha must not think too highly of you," Ásbjörn said, breaking the silence. "Sending a Beta into the heart of enemy territory as a scant messenger? Doesn't scream a whole lot of confidence to me."

"On the contrary," Wolfrick replied conceitedly. "I think of it as a challenge, one of many that the Alpha presents."

The two continued their exchange, Ásbjörn flapping his fingers like a pretend mouth. As they did so, Dax inched his way over to the emissary, his silver hammer glinting orange in the night.

"So, you think of being here as a challenge?" the Journeyman asked once he was close enough, and Wolfrick abruptly stopped talking. "Sort of like trying to hit a home run during a baseball game?"

Wolfrick bore an expression of unease mixed with confusion.

How had this human gotten so close? it asked, consuming him to such a point that he didn't notice Dax's grip on the sledgehammer's handle.

"Human games cannot begin to compare to the greatness of the Shadow Alpha's challenges."

"Well, I'm sure they can't," Dax replied, raising the hammer like a baseball bat. "But both are worth trying, right?"

None of them winced or turned away as the hammer struck Wolfrick's head. Not even for a second.

"What now? asked Dax, setting the bloody hammer head on the ground.

"The answer to that is simple: I'm going to get my son back and stop Lance while I'm at it," Grayson said. "This has gone on for long enough."

Before anyone could stop him or say another word, the Alpha was already walking toward a car that was parked nearby.

Dax, Ásbjörn, and Cooper all exchanged glances.

"Duty calls yet again," said Dax, slinging the hammer over his shoulders. He secured the handle with both of his hands and followed Grayson.

Ásbjörn and Cooper stayed behind, still looking at each other.

"I know your answer but I'm going to do my part and say: you don't have to come along."

Cooper smiled, looking up at the bear shifter's eyes nearly eight inches above his own.

"But I will," he replied. "We all have a score to settle with Lance, and I'm not missing my opportunity."

"Good man," Ásbjörn said, and after placing a large hand on Cooper's shoulder, he made way for the car. "See you shortly."

Cooper turned, seeing Alyssa and Billy still perched on one of the picnic tables. They'd watched the scene unfold from a safe distance, where Cooper believed they should remain. He walked over to them briskly but wanted to take all the time in the world, knowing that he had to leave.

"So where are we going?" Billy asked as Cooper walked up.

"*We* aren't going anywhere," he replied and Billy's smile became a frown. "Look, I need you two to stay here where it's safe. Things are going to get dangerous…"

"But you're going with them?" Alyssa asked, her voice wavering since she already knew the answer.

Cooper nodded and Alyssa hugged him, then reluctantly pulled herself away.

"I understand," she said.

Billy gave him a hug too, asking where they were headed.

"A vault of some kind. Apparently, Lance has gotten inside and has…" Cooper hesitated, not knowing if he should be happy or sad at his next words. "He has Liam as prisoner."

Billy and Alyssa both looked downtrodden. Cooper joined them. He supposed if they'd been happy about the situation, they'd be more like Lance than any of them would care to admit.

"What amazes me is that there's even a place like that under the town," said Billy.

"I know," Cooper replied, "and for all these years we've hung out right beside the entrance… Monument Park. It's where the attacking waves of wolves converged."

Billy shook his head in disbelief and Alyssa trembled. Cooper looked anxiously over his shoulder toward the car. The other shifters were waiting.

"I have to go," he said, giving each of them one last embrace. "I'll do my best to see you soon."

"You better," Billy said.

Alyssa remained silent. Had she said anything, she'd turn herself into a sobbing mess.

Cooper smiled at the two of them, turned, then sprinted for the car.

Moments later, he was climbing into the back seat with Dax.

Billy watched the door close and the car head off into the foggy smoke, disappearing around a bend seconds later.

"So, Alyssa," he muttered like a mischievous child left in a room after the grownups had left. "Are you up for a little walk?"

Her sadness seemed to dissipate quickly. Regardless of what Cooper said, she couldn't just sit around and wait while he was out their fighting for his life and theirs. She needed to do something. They both did.

"What do you have in mind?" she asked.

"I've no idea," Billy replied, the last remnants of a chuckle on his lips. He pulled a silver switchblade from his pocket. Showed it to her. The blade seemed to dance with enthusiasm, or perhaps it was just because his hand was shaking so much due to his nerves. Either way, he was ready.

"I think we should to go to the park," she said. "See if we can do anything to help."

Billy didn't think that was a bad idea, but Alyssa would need a weapon, and suddenly an idea hit him like a runaway train.

"Alrighty, we'll head there, but we need to get you something sharp and silver, plus I need to pay a visit to the camera store..."

2

386

The shadow pack howled ominously, Lance approaching the bronze statue in Monument Park dressed in a suit, less its black jacket. All around them were bodies of the respectable people of Goodman, left where they fell like a grim line of dominoes dressed in green. He stepped over them as he got closer, staring at the mighty warrior that represented the town's founder.

Humans, he thought. *How wonderful it will be address the lingering disease that is you, once I am reunited with...*

A scream came from behind, turning into an agonizing, inhuman screech. It was Liam, his numerous wounds festering from being denied the Change. Held by the collar of his jacket, two brutish men drug him along, not caring what their hostage bumped or scraped along the way.

Lance closed his eyes momentarily, then refocused on the unsightly creature the heroic human figure was battling. He spat on the ground in disgust.

Soon they will all see, he thought, shooting a glance over his shoulder.

"Bring him!" he commanded.

Liam was carried forward at once, then dumped between the Alpha and the statue. Lance looked down at the pathetic wretch that used to be a high school bully without pity.

"It seems that you're serving us in multiple ways today, Mr. Manning,"

Lance said callously, removing the key from his suit pocket.

Liam was listless, fading in and out of consciousness. A ringing sound had conquered his senses.

Lance kneeled, pulling back the protective wrappings around the silver cylinder. He pressed the cold metal against Liam's face and it sizzled like a steak on a grill.

The brutes held Liam still as a series of howls came gushing out of his mouth. His lips were curled over his teeth, eyes shut tight in misery. While he gasped for air in chugging swells between each nightmarish wail, Lance proceeded to roll the cylinder over his captive's skin. It left burns behind in the rough shape of the Fifth Pentacle of Mercury, though it was more a swollen, pink region that wept clear, scalding fluid. Holding out a single finger, Lance punctured the center of the seal with a claw. Liam's face knotted up, Lance pushing deeper. Blood poured across the bubbled skin in a thick streak of shocking red.

"*Aperio*," he mumbled, knowing the Order liked to use Latin in their spells.

The ground trembled and the statues started to move apart. Behind them an immense door opened down the middle of the park, grass and dirt spilling down stairs that plunged underground. An overwhelming smell filled the park area, mingling with the metallic scent of blood and the pungent odor of wet clothes and raw meat. It was the perfume of providence, and riding on those draughts of stale air was the scent of the thing Lance desired above all else: Her.

The Shadow Alpha stood triumphantly, taking a large breath. The hole in the ground called to him, but before he entered, he thanked Liam and gave his hair a playful rub. Stripping off his coat, he threw it towards Wolfrick, who fumbled to catch it.

"Take that to Grayson and tell him I am waiting for him inside."

"What if he doesn't come, my Alpha?"

"Oh, I think he will," Lance said. "The life of his one and only son hangs in the balance."

Wolfrick looked at the coat, a second thought crossing his mind. He hesitated for a moment, fearful of what might happen should he say anything.

"My... Alpha... surely this task is better suited for one of the subordinate envoys?"

"Perhaps, but this message coming from a Beta will carry far more weight. Do this for me, Wolfrick, and you'll guarantee your position as my successor." Lance's words were cold and calculated, but convincing to the right ears. Wolfrick had those, and Lance solidified his intent with a friendly smile.

Wolfrick bowed and made his way for Grayson's home, Lance turning his attention to the pack.

"Go to the borders of town and keep the Order away at all costs."

Barks and howls rung out through the otherwise silent streets, not even the birds singing their songs that day. There was a mad rush of paws and panting, thinning with the pack until they were gone.

Lance remained, there with Liam and his two guards. He gave a signal and they grabbed hold of Liam, jerking his flaccid body upright. The boy floundered like a fish on a hook, teetering on the verge of unconsciousness as the four descended towards their respective destinies deep in the earth.

Lance Goddard lead them, his yellow eyes shining as the light began to fade away.

3

A large shaft of light cascaded down the stone steps from the world above. It was quickly fading, the thought of bringing a torch or even matches escaping Lance's mind. Behind him, the guards struggled to keep their balance in check on the steep incline, Liam Manning's unconscious body an awkward load to bear. The four of them continued their descent and soon the light had diminished to a faint whisper of its former self, like the brightness of a full moon dwindling to nothing as it was renewed. The day had become gray and Lance was in twilight – ahead the black of utter darkness, behind thin strands of light still percolating down from Monument Park.

Suddenly, as if answering his thoughts on how much further they had to go until reaching the bottom, the stairs ended. Lance could tell a larger space was ahead, even though it was too dark to see. Taking a blind step forward, his foot came into contact with what felt like a stone floor and to his surprise, a light illuminated a small area around him. Taking another step, the light grew brighter and looking down, it seemed to come from where his feet were touching the floor, shimmering like the surface of a lake in the sun.

From what he could see they had entered a very large chamber, roughly the size of Grand Central Station in New York City, stretching out into darkness at the fringes. Inside were weapons and shields, crowns and amulets, tomes and grimoires, along with obelisks the size of buses turned on end. Those were but a fraction what the space contained from all corners of the world, stored in that one place, which in turn was one of many such places the Order had to keep nefarious things out of sight, out of mind, and out of reach. A cavernous ceiling rose above it all, its arched shape reminiscent of a cathedral. Along the outer walls were more passageways, and through the centermost one Lance moved, entering chamber after chamber like the one before.

The pinnacle of human avarice indeed, he thought, viewing the space not as a place to keep these things safe, but more so a place to ensure human dominion.

As much as the chambers were swollen with things, they were also sated with sounds of all sorts, the height of the different chambers magnifying them. Lance could hear Liam's inactive feet being dragged across the stone floor, the monotone noise underlying the erratic *tap-tap* of his guard's steps. There was also breathing – not any of their own – from the dark corners, and for a moment Lance believed it to be Grayson and his ilk... but that would not have been possible since they were behind, hopefully coming, while these noises were coming from places ahead that none of them had been. Erratic chittering then followed, coming out of the rim of darkness like large and monstrous crickets, and even distant whispers that begged for both aid and death.

Lance ignored them; all were distractions from his intentions. Pressing forward, he led the group into one final chamber which turned out to be his final destination.

This room was nearly empty and weeping. Water from a large, underground karst spring wetted the black and crumbling walls, covering them and the floor with a spongy layer of drab green mold. A trickling sound came from everywhere, and beneath it like the booming bass of a song, was a roar like thundering rain. Lance's attention wasn't on any of that, instead it was transfixed in sheer awe ahead.

There was a towering wolf statue, similar in appearance to the one on the surface in Monument Park. This one stood a good twenty feet or more above the four of them, its abnormally long arms outstretched like the letter T while its powerful legs were bound together in a pose reminiscent of a crucifix.

Lance howled softly, a single tear escaping his golden eyes as he craned his neck to speak to Her.

"Mother...I have come."

Chapter 23: Goodbye

1

The guards dragged Liam's body towards the statue, dropping him in a heap atop a platform that was part of the front. They fell to their knees in reverence while Lance paced along that same dais, his patience in waiting for Grayson getting quite thin.

Yanking a Colt revolver out of its holster on his hip, he checked the rounds anxiously. They were all there, just like the last five times he looked. Irritated, he flicked the cylinder closed and upon hearing that satisfying *click*, he could make out additional footsteps approaching.

At last.

The guards had just gotten to their feet when Grayson ran into the chamber, followed by Dax, Cooper, and Ásbjörn. They were all initially struck by presence and size of the wolf statue, but Grayson's attention soon fell to ground level, where Liam's unconscious body had been slumped.

"What have you done?" Grayson shouted, the energy in his voice seeming to stir some distant part of Liam to consciousness. He started to crawl aimlessly, moaning "Dad" and "help" in the lowest tones. It was all his body could muster.

"Relax, Grayson," Lance urged, casually walking up to Liam's scrabbling body. He placed one of his feet on the upper part of his back, then pushed down on it. "Your pretty boy is still alive…"

"Release him then!" Grayson demanded, and Lance did nothing but smile in reply.

"Oh, come now *Lichtträger*, where would the fun in that be?" Lance's voice was loud and broken, his face inflamed with joy. "Besides, we have someone else who requires our attention! Now, let's take care of all these distractions, shall we?"

What happened next unfolded to all in dirty slow motion but in reality, it was swift and clean.

Grayson watched Lance pull out that dark gray six-shooter, aiming it toward Liam's body.

BANG!

A silver bullet, the first of six, streaked from the barrel and punctured Liam's left buttock. He cried out as it smoldered like the first inklings of a campfire.

Grayson's eyes took it in, pupils wide as they could be, focused on the thin column of smoke rising from his son's helpless body.

BANG!

The second bullet entered Liam's right hand, which was extended at the time.

Grayson heard the muffled cries of his son, whose face was turned away toward the statue. He was frozen with anger, and sadness, and...

BANG!

The third bullet punctured Liam's leg at the knee, shattering it.

Grayson's eyes finally narrowed, anger driving his feet toward the Shadow Alpha and that godforsaken, smug expression.

The shadow guards rushed toward Grayson, but Ásbjörn and Dax leapt into action.

BANG!

The fourth bullet dove into Liam's shoulder, causing him to jerk up and flop his head over in the other direction. He stared at his father, crying.

Grayson saw him out of the corner of his eye, having made it to the base of the platform Lance was standing on.

Ásbjörn shifted into his massive bear form, bounding at the closest guard with all his might. He grabbed the still shifting wolf in his jaws, biting down as hard as he could. The taste of warm blood filled his mouth. It was disgusting, yet satisfying. The guard was dead.

BANG!

A fifth bullet pierced Liam's spine, ensuring the boy would never play football again, even if he were to make it out of there alive. His college and national dreams were over before the sound faded, but that wasn't the last gift Lance had for him.

Dax reached the second guard, dropping to his knees as he skidded across the floor. The guard had shifted, jumping in his agile wolf body to avoid Dax, but the big man swung the hammer in a downward arc that struck the werewolf hard between the neck and shoulder. The bones were destroyed, the wolf's head listing all the way to the side, attached only by muscle fibers and skin.

Cooper felt his own rage building, racing toward Lance – the cause of all this added heartache and grief.

Grayson reached his adversary, knocking him backward with a mighty punch to the face.

As he fell, Lance pulled the trigger…

BANG!

… launching the last, fatal silver bullet into the back of Liam's head. His skull cracked where the bullet entered his brain, blood oozing out of the wound and down the sides of his face, coating those pretty blue eyes.

Grayson's heart sank, and with it any sense of hope he had. He went into a rage, engaging Lance in a colossal brawl.

"Wait," Ásbjörn said, holding Cooper and Dax back to allow the two Alphas to battle it out. "They must do this themselves."

"LANCE!" Grayson screamed as he knocked him onto his back.

Dropping to the ground, Grayson spread his legs across the Shadow Alpha's upper chest, pining his arms while striking him repeatedly across the face. The blows were powerful, their thuds sending vibrations up Grayson's arms to the elbow, some to his shoulder.

"YOU TOOK MY SON YOU BASTARD!"

"I would do it again if I could!" Lance shouted, quickly turning up his right shoulder.

Grayson overbalanced and toppled, jutting out an arm to brace for the impact. He didn't time it correctly, his arm twisting slightly and his wrist surged with pain.

Lance scrambled to his feet and moved in front of the White Wolf

Alpha, kicking him in the jaw with one of his well-crafted dress shoes.

It drove Grayson backwards like a bop bag and as he righted himself, he cupped a hand over his mouth, unable to stop the blood seeping between his throbbing fingers.

"Come on Lance," Grayson prodded through his swollen and ruptured lips. "Let's end this!"

The two were on their feet again, crashing into each other with a flurry of pummeling fists and claws. They tore at their blood-soaked suits until both were nothing but wet tatters.

Lance got in an uppercut, which sent Grayson tumbling – feet over head and head over feet – until he came to rest under the statue's right arm.

The impact had torn away a section of moss that was loosened by all the fighting, revealing part of an intricate set of symbols beneath the years of overgrowth. Attempting to get up and continue the fight until either he or Lance was dead, Grayson's bloody hand touched some of the outlines, and a low hum resonated throughout the chamber as if some magic spell was spooling.

Lance grinned, his yellow eyes sparkling with pleasure as he kicked away a segment of moss where he stood. There were similar but darker runes beneath the statue's left hand.

"At last both light and shadow bearers can fulfill their roles!" Lance pronounced as he crouched, claws at the ready to spill his own blood on the seal. "Mother, I call to you! Soon you will be freed, and we shall remake the world in your image!"

Grayson's head spun in dizzying fits. The wall blocking his memories dissolved and then, unexpectedly and quite shockingly, he relived those horrifying days from centuries ago...

2

The Gray Mother is Her name.

Before there were none and after there were all.

***

The sixteenth century countryside around Bedburg, Germany sits beneath a dreary sky, rain falling in steely sheets that render the ground a thick, brown soup. In the town itself, down a narrow and stinking alleyway, a crowd is gathered around a large wolf-like creature. They jeer and scream, thrusting weapons at the unsightly thing. Wiry hair covers its large body while green eyes look out, the night sparkling in them like fire. A gaping mouth snarls with cruel teeth, and mighty claws tremble at the end of long, powerful arms.

The creature is relentless, but after unleashing several dogs on the foul thing, it succumbs. The people are shocked to discover that what they've cornered is actually no wolf at all, but a local man named Peter Stumpp.

***

The year is 1589 and Peter Stumpp is in the midst of a garish trial, not only accused of being the wolf-monster, but also witchcraft (allowing him to make such a transformation) and cannibalism (wherein he devoured his victims).

After being tortured on a rack, Stumpp confesses to practicing black magic since he was twelve years old. That sparked an interest in several legends across Germany, and his hunt for a sorceress by the name of Sidonia. As far as his ability to transform into a gluttonous wolf, Stumpp claims he is able to do so because he was bitten by another creature in the lands around Colongne twenty-five years earlier.

Stumpp had been a voracious eater before being caught, feasting on livestock, as well as humans – men, women, and children alike. Threatened with even more torture, he confesses to consuming eighteen people in all. Fourteen of them were children (including his own son, whose brain was spooned out as if from a bowl). The others were pregnant women, whose babies were torn fresh from their bellies and eaten raw.

***

Stumpp is brutally executed on Halloween, 1589, along with his daughter and mistress. After a series of violent and bloody steps, his severed head is placed in the very top of a pole – the torture wheel and the figure of a wolf on it – as a warning against similar behavior.

If only it had worked...

***

The Gray Mother roams the countryside, Her wails beneath a cloudy full moon are somber and frightful. She is a vile thing, the first of Her kind long in slumber since the dawn of monsters across the Earth.

This night in 1591, She gives birth to a savage species of Primal werewolves, spitting them out onto the Earth in disgusting splendor. Like Peter Stumpp and the werewolves before him, they are huge and monstrous, their greens eyes burning with strength, their bellies eternally hungry.

They are the pinnacle of werewolf kind.

They are Her children...

***

The birthing yields lesser mutations: seven normal looking pups without the spark of Primal greatness. Without warning, She consumes those pups, their newborn flesh tender and bones soft in Her formidable jaws.

There had been times before where an infant or two might escape, an issue which, over centuries, would lead to the various subspecies of werewolf kind.

But tonight, that didn't happen. All the offenders were gone, melting in the Gray Mother's stomach.

***

The sorceress Sidonia watches her home burning in the night, the howls of Primal werewolves filling the sky along with the rising smoke. Her family's screams echo from the fire into the darkness. She is driven to weep.

Later, in the distant countryside veiled in shadow, she can see the immense body of the Gray Mother devastating another small community with Her brood.

The look in Sidonia's eyes is no longer sadness but revenge... and she would have it.

***

A group of mutated pups is rescued the night of October 17, 1591. There are six in all, four of them spotted with brown eyes. Yet the last two are special and rare. One is pure white like a fresh snowfall, its eyes crystal blue like the cold. The other is darker than the night during a new moon, yet its eyes are bright yellow like the sun.

Taking the names Grayson and Lance after a pair of friendly souls that helped them along the way, the two pure werewolves grow up strong, leading large packs of their very own.

***

The time came for Sidonia to exact her revenge, learning that The Gray Mother had fallen ill after some townsfolk from one of Her recent attacks fought back. She consumed the attackers, but their clothes were stuffed full of wolfsbane, the plant taking a tremendous toll on Her body. She was weakened by it, and the latest birthing miscarried.

Rallying the White Wolf and Shadow Wolf packs to her aid, Sidonia leads an attack directly against the Gray Mother with the intent to kill Her. However, the fight is bloody and hard, the Primal horde still strong even though She was not. With losses amassing on the allied side, Sidonia decides the only way to succeed is to imprison the creature instead, hopefully an act that would last forever.

Using Grayson and Lance as the keys – the Light Bearer and the Shadow Bearer for balance – Sidonia uses blood magic and Solomon seals to imprison the mother of all werewolves within the stoniness of Her own heart.

***

Sidonia watches as the Gray Mother's statue is buried, and to ensure

She would never awaken (a thing that could happen if the two brothers were forced to use their blood to break the seals she had placed), Grayson and Lance agree to have their memories sealed and new lives started in America.

***

Grayson looks out over the Blue Ridge Mountains with his brother Lance at his side. The valley below is majestic and beautiful, a place that will eventually come to be occupied by a town named Goodman.

But for now, it is a quiet place, and the young Grayson shifts into his gleaming white wolf form, waiting for his brother to do the same. The two run off into the woods together, and between the howls and barks, there is playful laughter.

***

She is evil and must never be allowed to walk the Earth again.

Remember, the Gray Mother is Her name.

Before there were none and after there were...

3

"All..." Grayson muttered, his eyes opening at the moment Lance punctured his right hand.

Blood began to ooze, pooling in the shallow depression of his palm, and the Shadow Alpha held that bleeding hand out over the symbols.

Cooper was awestruck by what was happening, wanting to help in some way, but Ásbjörn's grip was still holding strong. Then, as if his worst fears had manifested – like Grayson had witnessed first-hand with Liam – he smelled something that he shouldn't have down in that vault. Ásbjörn sensed it too. Relaxing his grasp on Cooper and Dax, they all turned to see Alyssa and Billy arriving in the room, brandishing their tiny silver blades.

Billy lowered his weapon; gawking at the immense statue towering overhead. From his current perspective, it made him feel like a child again. Cooper's panicked voice would, too, sounding like his dad whenever Billy did something stupid – like showing up in the middle of a shifter battle deep within the bowels of a supernatural organization's storage facility.

That level of stupid.

"No, no, no!" Cooper screamed, rushing to them. "You shouldn't be here! I told you two you couldn't be here!"

Billy apologized, but Alyssa was looking at Liam's dead body.

"Baby... Alyssa... hey!" Cooper said, snapping his fingers. She came out of her stupor and he stepped over, blocking the view of Liam's body. "Why on Earth did you come?"

"W-we wanted to h-help," she stuttered, trying to peer around Cooper's shoulder. He adjusted himself to block her. "The three of us together, rremember?"

Cooper sighed, then quickly breathed in again.

"Right, and I agree, but believe me: you both could NOT be in a more dangerous place right now. I have no idea if us shifters have the power to –

"

"Lance! You must stop!" Grayson called.

"You told me the same thing nearly twenty years ago," Lance retorted, "and now that I'm standing in the very place I've desired to be all that time, you think I'm going to stop?"

"You have to!" Grayson's voice was cracking as he tried to force reason through each word, syllable, then letter. "Mother is *not* what She appears to be! She was imprisoned for a reason!"

"Yes! Because of the Order! Now stop trying to distract me Grayson! Just face it, your time is at an end!"

For all of Grayson's attempts to make Lance see...

Drip...

... and for all the attempts Lance made to free their powerful mother from Her stone prison...

Drip...

... the Shadow Alpha *still* could not remember Her true nature...

Drip...

... until the blood in his palm spilled over the edges, drops of it falling onto the symbol beneath. There was a flicker of light. Then, like Grayson, all those blocked memories came back as the walls around them crashed down. The flood of images, sights, and sounds were like a torrent of water after a dam collapse.

"Grayson?" Lance said, his voice like a different person. It was lost and confused, but good natured. His face was gentle, eyes still yellow but soft like butter. "Brother... I ... I see it all now! We must –"

"NOOOO!" Grayson screamed.

One of Her hands crashed down on Lance, crushing him to death with a single, heavy blow.

Grayson stood in horror as the Vault key rolled out from a gap under her palm, and he snatched it before it managed to roll off the edge of the platform into a deep crevice.

Everyone in the room fell into a stunned silence. Ásbjörn, Dax, Alyssa, Billy, Cooper, and Grayson gathered themselves near the exit, all twelve of their eyes watching helplessly as She lifted Her left arm. Lance's hot remains were there, a gruesome paste stretching like a wad of chewing gum stuck to the bottom of a blood-stained shoe. It was vile. Grayson saw an eye, still whole, affixed to a scrap of white bone. It stared at him, almost saying *sorry*.

Then Her other arm dropped free of the stone prison, shaking the entire Vault chamber. Thin tendrils of debris fell from the ceiling high above, worming their way toward the floor. It was a sure sign if one was ever needed that the place was not built for whatever She had planned. From what little was already done, fissures ran along the chamber walls like cracked glass, the water from beyond starting to force its way in.

"That is only going to get worse!" Grayson shouted. "We need to get out of here. Hammer, take the key and the children... use it to seal Her inside. Cooper and I will follow, so I need you to wait until the last possible moment. But should something happen and She reaches the door before us, you know what you have to do."

With that said Grayson handed the cylindrical key over to Dax, holding it with his bare hand. It smoked as the silver burned his skin, giving Billy a sudden and *really* stupid idea.

"Roger that," Dax said with a nod, shoving the key into his pocket. "Hey buddy, do you think you could give us a faster ride?"

"You bet," Ásbjörn replied, already transforming into his enormous bear form. Once the Change was complete, he crouched, and the humans climbed up onto his back.

"You know, I thought your fur would be a lot rougher," Dax said as he settled into position on Ásbjörn's topline.

"Whatever, little man," the bear replied. "Now stop rubbing me down. I don't need those kinds of rumors getting started."

"Billy!" Alyssa shouted, holding out her hand to help him up.

"I'll catch up to you," he replied somewhat confidently, but he was scared shitless. He stepped back. "Now go!"

"What are you doing, Billy?" she asked, but before he could answer, Ásbjörn had taken off.

Watching as the big bear dashed away with great speed, Billy cursed himself, wishing that he'd just climbed on.

Jesus, William, what have you gotten yourself into now?

"We have to try and anger Her a little more – cause some extra damage to this room," Grayson said to Cooper, both unaware Billy was still around due to their focus on the Gray Mother. "That should let in more water, hopefully enough to flood the Vault. Then, if we shut Her inside…"

"She'll drown!" Cooper said eagerly, and he started to shift into his monstrous beast form. "Let's go!"

There was a terrible roar, the Gray Mother shattering the rest of Her bonds, which fell off like boulders striking the side of a mountain during a rockslide. As more water spewed out from the enlarged cracks in the walls and now the floor, Her rotund gut slipped out of those stony confines like a massive gelatin mold emerging from a corset. It was much larger than what the size of the statue indicated, unnatural and vile.

"Oh my God," Grayson said with loathing. He saw that plump belly-sack moving, Primal werewolf arms and faces protruding through Her thin, veiny skin.

The bitch is pregnant?! Oh, shit! Billy thought, the hairs on the nape of his neck standing on end.

Eyes wide open, he spied one of the obelisks they'd passed on their way down. Racing over to it, his footsteps cast those eerie, rippling shapes of lights and shadows across the artifacts and walls. Finding some footholds, he climbed up the side like his life depended on it. Little did he know then that it would.

Back in the chamber, Grayson felt his mother's tight embrace around his stomach just before She threw him across the room. His back slammed against the cold stone, more cracks forming. Plummeting toward the ground, Grayson shifted mid-fall into a gleaming white wolf, landing on all fours. He shook off his weariness and the shower of water spraying from the walls, then charged back into the fray howling like the full moon was shining above.

The Gray Mother looked around, noticing the room collapsing. Despite not knowing where She was, She lumbered out of that end chamber into the next one. Along the way, priceless and powerful artifacts ended up beneath

Her massive weight, lost forever as they were reduced to broken fragments.

"Oh no, I don't think so lady!" Cooper roared, racing out of the end chamber. "Where do you think you're going?"

He dove, latching onto her weird arm with tooth and nail. He squeezed everything with all his strength and the Gray Mother shrieked in tremendous pain.

Her free hand came down, Cooper's eyes on it, tracking.

"Got ya!" he said, and at the last possible moment, Cooper dropped off, Her toughened skin whacking against those new rips and tears. It stung mercilessly, blood splattering everywhere, and She cried out once again.

Grayson seized the chance while She was distracted. Jumping high, he crashed into his mother's back, scraping and clawing his way up toward Her monstrous head. He planned to gouge out Her eyes, but before he got there, those gangly arms of Hers flapped then snapped, bending in the *wrong* direction to snatch him.

Fuck! Grayson thought, losing his breath quickly. He was being squeezed so tightly that his ribcage started to buckle.

"No!" Cooper bellowed – so loudly that he caused some of the chamber to crumble himself.

Then she flung Grayson's body again, this time at Cooper. Though he whooshed by – missing entirely – the white wolf struck the hard floor in the far reaches of the chamber with no bounce or roll. Just a flat-out *thud* amidst the spangled floor lights. It hurt to even think about.

"C-Cooper..." Grayson wheezed, barely audible as he slowly got up to retreat. "I'm g-getting too old for this shit. It's up to you... I'll be sure to see you topside..."

Cooper nodded, seeing Grayson's small, white body limp down a connecting passage. He then surveyed the rooms; just a little more of Her heavy ass crashing around should send the place crumbling.

The Gray Mother snarled, making a beeline toward the passage where Grayson went.

I need to slow her down!

Cooper was thinking desperately, looking for anything to help. Anything at all. Hell, at this point he could even wish for something insane like...

No way... no fucking way!

The very thing he thought about had appeared in front of him, perched atop an obelisk near the passageway. It had been a completely insane thought, one that he had no business thinking when easier and more effective solutions were available. But now his reality was better than fantasy, and with one more resounding thought he opened his beastly mouth and roared.

Billy had no idea what he was doing up there on the obelisk, watching that gigantic gray monstrosity get closer. She was bulging and veiny all over, except in Her sinewy arms and especially in Her distended belly, so ladened down with spawn that it started to drag across the chamber floor. Billy heard Cooper roar in the distance – surely rushing at Her now – so he reached into his pockets. Out came the silver blade and a bottle of silver nitrate from the camera store.

What the hell, silver is silver right? he thought, being the extent of his knowledge on werewolves.

He waited for Her to get close, and She was nearly close enough for him to do this incredibly stupid thing he'd thought of. It seemed far less appealing now, Her larger than life veracity thinning his confidence.

Gosh, She's a lot bigger up close...

"Come on Billy... you got this..." he said aloud. "Don't be afraid... it's time for you to finally rise up... time for Billy Arnett to meet the occasion.... it's time ... for... you... to... *shine!*"

He leapt from the top of the obelisk as the Gray Mother ambled by, the blade of his knife plunging deep into her left eye. She yowled, the sticky core gushing hot fluid over Billy's hand and down his arm. He was holding onto the embedded blade for dear life.

"Take that bitch!" he shouted, almost laughing as his legs swung like a pendulum. Yet tears of laughter can quickly turn to sadness.

The Gray Mother grabbed Billy and he screamed – a hopeless sound that was quickly shadowed by appalling things.

He could hear a nasty crunching noise, loud at the first *pop* but then softer as the seconds wore on. He could smell Her putrid breath and something patently meaty in his flared nostrils. He could taste blood and bile in the back of his throat, his heart beating in it, churning the flavors together.

Yet Billy Arnett felt absolutely nothing, like his brain had said *no thank you* to the pain salesman*, we don't want to purchase anything today!*

Then Billy happened to look down, his vision fading to black at the edges, and dimly he noticed that his right leg was missing below the knee. It was like a surreal dream in stunningly saturated colors.

He should probably wake up soon, or perhaps he should go back to sleep. A deep sleep… to relax…

No! The Silver nitrate! urged himself, and with his last bit of energy, he opened the vial and splashed it over her face.

Most of it did absolutely nothing, fizzing weakly, but the part that met Her freshly stabbed eye exploded with pain. The entire socket, then side of Her face bubbled up and burned, steam rising from the splitting skin. Red, pulsating gashes followed the lines of Her veins, spreading over the entire body as She collapsed in spasms, the very ground quivering with pain itself.

That forced the walls of the end chamber to buckle, then finally give way, sending a river's worth of spring water into the Vault.

The Gray Mother had dropped Billy's body on the floor, Cooper sweeping in to collect him. There he froze, stunned to see his best friend laying there with half a leg gone. A jagged and bloody stump was in its place.

"Fuck! Fuck! FUCK!" Cooper screamed loudly, gingerly picking up Billy's limp body in his large hand.

Lifting him to his nose, Cooper sniffed and checked him for signs of life. They were there but incredibly faint, akin to the last embers of a dying fire that were just about to go out. He needed medical attention, now, and they needed to get out of the flooding chamber else it wouldn't matter.

That's when the howls of many wolves rose up with a hunger he'd never heard before. It was an evil sound, shrouding the area with a darkness the world hadn't seen in centuries.

The Gray Mother's spasms had forced her to give birth to some of her brood. Primal werewolves, weakened by the attack but still powerful nonetheless, rose between her juddering legs. They were sickening grotesqueries illuminated in the weird light cast by the floor.

There were already too many for Cooper to handle, too many to count, yet they continued to emerge. Oh they were hungry, too, and they smelled prey in Billy and Cooper.

With Billy secure in his arms, Cooper turned tail and ran down the passageway into the adjoining chambers. Water continued to pour into the Vault, the horde of Primal werewolves splashing through it as they chased him down for their first meal.

"Close the doors!" Cooper shouted as he reached the base of the stairs, water starting to climb each one. "Dax! Grayson! Anyone! If you can hear me close them now!"

Nothing happened at first, and Cooper thought all was lost. Then, the colossal entrance began to seal itself above, its doors of thick rock, soil, and grass sliding toward each other.

"You're going to make it, Coop," he said to himself, looking down at Billy in his arms. "Almost... you're going to make it! For him!"

The entrance was now a thin sliver – still tightening – and using every muscle fiber he had, Cooper plowed up the stairs and through the gap into the world above.

YOU DID IT! his brain screamed as the doors closed.

Cooper looked back to see Dax and Ásbjörn – in bear form – taking care of the single Primal that made it through.

"Fifty-three, but who's counting," he could hear Dax saying proudly in the distance, Ásbjörn saying something smart-assed back to him.

Cooper didn't know what was said, his attention diverted back to Billy as his body transformed back into a human. Cooper then hugged him tightly, tears streaming down his face. He kissed Billy on the lips, stopped, then did it again as if the love of his life was departing.

"I love you, Billy Arnett, always have and always will," Cooper said solemnly. "I know that everything's going to be okay. Just hang tight brother. Hang tight."

The look of that mangy leg injury made Cooper think otherwise – casting a very dark cloud on their future – but with Alyssa crashing into the two of them, bringing generous hugs of her own, and Grayson Manning limping over with a proud look on his face, Cooper suspected that things would be okay in the end.

All he could hope for was to be right.

Chapter 24: Then Dawn Touched the Sky

Wednesday, March 20, 2013

1

Over the next few days, a lot of things transpired – more activity and hassle (and burials) than the town had seen since the massive construction project at Monument Park began in the spring of 1967.

"Are you deaf?" Chief O'Carroll asked tersely, standing with a forward lean. His right arm was braced against a desk, fingers tapping impatiently against the stacks of papers on top of it. "Are you with the Feds or not?"

O'Carroll was addressing the leading man of a group of black-suited agents (*If they were agents of anything at all,* his mind wondered suspiciously, thinking their outfits were far too on-the-nose).

His old, Irish eyes were wide and gleaming while waiting for an answer. They were the color of a field of clovers, the perfect accompaniment for any Saint Patrick's Day outfit had the entire downtown area not fallen into – or rather become – the largest pile of shit he had seen in his entire thirty years on the force.

The staunch agent did not reply during their meeting in Mayor Ryan Reiss' office, even when addressed by the Mayor himself a short time later. Instead, he took a single step to the side and a small-framed woman who'd been hidden stepped forward. Her hair was drawn back into a silvery bun so taut that it smoothed out her stern features like a clamp.

Wait a minute, Chief O'Carroll thought after a few quick-fire blinks. *Had she been there the whole time?*

Surely so, he further supposed, otherwise his mind was playing tricks on him and he'd rather keep tight-lipped about that.

The Mayor folded his arms behind his desk, lips parting while his brain formed a string of words to catapult her way. But as her flat black loafers inched forward along the unsightly carpet, he closed them up again. There was something about her – more *in* her – that garnered respect and even a slime ball like Mayor Reiss was not going to see what happened if he challenged that.

"Mr. Mayor," she said with eyes full of dismay, saddened that they had to have this dialog after such a terrible disaster. "My name is Councilor Jane Carter, and cutting right to the chase: we have a lot of things to discuss."

"Forgive me, but Councilor?" the Mayor questioned, having had his fill of strange shit for the month. "What exactly are you a Councilor of?"

"Well since you asked," Jane replied with a smirk. "The world is full of nightmares, and the Order Council and its Journeymen are what stands, or rather *fights,* against the night…"

Thus – after convincing the irate Mayor and Chief of Police to let those that know how to contain such "incidents" do their job – elite Order operatives began to descend upon the town from across the United States, containing the awful supernatural event and restoring a thin veneer of normalcy around Goodman for at least the next few years.

2

Meanwhile, Grayson Manning sat alone in the front lawn of his former home, its remains even more skeletal than before now that the smoke had cleared away and the late March sun shined down on the ruins.

In his hand, trembling, was a photo given to him by Fridolf. He had found it in the ruins, the photo itself taken right after Liam was born. Also in it was his beautiful mate Freya, smiling as she held the "Heir to the White Wolf Pack" in her arms. That was what they were known as to the pack you see – the Alpha's mate and Beta – but to Grayson, then, now, and forevermore they were just Freya and Liam. Far more than any title alone could bestow.

Gosh, I miss you both terribly, he thought, wishing more than anything in the world to have them back, even for a moment, outside of remembrance.

As he continued to stare at the photo, tiny specks of tears fell on its glossy coating. At the time it was taken, he had no idea that a couple of days later she would be gone, and her absence would send father and son on a dark path where their relationship never became more than aggravation wrapped in hope.

He had learned once in January 1994, and again in March 2013, that things can be replaced, but people: no, their uniqueness is forever lost to darkness once their lights go out...

3

As the elite operatives continued their operations in Goodman, the

Journeymen that were stationed there had been summoned to the headquarters building in New York City. There, they underwent a debriefing on the incredible amount of damage sustained in the Vault and throughout the town.

Dax "Hammer" Wallace and the shifter Ásbjörn were interviewed by a man named Lawrence Robinson, who had just completed a similar meeting with Doctor Wen Ross – also from Goodman. The doctor and Journeymen met briefly in the hallway between the meetings, later rumors suggesting the doctor was offered a position in the hospital ward right there in HQ due to his exceptional work on the Cooper Bennett case. Sadly, neither Dax or Ásbjörn ever saw him again, though others would in time.

Robinson was the opposite of Dr. Ross: an abrasive, stump-like security officer with a balding head who seemed to place more value on those *things* in the Vault than the people who lost their lives due to its presence. Years from then, that rude little man would become an interim Head of Security for the Order during a major time of crisis, displaying the same level of biased incompetency that he showed then. Time changed some things, whereas others resisted to the end.

After their meetings and one last drink at a local bar, Dax resumed his mission to Ireland, while Ásbjörn returned to Goodman alone. Some say he eventually wandered north towards the Great Smoky Mountains, but the details of that journey remain lost to time.

4

Wednesday, March 27, 2013

Cooper Bennett, who wore a pair dirty boots, ripped jeans, and a white wife-beater, met Alyssa Noble, dressed in a crop top, snug jeans, and boots herself, down on Wolf's Ridge Greenway. The place was familiar and secluded, something both of them needed as they tried to piece their lives back together...

Alyssa's parents had shuttered themselves in their house during the attacks, managing to escape the carnage relatively unharmed (though her mother seemed to have a new perspective on life – one Alyssa hoped would last more than a fleeting fashion trend).

Cooper's father did not survive after all, apparently assailed in the front lawn as the werewolves flowed through the streets. Cooper suspected, though never told anyone other than Alyssa, that he was already drunk (when Cooper left that morning, Roland was already downing the first beer of several six packs he had in the fridge), and that his end was due to his suppressed thinking capacity.

On the other hand, Billy Arnett was recovering from his grave injuries in Goodman Hospital, overseen by Dr. Ross – returned from New York – and his assistants. Alyssa and Cooper wondered if his missing leg would make him turn and if so, into what, considering the wound was from the Gray Mother Herself.

"Well, we'll find out tonight actually," Cooper mentioned as they walked beside the creek. "There's a full moon, and if he's not in a medically induced sleep, we should be there for him should anything happen."

"We should go regardless," Alyssa said, holding Cooper tightly.

They walked a good distance without saying anything else, simply enjoying the time in each other's company. Cooper even noticed Alyssa's nails, painted a glossy lilac color, while the birds sang cheerily and the creek gurgled gently. However, the way the sun glinted off its flowing water reminded Cooper of the eerie lights in the Vault, and that sent a shiver down his spine that Alyssa could feel.

"Everything okay?" she asked calmly over her shoulder, knowing that it probably wasn't.

"Not really," Cooper replied, closing his eyes. Using two fingers, he rubbed the sides of his nose before letting out a sigh.

"I…" he started, debating whether he should continue. "I don't know what to do about…"

"The future?"

"Yeah. I know we all talked about that, but it was before things changed – so much so that I'm lost."

"How?" Alyssa asked, stopping at the next bench. They both took a seat, Alyssa placing a caring hand on Cooper's thigh as he spoke.

"Well, with Lance dead and no apparent heir, I suppose I could... *should*... assume the role of Alpha for the Shadow Wolves."

"Would you *want* to do that?"

"You see, I don't know..." Cooper replied, one of his hands hitting his knee out of frustration. It wasn't because he didn't want to explore that life, of course, he just didn't want to do it *without* Alyssa there with him.

"You don't want to turn me into one of you..." Alyssa stated.

Sure, as an Alpha he could have a mate, but to ask her to give everything up just for him was too much. Besides, if he remained a lone wolf and stayed with her anyway, danger would flock to him like moths to a flame. It appeared to be a lose-lose situation.

"You've seen what this life entails," he replied, thinking of all the death they'd witnessed, "and you deserve something far more normal – without all the added burdens of pain and impending death."

"I might like those burdens," she said jokingly.

"Baby, you don't know what you're saying. I can't bring myself to do that to you, or even ask…"

Alyssa nodded alongside a sigh of her own.

"I agree," she said, swiping fingers through her disobedient hair. It seemed far more magical before. "You can't be asked to make that call."

Looking at Cooper's amazing face, it was made more appealing by the wonderful personality she knew shined from within. Rubbing the hand that she had on his thigh, he started to get visibly excited.

"Cooper, I just wanted to say: thank you for everything."

"Always," he replied, leaning in.

As their lips met and they kissed, Alyssa bit down on him, taking some of his blood into her mouth.

Cooper pulled away quickly, a look of shock on his face. His hands couldn't keep still for all the fidgeting he was doing: first on her shoulders… then up her neck… then her supple cheeks.

"What… what have you done?" His heart was racing. "Alyssa… no…"

She wasn't upset. In fact, there was a slight smile on her face. It reminded him of the first day they met.

"I made the choice for you," she replied, and it was such a casual statement that Cooper didn't know if he should be furious or not. He was leaning toward the former when she hugged him again. It was like morning's first light touching the night sky and with it, all his worries faded with the darkness.

As they pulled apart, Cooper looked deeply into Alyssa's eyes. Those blue gems were spangled, the slightest hint of green peeking through the shine.

He smiled.

You see, Cooper might have hated growing up in Goodman – living a hard and abusive life in that sleepy town – but knowing what he knew now, and holding such a gorgeous thing in his arms, he was glad that he had.

The secret life of Cooper Bennett might have ended, but a new one was just starting to dawn.

Made in the USA
Lexington, KY
19 August 2018